KILLING TIME

Wickes, David.

    Killing Time/by David Wickes

    ISBN 0-9687968-0-X

Printed and bound by University of Toronto Press Inc.

Toronto, Canada

10 9 8 7 6 5 4 3 2 1

Acknowledgements

Many people helped in producing this novel. Areas included research, proofreading, moral support, and all aspects of writing and publishing the work.

Many thanks to the following:

Karen Parlette, Denise Garvey, and Rick Sirisko for hours of reading and valued input.

Chief Rod Freeman, Orangeville Police Service, for countless discussions on policing and procedures.

Sergeant Debbie Backdahl, Crow Wing County Sheriff's Department, Brainerd, Minnesota, for not only information on Minnesota policing but being kind enough to organize meetings with Irv Tollefson, Chief John Backdahl, now retired, and Special Agent Dave Bjerga. All these officers willingly gave their time to brief me on their procedures.

Michael Tieber for coordinating the printing and jacket design.

Typography and proofreading by Dane Wong and Oscar Flores.

Jacket design by Boris Folkenfolk.

All the Garveys for their support and encouragement.

My son Stephen and daughter Lara, for always being there with help and advice.

Certainly to Michael Crawley, author, tutor, and friend, who has generously given his time to teach, counsel, advise, and critique the work.

And to my wife Maureen for providing assistance in all aspects, but especially for her love and support.

KILLING TIME

◇ ◇ ◇ ◇ ◇

David Wickes

For Michelle,
Best always,
David Wickes

1

Sharin felt the Jaguar hug the road as if the car and pavement were one. The smell of leather was intoxicating, as it always is in a new car. She glanced at the dress resting on the passenger's seat. Eric had given it to her just before leaving for Los Angeles today. What a difference in their life style since his business was doing so well.

The seat-belt tugged at her lap – her imagination? She was three months pregnant and not showing yet, but being so delighted with her condition, she could sense the changes in her body. She had dropped Eric off at the airport and to avoid Sunday traffic, had opted to take this side road home. The country store was just too tempting to pass, so she stopped for her favorite, a strawberry ice cream cone. Sharin looked forward to a leisurely drive on this winding road.

She bumped her head getting in the car and almost dropped the ice cream cone. What a klutz she was. How many times did she stub her toe or knock her shin or whatever? There seemed to be no way of slowing down her movements to avoid these minor accidents. She balanced the cone and managed to start the car without further incident.

The early October colors were magnificent, with the maples and oaks resplendent in shades of yellow, orange, red, and purple. It was a gorgeous, bright day, perfect for a fall drive. Autumn leaves were always a treat to view, even more so when the sun was out. The colors were so vibrant you would think the leaves were afire.

Friends often teased her and Eric about living in Minnesota with its two seasons, winter and road repair, but the change of seasons was a source of pleasure to them. Sharin's favorite was the fall. She opened the sun roof. Cool, fresh air prickled her senses. She marveled at the beauty of nature. The passing scenery reflected her contented state of mind, with the colorful pastels mirrored on the shiny hood of her car. An infinite blur of beauty presenting itself over and over again.

The road meandered for about twenty miles before intersecting with the main highway. With so many turns and her preoccupation with the fall colors, Sharin did not notice the Jeep until half way up the deserted route.

She was just about to round a curve when a glance in the rear view mirror showed the vehicle gaining on her rapidly. She accelerated for a new straight section of road, however the Jeep reappeared before she had covered half the distance to the next turn. Was this just a speeder taking chances? Probably. Sharin decided to slow down to let him pass.

As the Jeep neared it slowed and stayed right behind her, too close for comfort. Inexorably, the Jeep closed the short distance between them and bumped her. What was this idiot doing? Then another bump, this time harder than the first. The ice cream cone flew out of her hand, splattering across the dash on the passenger's side. It looked ridiculous against the posh, light beige leather.

Sharin had little trouble controlling her car but this was not only infuriating, it was terrifying. When they arrived at another turn in the road, Sharin accelerated in an effort to pull away from the Jeep. With several rapid turns coming up, maybe she could distance herself from this maniac and get to some help and safety.

The Jeep stayed with her and gradually closed again, this time hitting her hard enough to cause a minor fish-tailing. She fought to regain control, just managing to stay on the road. Again he hit her, jolting the car severely and throwing her forward so hard the safety-belt engaged, momentarily holding her captive against the seat. Sharin started to panic. It was another five or ten miles before reaching any built-up area and unless another car happened by, she was on her own.

What was happening to her baby? There was less risk after three months, yet with the force he was hitting her, could there be harm done? If only she could reach the cell phone and call for help. With her car being battered from behind, it was difficult just staying on the road.

Again he rammed into her. The sound of crunching metal was sickening. His vehicle had some sort of gear on the front, perhaps one of those off-road kits she had seen. This was doing considerable damage to her car without seemingly affecting his truck at all. In any event, nothing mattered now but how to extricate herself from this predicament and survive.

Regardless of how fast she drove into the turns she just couldn't shake him. Then without warning, in the middle of a sharp turn on a downward stretch, he hit her so hard she slid off the road on to the shoulder. Sharin fought hard to counter the side-ways skid by cranking the wheel quickly to the left and back to the right, barely getting back on the road.

Now extremely shaken and driving by reflex alone, Sharin thought she might not survive this ordeal. To hell with it. She floored the Jaguar. It leaped in response. She careened around a sharp right turn, ran a straight stretch, then another even sharper turn to the left. There was now a little distance between them!

Sharin struggled to maintain control. Her speed steadily increased to a dangerous level for this road. She negotiated another curve in a four-wheel skid. She desperately wanted out of here. Suddenly the road descended sharply. She had to decelerate or risk causing her own accident.

At that moment the Jeep came hurtling around the last turn and caught her full force, driving the Jaguar off the road. The wheels skidded along the gravel shoulder. Sharin wildly fought for control, wrenching the wheel to the left. She urged the car to get back on the road. It wouldn't. The wheels contacted a small rut in the gravel. The car flipped over and plunged down the steep embankment.

Sharin's car began to cartwheel down the slope. One minute she was upright, then on her side, upside down and over again. The noise was deafening. She heard metal scraping and glass breaking. A shard of glass ripped into her cheek. Sharin felt warm blood on her face.

Her head smacked against the door frame. The side air bags deployed, blinding her. The car filled with the acrid smell of powder. The sensation was unreal, as if it would never end. Abruptly the car's movement came to a resounding halt. It smashed into a hundred year old oak tree. Sharin started to lose consciousness. She thought of her baby, of Eric and the dogs, her parents being so happy with her pregnancy. Then everything went black.

Strawberry ice cream melted.

2

Lieutenant Jack Petersen had been policing for eighteen years, joining the force immediately upon graduation from college at the age of twenty-three. Now a homicide detective, he had been with the Bureau of Criminal Apprehension for the last twelve years, based in St Cloud.

Petersen was off duty and heading home when he saw the car at the bottom of the gully. He was not overly surprised, having witnessed too many accidents on this stretch of road.

After parking at the side of the road, he eased his six foot, one hundred and ninety pound frame out of the car. He was athletically lean and fit, having been a jock all his life, and still playing organized fast ball and touch football, at least when time permitted. However, his duties and hours were so unpredictable, he often missed scheduled games.

He made his way down the steep hill. The car was a new Jaguar but had taken a real beating. There was no one inside the vehicle. He noted the licence plate, then called dispatch to report the accident.

"St Cloud division, Patrolman Watson here."

"Bob, it's Jack Petersen. I'm on the Waverley road about seven miles west of the intersection with 94 and have a damaged vehicle off the road."

"That place sure takes its toll. How bad is it?"

"Quite serious. The car rolled down a steep hill, smashing into a large tree. Luckily it ended in an upright position. The driver must have got out okay because there's nobody around. You better run the plate. It's a new Jaguar." He gave him the plate number.

"Will do. What back-up do you need, Lieutenant?"

"Send me four officers. Also check around in case someone has called to report this. There's at least one person missing, the driver, who could easily have been injured by the look of this wreck."

"Okay. I'll have a team out to you right away."

"Bob, get an ambulance over here in case we find the injured party. I'm going to start looking around. Talk to you later."

It was almost five o'clock. He would be here for a while and not going to make dinner at home. A quick call to his wife explained the situation. She was understanding as always. Jack was very popular with fellow officers as well as their friends. He and Jennifer had been married for twenty years, spanning his entire police career. She knew what to expect and how to cope with his unusual hours.

He started by checking the area beside the driver's door, moving carefully so as not to disturb any ground that might yield some information. Somehow, the driver had got out of the car and there might be some clues to describe the individual and their condition. Fortunately the ground was reasonably soft, and as the leaves hadn't started falling yet they would be able to get some good impressions.

Next to the driver's door were well defined footprints as well as a series of scuff marks. From the size and indentation in the ground, they were made by a large man. Other markings appeared to indicate he had stumbled or slipped. Had his injuries affected his balance?

Petersen looked inside and saw some blood on the driver's seat. There must have been some kind of minor injury incurred by the driver, because the quantity of blood was minute. Most of the windows had been shattered during the crash. Possibly the driver had been cut by flying glass. The side air bags had deployed, so he doubted the driver had sustained any serious head injury.

He heard a car. His back-up had arrived. Sergeants Muir, Wilkins, and Jonsson came down the hill. They all respected Jack and enjoyed working with him. The Lieutenant was not only popular, he was good at his job.

Muir whistled. "What a waste of a good car. No sign of the driver yet, Lieutenant?"

"No. I have some imprints here that need a further going over so I'm going to continue with this. Muir, you and Wilson start searching the surrounding area for our missing driver. Jonsson, take a look at the spot where the Jaguar left the road. He must have been going at a hell of a clip to flip over like that."

"You want to leave the car for now?" asked Muir.

"Yeah, don't touch it till we know a little more," said Jack.

Petersen called dispatch. "Bob, I'm now positive the missing driver was injured, so check out the local hospitals. See if anyone has been admitted who might be our man. Also, find out if any local taxi companies picked up a fare from this location."

Jack continued to inspect the ground near the car where he had seen the footprints. There was a set of tracks leading to the Jaguar, and one leaving. That didn't add up. He marked the location for the specialist.

"Jack, you better have a look at this." It was Jonsson at the side of the road. He pointed to some long skid marks apparently left by the Jaguar.

"It looks like he skidded along the gravel, then flipped over, before rolling down the hill. Yet back here, look at these glass fragments. They're orange and red, so they're tail lights. I'd say there must have been contact from another vehicle. There's also a second set of tire marks to confirm this. See, these look like someone stopped, but those further up just skid and leave the road."

"If that's the case, we may have a hit and run. Keep on this and mark it for traffic. It looks like we'll need them, as well as forensics. I'm going to take another look at the Jaguar."

Jack returned to inspect the back of the car. It had taken such a beating from rolling over, it was difficult to sort out what caused the damage to determine if there was another vehicle involved. The rear lights were all broken, but that could have happened coming down the hill. Yet there was the presence of glass at the side of the road. He thought the trunk looked compacted but not in a way to indicate it had been struck by a car. This would need an expert from traffic to sort out, so he made another note. His portable rang. It was dispatch.

"Lieutenant, we have a trace on the Jaguar. It's leased to a Mrs Sharin Jensen. We have her home address and phone number."

"Christ, I don't like that."

"What's the problem?"

"It looks like the driver was a man. The car may have been stolen and the guy decides to beat it, or Mrs Jensen could have loaned her car to her husband or a friend, but I don't like it. Better get traffic and forensics over here, Bob. I'll take that phone number."

Jack had to make the call. It was one part of the job he didn't enjoy. It was not pleasant being the bearer of bad news. Either he was going to reach the husband, who would be distraught over his missing wife, or Mrs Jensen herself, who wouldn't be too happy either. He dialed the number.

"Frank Wilson here," a booming voice intoned.

"Mr Wilson, may I speak to Mrs Jensen please?"

"Mrs Jensen isn't here. Who is calling?"

"This is Lieutenant Jack Petersen from the Sheriff's office, St Cloud. Do you know where Mrs Jensen is?"

"She's on her way home from the airport. We've been expecting her for some time now. Why are the police looking for my daughter?" asked Wilson.

Well this explained who Mr Wilson was. It also ruled out the car theft. Jack didn't like the feeling he was getting. This could turn out to be quite nasty. He had a female driving a car that might have been forced off the road. Yet the only evidence he had so far pointed to a male at the scene.

"Mr Wilson, is there a Mr Jensen, and if so do you know where he is?"

"He's on an airplane heading for Los Angeles, or has already arrived there. Now, I asked you why you're looking for my daughter, and I want an answer."

"Yes, sir. Your daughter has been in an accident and is currently missing. Somehow she got out of the car, or was helped out, and we're now investigating."

"Good God, are you sure she's all right? Why can't you find her?"

Jack tried to explain the situation without going into full detail of his findings. He didn't want to release all the information at this time.

"We've just started the investigation. There may have been another car involved, but that's only speculation at this point. There is currently a team of four officers here with more being added. We've contacted local hospitals and will be issuing an All Points Bulletin immediately. Please give me a detailed description of your daughter."

"Yes. Let me see. Sharin is thirty-two, five feet, seven inches, and weighs about one hundred and thirty pounds. She's trim, with an athletic physique. Um, she has reddish brown hair, not too long. God, she's also pregnant, but hasn't started to show yet."

"That's a good start, Mr Wilson. What was she wearing when she left for the airport this morning?"

"Brown slacks, a white blouse, and uh, casual shoes I think. This isn't easy, Lieutenant," stammered Wilson. "Sharin, she's it in our family. There isn't anyone else."

"I understand, Mr Wilson. Do you remember if she took a coat or jacket with her?"

"Let me think. Yes, she did. Since it was a little cool this morning, she decided at the last minute to take a jacket. It's three-quarter length, light beige in color."

"Thank you, Mr Wilson. Do you have a recent photograph handy?"

"Yes, I'm sure we can find one here."

"We'll have an officer come by shortly to pick it up. Now, Mr Wilson, we have to contact Mr Jensen. We need the details of his trip and a number where he may be reached."

"Just a minute," Frank said. His muffled voice asked his wife Judy to get Eric's itinerary.

"To the best of your knowledge, Mr Wilson, would Mrs Jensen have been alone in her car on the way back from the airport?"

"Yes. Sharin was to drop Eric off at the airport and return home. We just arrived yesterday so she was anxious to get back here. Frankly we had expected her within the last hour, but thought she was probably caught in Sunday traffic. Do you think there was someone with her, Lieutenant?"

"No, just checking. Do you have the itinerary for Mr Jensen?"

"Yes, here it is. Eric was leaving Minneapolis at two o'clock, arriving in Los Angeles at three forty-five P.M., Los Angeles time." He gave him the phone number of the hotel where Eric was staying.

"Thank you, Mr Wilson. I'm sorry to bring you this bad news. We'll keep you up to date on our investigation. If you hear from your daughter or Mr Jensen, call immediately. You may reach me on my cell phone or at our headquarters." He gave him the numbers then hung up.

Petersen called Watson to have him check out Eric Jensen's booking and determine if he did board the flight to Los Angeles. If so, contact LAPD and get a detective over to his hotel to interview Jensen. It was now almost six-thirty here, making it four-thirty in L.A. As his flight was scheduled to arrive there at three forty-five, he was probably on his way to the hotel by now.

He had the officers cordon off the entire area as a crime scene. A team of two from forensics, headed by David Folk, had arrived to start their work. He went over his notes with them. They started in earnest as darkness was fast closing in. He noticed a traffic specialist was also on the scene working with Jonsson.

Jack stayed till the special agents finished their work, then asked dispatch to order a tow truck to take the Jaguar to their own compound. There was more work to be done on the car by forensics and traffic to help solve this case.

He called Jennifer to let her know he had to return to St Cloud headquarters to organize a team of detectives and officers for this investigation. He apologized saying he was going to be later than he originally thought.

3

Eric gazed at the cumulus clouds in the distance, as the plane leveled off at 39,000 feet on its way to Los Angeles. With his experience as a jet fighter pilot in the Canadian Air Force in the eighties, he was constantly aware of all the nuances of flight. Relaxing in first class, he fondly remembered the numerous times he had taken similar flights from Toronto to L.A.

He was traveling with Garry Timlin, his Sales Manager, who with his wife Jan, had become good friends. "Eric, Jan and I are delighted Sharin is pregnant. We know you badly wanted a family. Finally found out how, did you?"

"I guess so," Eric said with a chuckle. "It's almost three months, so I believe we're on safe ground now. Her parents are here, and are they happy! This will be their first grandchild."

A flight attendant came by with their drink orders.

"Here's to our meetings this week. I always enjoy working with these guys. It's a real pleasure dealing with them. Didn't you manage their operation in Canada before coming to the Twin Cities?" asked Garry.

"Yeah. It's the main reason we decided to move to the States. They offered me the exclusive rights for Minnesota and the Dakotas. It was an offer I couldn't refuse."

"You two seem to have adjusted very well to living here."

"We find the Cities quite similar to Toronto. Roughly the same size and population, but these winters are longer and colder."

"I've heard you mention that before, and it seems odd that Toronto has milder weather than we do. I guess all of us think Canada is north and cold," said Garry with a laugh.

"I know you do. Sharin and I are always amused when we tell people Toronto is south of Minneapolis. They just can't believe it."

Eric and Garry continued their business discussions, and before they knew it were on final descent into L.A. They arrived right on schedule at three forty-five P.M. and were met by a company limo which took them to the hotel. They met several friends in the lobby while checking in. Eric was pleased to learn dinner arrangements had been organized with a few of their closest associates.

He was in the midst of unpacking when the phone rang. It was the Assistant Manager explaining the front desk had neglected to give him an urgent message on his arrival. He apologized profusely. "We will make this up to you Mr Jensen," he asserted.

"Thank you. What's the message?" asked Eric.

"A Mr Wilson called at four-fifteen asking you to phone him at your home immediately. Again Mr Jensen, the hotel will take..."

"Thank you," interrupted Eric, who had had it with the apologies and was wondering what this could be. Frank Wilson was not one to overplay any situation. If he said urgent, it must certainly be important. He dialed his home number.

"Frank Wilson here."

"Hi, Dad. Just got your message. What's going on?" Eric had lost his mother and father in a tragic accident when he was in his late teens, and since his marriage had referred to Sharin's parents as Mom and Dad.

"Thank God you finally called. We tried your hotel nearly an hour ago after just missing you at the airport," Frank said hurriedly, quite unusual for him. "The police called us. They found Sharin's car off the road at the bottom of a hill. The car was badly damaged and there's been no sign of Sharin."

"Is Sharin all right, Dad?"

"They don't know for sure. In their opinion any injury sustained was not serious, certainly not life threatening, but Sharin is missing. The officer in charge, a Lieutenant Petersen, has the investigation underway, and promised to stay in touch."

"Why can't they find Sharin? Surely she wouldn't just wander off and not report to someone, especially if she's hurt," said Eric.

"I'm afraid there's more to this, Eric. Sharin's car may have been struck from behind by another vehicle and forced off the road. The police are not certain about that yet, but it's a possibility. The Lieutenant assured me they have a full team of officers on the investigation and are doing their best."

"Christ, Dad, I can't believe this. Have they checked the hospitals?"

"Yes. They started on that right away," said Frank.

"When did you last talk to the police?"

"They called about an hour ago. The accident occurred in a remote area and they haven't been able to talk to any witnesses. They tell me they're doing all they can, but I'm going to ensure we get a top priority on this."

Eric guessed it was said partly to make him feel better, but he also knew Frank was well connected from his political days, and this was not just an idle statement.

"Do the police know Sharin is pregnant?"

"Yes, I told this Petersen fellow."

Eric was numb. This couldn't be happening.

"What's this guy's number, Dad? I'm going to phone him. Then I'll book a flight home."

Frank gave him Petersen's number. "He should still be in his office. We'll be here for you, staying in touch with their investigation. Don't worry, Eric, we'll get to the bottom of this with the best people involved."

It was little consolation but Eric knew he meant well. Frank Wilson would muster all his resources and stay on this to the end, whatever that might be. Eric wouldn't let himself dwell on such thoughts as he dialed Petersen's number.

"St Cloud detachment, Patrolman Watson."

"Lieutenant Petersen please."

"He just left. Who's calling?"

"It's Eric Jensen. My wife was in an accident today and he's in charge of the investigation isn't he?"

"Yes, he is. May I have him call you?"

"Call me? My wife is missing. I want to talk to somebody who knows what the hell is going on."

"He should be back here soon. I can assure you he's the top guy here and has a full investigation underway now. You're in L.A. aren't you?"

"Yes," said Eric. "I'm God Damn well in L.A. and you can't find my wife."

"Mr Jensen, we're on top of this with a full team of officers out there. You get back here as soon as you can and we'll find your wife."

"That's not good enough. You say Petersen is due back soon. Just when is soon?"

"Sir, I appreciate your frustration, but the Lieutenant is out there working on your case right now. I can't tell you exactly when he'll return, but it should be within the hour. Why don't you call back then?"

"What do you think is going on?" asked Eric.

"We only know your wife's car left the road and rolled down a hill. The car's banged up but it appears your wife got out okay."

"If she's all right, why hasn't someone heard from her? It's been how long since the accident?"

"I don't know the exact time as yet. The Lieutenant first spotted your car about an hour ago," said Watson.

Eric knew it was time to organize his return flight and that he needed to talk to Petersen to get any useful information.

"Tell the Lieutenant I'll call from the airport in about an hour,"said Eric. He hung up, more frustrated and worried than ever.

4

Kurt eased the Jeep to a stop. The Jaguar had rolled down the hill and slammed into a huge tree. Nothing had happened. Why hadn't it exploded and caught fire or something? He had really planned to kill her but somehow she might have survived the crash.

He decided to take a quick look. If someone came by he could claim he was just helping out. He worked his way down the hill. The car was sitting perfectly upright as if it had been driven there and parked, although it was battered to hell. As he neared he saw her, slouched over against the deflated air bag. He tried the driver's door; it opened easily. She was out cold, but breathing. He felt the pulse in her neck. Okay.

She was quite beautiful actually. Her face wasn't perfect, it was striking, with fine chiselled features that made you want to look again. Deep green eyes blended perfectly with her auburn hair, trimmed and styled fashionably short. High cheek bones complemented a full, sensuous mouth.

He had followed her one day when she was grocery shopping with an obviously close friend. They had meandered up and down every aisle, having a great visit while filling their carts with provisions. That had been the closest contact he had experienced in the two weeks of following her.

He hoisted her out of the car and carried her up the hill. He laid the unconscious body across the back seat and secured the seat belts to keep her in place. The Jeep pulled away smoothly, leaving the scene undetected.

That new car was just too well built, protecting her while it rolled down the hill. He had carefully planned and executed this scenario only to be caught short by these bizarre circumstances. Damn it! Now he had this woman on his hands and didn't know what he wanted to do.

The house had been rented from a mutual friend. It was rather isolated and only a fifteen minute drive away. He drove carefully, not wanting to be apprehended with a body in the back seat. That would be a little difficult to explain. He arrived without incident and with no neighbors nearby, secreted Sharin inside to secure her for the time being.

She had a small cut from some glass but otherwise seemed to be okay.

His nurse's training allowed him to clean and dress her wound. He thought she would come around shortly.

Kurt made sure his captive was firmly bound. The tape he had was ideal for keeping her silent as well as securing her ankles and hands. Why not just put her away and not have all these problems? For some inexplicable reason he just didn't want to do that right now.

In the fridge there was the remnants of yesterday's pizza which he slapped on a plate, and finished off with a Coors light. He didn't enjoy eating this way but it would have to do for now. Normally he ate well, carefully balancing his intake with plenty of vegetables, fruits, protein, carbohydrates, and healthy drinks. His lean stomach was kept trim with a vigorous exercise routine.

After stacking the dishes he went down to the exercise room the owner had set up. It wasn't as complete as he would like, but enough to maintain his condition for this short period. He turned on all the lights, no dark basements for him anymore, not since...

He heard the screams. Who was it this time? He was seven or eight, his earliest recollection of those days of terror. The basement is pitch black as it always is, the pain of his earlier beating is beginning to ease, but he is consumed with fear. One of his brothers or sisters was now taking the brunt of their drunken parents' latest outburst. Or is his mother thrashing his father? Or vice versa? It was endless.

There were so few moments of peace. The only care came from his father. When sober he would feed them and ask their forgiveness. He would promise to protect them from their mother, who it seemed was never sober. Inevitably it would begin again. The beating, then the basement. Always dark, mostly cold.

There were four children, then three, then two. He never knew where the others went. They just weren't there one day. Then his father left. Somehow he knew there was no hope of surviving. He was twelve when it happened.

His mother had passed out in the living room after another evening of heavy drinking. It was dawn. Kurt took a screw driver and drove it into his mother's ear. He then used a bread knife to hack and slice until there was little resemblance to the human form that had been his mother. He dragged the corpse to the door leading to the basement, opened it, and pushed his mother down the stairs. He made sure the lights were turned off.

Kurt went outside and sat on the front door step. A passerby saw the young boy covered in blood, holding a knife in his hand. The authorities arrived and

Kurt was placed in an institution. His subsequent recovery appeared miraculous. He had a voracious appetite for reading. Although several years behind in formal schooling, he made up for the lost time by devouring the correspondence courses made available. At age nineteen he received his high school diploma. The following year he was released on probation.

Seven years later he was given a clean bill of health. He had beaten the system. Only he knew the anger remained. The idea of shift work appealed to Kurt, so he applied to a hospital to register in the nursing program. Thirty years later, the young boy's past seemed lost and forgotten. Not to Kurt.

The phone startled him, its shrill ring invading his reverie. He answered on the second ring.

"It's me. What the fuck's happening?"

This was not unusual. On occasion he was unnecessarily crass, had little or no social skills, but was amazingly brilliant. It was the latter that held the relationship together.

"I have a little dilemma," said Kurt. "My holiday has been interrupted. I've been following this woman for a couple of weeks. Today she had a little accident."

"You weren't going to do anyone in Minnesota. What the fuck are you saying now?"

"I changed my mind. Now, just listen. It'll take some time to resolve this situation, so I'll need some help with William."

"That piece of shit bugs me. He keeps bringing his new boyfriends to the shop to introduce them to me, as if I might care. That prick better leave town soon or I'll help him out if you know what I mean."

"You may get your chance to do just that," said Kurt.

"It'll be my pleasure. How'd you meet this fuck anyway?"

"It's a long story, but his house has come in handy. The problem is, William is due to come back next Saturday."

"Yeah, something like that. Why is that a problem?"

"I may need this house for longer than that and I don't want him arriving while we're still here."

"What the fuck is this 'we' stuff? You getting laid or something?"

"Don't get smart with me," snapped Kurt. "This is only Sunday, so I have almost a week to work this out before William is due to return. I'll call when I sort things out."

"Okay. The sooner the better if you want me to do this shit."

He thought he heard her stir. "I have to go now," said Kurt as he hung up.

5

Frank Wilson had been a Member of Parliament in Canada's federal government for twenty-eight years. He had served as a Cabinet Minister during his last seven years prior to retirement a year ago. During his tenure in politics he had naturally developed a wide base of friends and connections in both Canada and the United States.

His first call was to Don Taylor, who was a Deputy Commissioner with the Ontario Provincial Police in his home province in Canada. They had known each other for years and were regular golfing partners. Frank needed to get to a high ranking police official in Minnesota and Don would know how to accomplish this. He dialed his number.

"Don, Frank Wilson here. I'm in Minnesota and have to ask a favor."

"Don't know why you chose to go to Minnesota now," joked Taylor. "It was sixty-eight today and we played twenty-seven holes. May not get too many more days like this."

"Don, I've got a serious problem and need your help," said Frank, not reacting to the barb from his old friend.

"That doesn't sound like you, Frank. What's up?"

Frank brought him up to date on the accident and what he knew about the police investigation.

"Jesus, Frank, that's unbelievable. When did you first hear from the police?"

"They originally called around six o'clock, having discovered her car about an hour prior to that. It's now seven-thirty here and still nothing new on Sharin's whereabouts. Don, what can we do to get a top priority on this?"

"I know the Commissioner in Minnesota. We were on a course together several years ago when he was Deputy Commissioner. I heard he made Commissioner last year. I'll call him right away to let him know who you are, and that you're a close friend of mine. I'm sure he'll call you as soon as possible. Where can he reach you?"

"I appreciate this, Don," said Frank. He gave him the number.

Frank's second call was to Bob Johnston, a member of the Minnesota State Senate. He had worked with Bob on air pollution legislation in the early nineties and had remained in touch with him and his family ever since. His wife, Pat, was pleased to hear from Frank, but explained Bob was out of town till next Tuesday.

"Is there a number where I can reach him, Pat? It's extremely urgent."

"Is everything all right, Frank?"

He gave her a quick rundown and said he needed Bob's help.

"That's awful, Frank. Let me see. Bob is at the Peach Tree Plaza in Atlanta. His room number is 916." He thanked her and said he'd keep in touch.

Frank called the Peach Tree, got through to Bob's room, and an answering machine. He left a brief message with his Minneapolis number, saying it was important and to please call, regardless of the hour.

Judy had been hysterical with the news, and he had given her a sedative so she could get some sleep. His only company now were his daughter's two German Shepherds, King and Kayla. The bitch was now four and at eighty-five pounds was large for a female. King, a year younger, was over one hundred pounds of solid muscle. They were magnificent animals, well trained with marvelous dispositions.

Frank, picked up the portable phone, and took the dogs out for a walk. They immediately bounded off towards the brush. There were fifty acres here, heavily treed, and the dogs knew the property by heart. Tonight they were a little confused as Sharin was not home and they seemed to be looking for her. They were incredible companions. He realized how important they were to both his daughter and son-in-law.

The mood created by the calm, clear night and the joy the dogs displayed during their run, was marred by the thoughts of Sharin's plight. He would commit all his time and energy to ensure they had nothing but a top effort from the police in solving this mystery and finding her.

The police were certainly vague in describing the situation. With the added help and influence from the Commissioner's office, he would learn exactly what was happening.

He called the dogs who responded immediately, and returned to the house. The message light was flashing. How could he not have received that call? Maybe the portable had some kind of limiting range. Damn! He retrieved the message. It was Don Taylor. He called him right away.

"Don, sorry I missed your call. I was out with the dogs and thought I could receive any call with this portable, but apparently not. Did you reach the Commissioner?"

"Yes, and he was reasonably cooperative. He needed more information from the Lieutenant in charge of the investigation, then would decide how to proceed."

"Translate that for me, Don."

"Frank, they have many cases involving missing persons. There has to be some positive proof of foul play before assigning a sizeable number of detectives to any case. That would come from the investigative team's findings at the scene this afternoon. They are probably meeting now at headquarters to assess the situation."

"Hold on, Don, they called me, not the other way around. The police know Sharin is missing, there's no doubt of that."

"That's true, Frank, but they don't know why. She could have wandered off to a nearby home and received help, or was taken to a hospital or clinic if she required professional care."

"Don, it's been over three hours since the time of the accident. Surely Sharin would have called here by now."

"I agree, and understand your concern, but the police probably don't have enough information yet to know where this is going. I would imagine they're close to making a determination and assigning a team they believe suits the situation. Frank, once they suspect any foul play, a full complement of officers will be on the case. In the meantime let's not buy trouble."

"Still, we haven't heard from Sharin. It's been too long since the time of the accident. I just bloody well don't like it."

"Frank, I'm sure you'll hear from the Commissioner or the officer in charge shortly. He promised me you would be brought up to date. Now, please sit tight and try to maintain a positive outlook. Keep me posted, and if anything else crops up, give me a call. You know I'm here for you."

"Thanks. I hear you, but we better get some word soon."

"How is Judy taking this?"

"Not well at all. I gave her a sedative to put her out for a while, for her sake and mine. Don, there's an incoming call. Talk to you soon."

"Good luck, Frank."

He clicked over to receive the new call.

"Frank Wilson here."

"Mr Wilson, Lieutenant Petersen. We've completed the first phase of our investigation and wanted to bring you up to date."

"I've been anxious to hear from you, Lieutenant. What's going on?"

"We now have reason to believe there was contact with another vehicle, which resulted in your daughter's car leaving the road. Therefore we're treating this as a criminal investigation, but I don't want you to be alarmed by that term. It simply identifies there may have been contact causing the accident and we have to proceed on that basis. I've assembled an investigative unit. Our first briefing with the new officers is set to start in the next few minutes. Have you heard anything?"

"No, not about Sharin, but I have asked a friend to contact your Commissioner."

"Yes, the Commissioner called about half an hour ago. I understand your position and know you're trying to help. I reviewed the case with the Commissioner and he agreed with my plan of action. Our people are ready now so I must get to the briefing. If you hear anything about your daughter, Mr Wilson, call us immediately."

"I won't be resting for a minute until Sharin is found, Lieutenant."

They said their good-byes.

Frank went to the liquor cabinet for the bottle of Remy Martin VSOP. He was not much of a drinker but thought a small cognac would be very much in order right now. He poured an ounce and a half into a snifter and headed to Eric's den, sat down and started making notes on everything that had transpired since early evening. He was going to be totally prepared and had to keep busy, as the waiting was intolerable.

His notes were complete and the cognac finished. It had to be getting late. He couldn't believe it was close to midnight. The dogs, who had been at his side all night, let him know they wanted out.

King had a way of being very demonstrative about this. He would whack your arm or leg with his huge front paw and start wagging his tail enthusiastically. A few gruff barks told you he wanted something. Frank simply said, "Do you want to go out?" The ears went straight up, the head cocked to one side, the tail wagging increased, and both dogs began rapidly pacing and squealing in delight.

Frank let them out but remained at the door within earshot of the kitchen phone. He was not gong to miss any more calls.

Why was there no word of Sharin? It had been almost seven hours now. This was looking darker by the minute. If he was a religious man he would have prayed.

The dogs returned. The three went to the den and Frank settled into a comfortable reading chair. The one cognac was enough for now. He sat quietly and absently petted the Shepherds. How much did they understand? They certainly were as quiet and pensive as he was. Strange. He felt there was no way they could fully grasp the situation, but they certainly could sense his mood. It was some comfort.

He waited for the phone to ring.

6

Sharin felt something foreign straining at her ankles and wrists and also realized her mouth was taped. She was confused and disoriented. Slowly it started to come back to her. Some idiot had forced her off the road. The sensation of rolling down the hill revisited her.

Her body must have taken a fair degree of punishment from the assorted aches and pains she could feel, which would only worsen in a day or two. Had anything happened to the baby? With the incredible forces put on her body during the tumble down the hill, God only knows what may have occurred. She had no way of knowing that right now. She was not aborting. The cramps would be much different, more severe, and there was no sign of labor pains.

The room was somebody's bedroom. It was rather small, but neat and clean. The one window had curtains drawn, preventing her from seeing outside. Sharin could not make any sound with the heavy tape on her mouth. Both hands and legs were bound, and her shoulders were strapped down, holding her against the bed while totally restricting any movement. The tape binding her ankles was fastened to the end of the bed.

Whoever this was, he was thorough. Sharin definitely wasn't going anywhere and with that reality setting in, fear took over. There was a man's voice in another room. By the sound of it, he was talking on the telephone. This probably was her captor. Was it the same idiot who had forced her off the road? If so, what on earth did he want with her? This was a living nightmare and Sharin knew to have any chance of surviving she would have to keep her wits about her, for both herself and the baby. That didn't lessen the fear overcoming her.

The man stopped talking. She could hear the sound of someone approaching her room. The hallway must be bare hardwood floor because his footsteps were clearly audible. They sounded heavy and deliberate. He had to be a large man. Her heart was pounding. Cold sweat covered her body. Christ!

Large he was. He arrived at the door and stood there. Well over six feet tall with a muscular frame, he just stared at her. God, this was nerve-racking. Sharin had never known such fear.

"Don't know what to do with you," he said laconically.

What the hell does he mean by that? Tears welled in her eyes. She couldn't stop. Instant anger overcame her. You could set me free, you son of a bitch. First of all you nearly killed me, and secondly, I'm pregnant. The tape seemed to tighten. It grabbed at her wrists and ankles. Saliva built up in her mouth. She swallowed once, twice, several times, till there was no saliva. The anger dissipated. The fear totally absorbed her.

His eyes were scary. They were almost colorless and devoid of any emotion. What did he want? Was he a kidnapper looking for a ransom?

Finally he moved, lazily approached the end of the bed, leaned over and placed his hands on the base board. His hands were *huge*. She thought her heart would stop. Suddenly he picked up the end of the bed, lifting it off the floor a couple of feet, then let it drop. Her entire body shook with the impact and she shuddered.

He still showed no emotion. Don't tell me he's a psycho. More cold sweat.

He turned and walked out of the room, closing the door softly. The sound of his retreating footsteps echoed down the hall. Then all was quiet.

There wasn't a sound in the house. She could hear her heart beat. It didn't beat, it pounded. It felt like it was going to burst through her chest. She started to shake. How to control the panic? The restraints were so confining. The knot in her stomach tightened as she struggled against the tape. Would she ever get out of here? She clenched her fists so tightly, her nails dug into the flesh, stinging the palms of her hands.

After several minutes she tired. Sharin just lay there, not moving a muscle, afraid to do anything. Why did this maniac force me off the road? What is he going to do to me? Was there more than one person involved? She had heard him talking on the phone – to an accomplice?

The headache started, accompanying the other hurts she was feeling all over her body. She felt groggy, but not nauseous. How long had she been unconscious? It couldn't have been more than a couple of hours, or she would have different symptoms and be in big trouble. It probably was a mild concussion.

It was dark outside but he had left a light on in the bedroom. Thoughts of Eric, the baby, the dogs, her parents, all came to her. She began to cry, softly at first, then full body shaking sobbing. She had to stop. She was in trouble, and to survive meant to be under control, regardless of how dark or desperate the situation may be.

Her background and training would definitely help her. Three years of her nursing career had been spent in a psychiatric ward, giving her an understanding of what she may be dealing with.

Staying awake was imperative if she had indeed suffered a concussion. That was going to be a challenge. She was aching and fatigued from the accident but felt she had to muster the will to handle this, for everyone concerned. She hadn't run today. With Eric, they had a regular routine, which they recorded faithfully, listing their running mileage daily. She averaged twenty-five miles a week, keeping her fit and trim. Why was she thinking about that now?

Where was this house located? She could have been unconscious for two hours at the most, otherwise she wouldn't be awake now and reasonably alert. It would have taken at least half an hour to move her to his Jeep, (she remembered the Jeep!), bring her inside this house, then tie and secure her. That would leave driving time of about an hour and a half at the outside, more likely less.

She had been run off the road about five to ten miles west of Highway 94. So this house was somewhere within a one hour radius from that location. Did that help? Sharin didn't know yet but she had to keep working on information that might make a difference. At least it would keep the mind occupied and help her stay awake. It also eased the panic that was threatening to overcome her.

She began to think about tomorrow. Every Monday she went to the General Hospital for volunteer work. It was comfortable surroundings for her, to be back in a hospital which certainly needed all the help they could get. What were her chances of being there tomorrow? Not likely.

And the next day was even more critical. Every Tuesday she and Eric helped out at a shelter in the Cities. A city wide organization offered meals and beds for the homeless. They had been involved now for three years and seldom missed a Tuesday. The work was rewarding and needed. Sharin helped out in the kitchen, preparing and serving meals, while Eric assisted in admitting and registering. It was well organized, complete with Security Staff and nursing. They started at three-thirty, and by the time the meals had been served and cleanup was complete, it was usually eight o'clock before they left.

Afterwards they would head out together on a 'date.' Tuesdays were an important day in their lives. What would happen this Tuesday? She thought of the homeless people waiting for their meal. Would someone take her place and take care of them? She and Eric had come to know many of those seeking refuge. The crying started again. Was she feeling sorry for the people at the shelter or herself?

Sharin was determined not to feel sorry for herself, despite her current situation. She was scared. That's allowed. Allowed? She had no choice. She was absolutely terrified but had to find a way to keep thinking and planning. Her love for Eric would help her through this. They were going to be parents! More incentive to survive.

A door closed. Did he leave? If so, how long would she have to try to free herself? The tape on her wrists was secure, yet there was some small amount of play. If she worked her hands back and forth maybe she could loosen it even more.

7

It took some time to organize his return. The best Eric could do was fly to Chicago and overnight there, getting the first flight out the following morning. Minneapolis flights were being diverted due to weather. It was better to at least get to Chicago tonight, leaving only an hour and a half flight the next day. A quick call home revealed there was no further news about Sharin.

He called Garry who was not in his room. With only an hour or so to his Chicago flight, he began re-packing and called the Bell Captain for a taxi and luggage service. Two friends dropped by, saying they had tried to call him during the last hour to come to dinner but kept getting a busy signal. Eric had completely forgotten about those arrangements. He briefly explained the situation and asked them to contact Garry. They assured him they would and offered their sympathy.

Two detectives arrived, introduced themselves, and said they needed to talk. Eric explained he had a plane to catch as he had to get back to Minneapolis. They understood but there were a few questions.

"I'm Lieutenant Callahan, and this is my partner, Sergeant Dixon. We better do this in private," he said and closed the door. They all shook hands.

"Jesus, I've just learned my wife has been in an accident and is missing. I have to get out of here."

"We have only a few questions that won't take long. If necessary we'll help you get to the airport, but we have to know your whereabouts over the last few hours."

These guys were serious. Did they think he had anything to do with Sharin's disappearance? This was nuts.

"Look I'll be pleased to cooperate with you but this is my last chance to get back east tonight."

"We'll be as brief as possible. Let's start with the last time you saw your wife."

Eric explained in detail the trip to the airport with Sharin. She had dropped him at the terminal about an hour prior to his flight. Her parents were visiting so she let him off at the terminal rather than park and stay till flight time. He had insisted on this, knowing she was excited to get back to her folks.

He had checked in, and spent approximately thirty minutes prior to the flight in the First Class lounge. This could easily be verified as all visitors to the lounge were checked in by name. He was also with his Sales Manager who flew out with him and was now in the hotel.

"What's your Sales Manager's name?"

"Garry Timlin. I called him a few minutes ago but he wasn't in his room. I suspect he's in the bar or dining room. We were to have dinner with two friends."

There was a knock on the door. It was the bellman. Eric pointed to his luggage, looking at the detectives. They nodded and a rather puzzled bellman took the bag, saying his taxi was ready.

Callahan asked if he had made any calls from the lounge. "No, I didn't make any calls. Now I have to go," said Eric, who was not only agitated but nervous.

Callahan persisted. "How long have you been married, Mr Jensen?"

"We've been married eight years, and very happily thank you."

"Have you had any fights or quarrels lately?"

"Not really, a couple of small spats, but nothing serious." Eric looked at his watch.

"We won't be much longer, Mr Jensen. How was your wife when she dropped you off? Did she seem upset or display any nervousness at all?"

"No. On the contrary, she was excited about getting back home to be with her folks. They had just arrived yesterday to stay with us for two weeks."

"Did you notice anything suspicious or out of the ordinary at the airport when your wife left you?"

"Look, we were both very up-beat and had a loving good-bye. I then took my suitcase and entered the terminal. Why would I be looking for something unusual?"

"We understand, Mr Jensen, but we have to check all the details. Just fill in the rest of the trip and we can wrap this up."

"I boarded the flight, we left on time, arriving in L.A. right on schedule. A limo had been reserved to bring us to the hotel. We came directly here, where I've been through a living hell ever since."

The detectives seemed satisfied with Eric's reaction and story. They told him he was free to return to Minneapolis. He still had almost an hour to make his flight.

The trip to the airport was a blur. First the stunning news of Sharin's accident and her disappearance, then the LAPD detectives questioning him. The adrenalin rush was incredible, but he was also just plain frightened.

On arrival, Eric purchased new tickets, checked his luggage, went through security, and down to the departure gate. He had about ten minutes to spare so he called the police. Lieutenant Petersen was still not available. Frustrated, he called home.

"Dad, I can't get through to the Lieutenant. He's not there or won't come to the phone."

"That doesn't sound like Petersen, Eric. I've talked to him only twice, but he seems straightforward and helpful. He called less than half an hour ago but had nothing new to report. Their investigation is well under way. They were back tracking Sharin's possible route to see if anyone along the way had seen her car or her pursuer's. I'm still working on my connections here."

"Thanks, Dad. I appreciate it. My flight's in final boarding now so I'll have to call you later."

Eric's first class seat was in the bulkhead and luckily no one was beside him. He wasn't in the mood for conversation. He could tell by the way the flight attendant eyed him, she knew he was troubled. Eric realized he had not paused for a moment during the last several hours. It had been one continuous series of events after another. Could this really be happening? It seemed impossible.

"May I get you something, sir?" the flight attendant asked. He barely heard her. Due to the late departure time there would not be a meal service. It didn't concern Eric, who hardly felt like tying into a full dinner. He said some coffee after take-off would be fine. He would call home again and maybe try to get some sleep, although he didn't like his chances of nodding off.

The take-off roll was smooth and uneventful. After lift-off the pilot began cleaning up, retracting wheels and flaps. There was the usual slight settling, then the jet began to accelerate, soon achieving its regular climbing speed and attitude. The city of Los Angeles slowly faded away as they turned on to the easterly heading for Chicago.

You don't think this kind of thing is ever going to happen to you. It only occurs in movies and books, or to complete strangers, in other cities or states or countries. Not to you or your family, or your friends, or to anyone you know. He was upset, angry, and afraid. His stomach churned while he willed the flight to be over. He realized he would not be in Minneapolis till tomorrow morning, which only heightened his anxiety.

What has happened to Sharin? They say she was run off the road and injured in the accident. She has been missing for several hours now. Sharin would never stay out of contact in a situation like this unless something prevented her from doing so. She had to be alive, he could not begin to accept the alternative. Not only that, they had to be alive. There was more than one life at stake now. She was his entire life, and now there were two.

The week had begun with nothing but good news about the pregnancy. They were incredibly happy as they both had wanted children from the beginning. She was nearing three months and the doctor had confirmed everything was normal. The enthusiastic reaction of her parents had only added to their happiness.

"How would you like your coffee, sir?" The flight attendant's voice brought him back.

"Just as it is please," Eric replied.

"May I get you anything else before our light snack, which will be available shortly?"

"I'll just settle for coffee." Eric turned to the window, ending the conversation.

He tried to imagine Sharin. Where she was, what she was doing. He thought of King and Kayla, who absolutely adored her. With their new home and land, they had immediately set out to find two large dogs, since they now had ample space for them to roam and exercise. As working dogs, shepherds need sufficient space to expend their high energy. Extremely loyal and loving, they are also perfect companions and protectors. Although Eric no longer traveled extensively, he was still away occasionally, thus the dogs were a comfort to both him and Sharin.

As it was getting late, he decided to call home again in case Frank wanted to get some sleep, although he rather doubted that. Frank had heard again from Lieutenant Petersen who unfortunately had nothing new to report.

"This Petersen seems like a thorough fellow, Eric, covering all the bases. He did apologize for missing your calls but will see us as soon as you arrive in Minneapolis. So far I like his attitude and perseverance."

Coming from Frank, this was a hell of a compliment.

"I'll call you from Chicago when I arrive," Eric said. "I plan to stay right beside O'Hare. How are you two holding up?"

"I gave Judy a couple of sleeping pills. She was becoming a little unraveled. How are you doing?"

"I really don't know, Dad. I love Sharin so much, it's difficult coming to grips with this. Why haven't we heard from her? That keeps haunting me. I'm just going through the motions right now. It's difficult to think straight. I'll call you when I get settled, with my room and phone numbers. I'm glad you're here." They said good-bye.

This was getting worse by the minute. It had now been over seven hours since the police had discovered Sharin's car with still no word of her whereabouts.

Eric must have dozed off because the next thing he realized the flight attendant was nudging him to say they were landing momentarily. She explained she hadn't wanted to disturb him when he had fallen asleep because it looked like he badly needed the rest. He could see the lights of Chicago as they turned on to final approach for O'Hare. The reality of his current situation came flooding back to him.

While waiting in the baggage claim area, he had telephoned the nearest hotel and yes, they did have a room available for the night. He said he would arrive shortly.

Numbly he watched the baggage carousel come to a stop. All other passengers were gone. He realized his bag had not made the flight. Now he had to stop at baggage services to report his missing luggage. He was not in a patient or understanding mood as the agent went through the routine of locating his luggage. They found his bag. It hadn't made his flight but would arrive in Chicago early in the morning.

"You must have been running a little late, were you?" asked the agent.

"Yes, I guess I was," snapped Eric. "Just send it to my hotel will you." Eric told him where he was staying, turned and left.

He took the shuttle to the hotel. He realized how short he had been with the airline agent. Not normal for him. The stress and weariness were taking over.

If the front desk clerk wondered about this guest checking in at one-thirty A.M. without any luggage, she didn't show it. He was politely given his key and pointed in the direction of the elevators. The room was on the twenty-fourth floor with a view of O'Hare.

He sat on the edge of the bed watching the arrivals and departures. He suddenly felt very alone and helpless. Where was Sharin? How could he help? He knew he must try to get some rest, as short as it might be, before leaving for Minneapolis on the six A.M. flight. Would his bags arrive in time? That was the least of his worries.

8

Kurt needed a diversion. The pressure was starting to build again and he knew he had to get out of the house. After driving north for about an hour he spotted a flashing neon sign off the highway. It was some kind of bar as the sign was plugging a local beer. Everything's so fucking commercialized.

He took the next exit, then doubled back in the direction of the sign, finding it easily. It was a simple building that looked like a run down shack. There was a garage next door with one fuel pump and a small service bay. It looked like the business had seen better days. The front of the bar was weathered clapboard that someone had painted a dull brown a few years ago. It was a two story building with what was probably a small apartment upstairs.

The beer sign blinked on and off. The whole place appeared – monotonous. He walked into an even more boring interior. There were two tables with a few chairs, a pool table that looked like it was never used, and a small bar with four stools, one of which was broken. There was barely enough light to make out the dull features. One customer at the bar was nursing a beer and talking to the bartender. There was no one else in sight.

He thought he might have one beer and leave, until he got a closer look at the woman behind the bar. The bartender was not only young, perhaps late twenties, but quite attractive. She was tiny, perhaps five feet tall. She wore a tight fitting white tank top and blue slacks which rode low on her hips, showing off a firm, slim waist. Her light brown hair was cut short and streaked blond from the sun. Had she been in a different setting, with decent make-up, she would have turned a few heads. Not that any of this mattered to him. He could have cared less, but she did represent a potential candidate.

"We'll be closing soon. What can I get ya?"

"I'll have a Coors light please," said Kurt with a soft smile.

She fished the beer from the cooler, and slid it down the bar.

"Need a glass?"

"No, the bottle's fine, thank you." Kurt flashed another smile. She didn't seem to notice, returning to her conversation with the customer. Kurt drank half the beer, and got up to go to the washroom. It was off to the right at his end of the bar. He lingered, freshening up as best he could. There was no soap, only cold water and a few paper towels. He made do, then returned to his seat at the bar.

The other customer was older, sixty going on seventy. He obviously knew the bartender well, as their conversation had that tone of familiarity. She seemed kind and attentive, as well as touchy-feely. She constantly put a hand on his arm while chatting and smiling. She was a charmer, extremely friendly and likeable.

Kurt felt a cool draft on his back as the front door opened. A couple entered and saluted a greeting while sitting at one of the tables.

"What's on tap tonight, Ginny?"

"Budweiser, the same as every night, Albert."

"Then we better have two, one for me and one for the missus."

Ginny took two mugs, filled them from the Bud tap, then swished out from behind the bar to serve her two new customers. Her movements were fluid, with a gentle sway of her well proportioned hips. Everyone knew each other. The bar's main business undoubtedly came from its regular clientele.

"Just have time for a quick one, Ginny. Early day tomorrow."

"It always is for you, Albert," said Ginny. She smiled and gently stroked the back of his head and neck, letting her hand linger there. It appeared so natural for her. If this flirtatious act bothered Albert's wife, she didn't show it. Ginny was so friendly and naturally out-going, the customers adored her.

She returned to the bar and glanced at Kurt.

"Care for another, mister?"

Kurt beamed his best smile and shrugged. "Don't mind if I do."

This time she brought the beer to him. She picked up the empty bottle and touched his arm lightly.

"Didn't take you long to down that one." She smiled.

Kurt began to think this might work out very well indeed, providing the others didn't stay too much longer. Sooner or later the owner would have to show up and that could alter his plans.

"Guess I was pretty thirsty. It's been a long day on the road."

Ginny smiled again. "Catch you a little later. Have to get back to Fred."

"As long as you have some time for me, I'll gladly wait," Kurt said with a grin.

She paused, increasing the pressure on his arm slightly, then moved back along the bar.

Fred was trying to decide whether or not to have another beer. Christ, time could run out on Kurt if the old fart had another. Ginny offered to flip a coin for him.

"Heads you have another, tails you go, okay?"

Fred chuckled and nodded. They had been through this many times before, Kurt guessed.

"Heads it is, Fred. One more for the road."

Fred giggled and bashfully accepted the beer. How long would it take the old bastard to drink it?

Albert and his wife got up to leave, said their good nights and promised to be back tomorrow. Ginny cheerily waved good-bye while picking up their empty glasses and wiping down the table. When they reached the front door, they stopped and called for Ginny.

The three huddled at the door talking, while Albert's wife kept stealing glances in Kurt's direction. Ginny laughed and patted Albert on the back, giving his wife a good night peck.

"Get straight home you two." Ginny smiled.

Fred was sipping his beer. He wasn't in any hurry. Occasionally he glanced at Kurt, as if mildly concerned about this stranger in their bar. He was now in deep conversation with Ginny, who seemed to be appeasing him in her confident way. Fred excused himself and headed for the washroom.

"Do I have time for one more?" asked Kurt.

"All right, but that will have to be it. I've had a long day and we'll be closing now."

"Oh, I understand," Kurt said. "I've been on the road all day myself and know how you must feel. Actually, I'd been hoping to find a motel along here. Is there something up the way?"

"You heading north?"

"Yes. I'm on my way to Grand Forks, but won't get that far tonight."

"Yeah, well another ten miles or so, there's a motel just off the highway. This time of year there'll be a room for sure." She moved off to clean the bar and put away the empties.

"Must be kind of lonely, way out here. Where do you go for entertainment?"

"Hmpf. Entertainment? This is it for me. Work the bar day and night while my husband goes off fishing, or whatever."

"He can't very well be fishing at this hour, so is this the 'whatever?'"

She shrugged.

"I can't understand how any man could leave you alone for very long. He doesn't realize how lucky he is to have someone like you."

"You making a pass at me?"

"A guy would be crazy not to."

"You say a lotta nice things, mister, but I'm a married woman, so its just business with me."

"Then may I buy you a beer? I know you have to close, but surely you could treat yourself to having an after-work drink."

Fred came ambling back to his seat at the bar.

"That's good of you to offer, but after you boys finish up, I'm closing for the night."

She started tidying up, what little there was. She wiped the two tables, arranged the chairs neatly, and returned behind the bar to straighten out a few bottles. She stole a look at him and smiled.

"You're not from around here, are you?"

"No, I'm just passing through. I'm on the road a lot, kind of a traveling salesman I guess."

Fred had finally finished his beer. He seemed hesitant to leave but Ginny took him by the arm and escorted him to the door. He was unsteady, but with a last look at Kurt and a good night hug from Ginny, he left.

"You sure are a friendly sort," said Kurt.

"Guess I've been that way all my life. Don't take it the wrong way though. As I told you I'm married, and friendly is as far as it goes."

"You said there's never any time for fun. Surely you could use a little fooling around." He reached for her hand.

"Look, Roy's due back soon and we both don't want that to happen. You look like you could handle yourself, but you don't want to tangle with my husband."

"Why not show me that motel you mentioned?"

"I think it's time you left, mister. Nice as you are, I'm not interested."

A change came over him. His eyes turned cold and threatening.

Ginny moved away, behind the bar. He knew he had frightened her and decided to soften.

Kurt stood up slowly and grinned. "Look, I didn't mean to come on too strong. You just seemed like you might be receptive to...well you know, a guy gets awfully lonely on the road."

"I'm sorry if I gave you the wrong impression, but it's still no."

His look darkened. Again he abruptly changed, smiled, and shrugged.

"Well, guess I'll be on my way."

Relieved, she came out from the bar to lock the door behind him.

He took the gloves out of his jacket and put them on. This was the part he enjoyed. The anticipation of the event. He needed this right now. He started to turn towards her when the phone rang. She whirled, and in an instant was off to the bar.

"Go ahead, mister, I'll lock the door later."

He left, but was not happy. He sat in the Jeep for a few minutes, thinking about leaving, but the anger continued to build. He looked through the window. She was still on the phone.

9

Ginny was talking to Roy on the phone. The poker game with the boys would be a while yet. He asked her to cash out and put the money in the safe. She agreed, and afterwards was going straight to bed. She was too tired to wait up for him.

Ginny took the cash, put it all in a large envelope, and went to the back room. There was a small office at the rear of the building where they kept the safe and various odds and ends. She sat at the lone desk where the company's books were kept, feeling tired and lonely. The day had been long and draining, like so many lately.

Roy wasn't a bad husband, but recently he just didn't seem to have any time for her. They not only hadn't taken a holiday for years, he seldom helped out running the bar. She was putting in too many seven day weeks. Eight years ago at the tender age of nineteen, after a whirlwind two month courtship, they had married. It seemed so wonderful. He owned a bar and Ginny loved people. It would give her the opportunity to meet and serve the public. Most of the customers were local, who knew and liked Ginny. She'd be a great draw for the business.

She thought she heard a noise from the bar. It dawned on her she hadn't locked the front door. How stupid of her. That newcomer had been a little strange at the end of the evening. She waited but there were no further sounds from the front. Ginny decided to balance the cash in the morning.

Despite the long working hours, there were many redeeming factors to help her through the days. Fred was a good example. He was like a father to her, and always entertaining company. His stories were endless, sprinkled with large doses of humor, all in his inimitable style. He loved to reminisce about his early working days, like when he delivered telegrams by bicycle and earned the grand sum of three cents per delivery! Fred's insight into life and understanding people provided a wide source of knowledge for Ginny, who leaned on his every word.

Ginny bent over to open the safe and was fiddling with the combination. The light was so bad she always had a problem opening it. Another sound reached her. It was a slight creak, like a floor board announcing a foot step. Then another. Ginny didn't like this. Why hadn't she locked the damn door?

It was silent again. Maybe it was just her imagination. She waited a few seconds before continuing with the safe. Stay busy and try not to think what could be there. This safe never cooperates! Got the wrong numbers again. She whirled the dial back to zero and started over. What if someone is out there? There was nothing here to protect her.

The ladies room was off the hall leading back to the bar. Time to check this out. She got up and walked along the darkened hall. Nothing. She entered the washroom and turned on the light. After rinsing her hands and splashing cold water on her face, she felt better. Ginny returned to the office to finish up.

She'd have another go with the recalcitrant safe, although it was difficult having to crouch over to open the damn thing. How many times had she asked Roy to put the safe on a table and get proper lighting in here? Both of which would make this job a lot easier. Maybe next week.

A full moon shone brightly over the tree tops at the edge of their property. More light out there than in this office. The window offered a pleasant view of the country side. It reminded her of their honeymoon. Roy had suggested they rent a small trailer and just take off for parts unknown. There was no itinerary. It was marvelous. Just get up in the morning and decide what to do. Stay put and fish, which they both loved, or drive to another spot. The trip took them through northern Wisconsin, over into Canada, and back home.

Another sound broke her reverie. Yet she had just checked the hall and there was no one there. God, Roy wasn't coming home for a while yet and the only phone was at the bar. Why hadn't she mentioned the guy to Roy, that there might be a problem? More fidgeting with the safe.

She felt something behind her, stood and turned quickly. There he was, looming over her. She gasped and stepped back. The look in his eyes was absolutely terrifying. She tried to catch her breath.

"Look, I don't know what you want, but that was my husband on the phone. He'll be here any minute. It would be best if you didn't try anything."

He struck suddenly, taking her by the throat in a strangle hold. She was totally bewildered and stunned. She grabbed at his arms but couldn't budge them. Christ, he was strong.

He stared into her eyes, increasing the pressure. She squirmed and clawed at him. Fear turned to rage as she fought him. He held his arms out straight, maintaining his death hold.

She reached for the envelope of cash on top of the safe, grabbed it and swung at his head. It split open, coins raining on his shoulders, bills fluttering to the ground. He grinned and increased the pressure, pushing her back against the desk.

Ginny swept her hand across the top of the desk looking for something, anything, to help. Her hand closed on a letter opener. She swung wildly, driving the opener into his arm. He winced, releasing his strangle hold. She raised her arm to strike again but he stopped the thrust in midair. He held her wrist and increased the pressure. Eventually the opener fell harmlessly to the floor.

Ginny kicked him and made contact with his knee. It didn't seem to phase him. He then knocked her to the floor with a vicious blow to the head. She was dazed and barely conscious. Kurt knelt down and pinned her to the floor. He ripped off her blouse, took out his knife, and slowly went to work.

Nobody heard Ginny's screams. The pain was excruciating as he continued slicing and stabbing. Her young life had been full of unhappiness, now she just wanted to die. Eventually and mercifully she lost consciousness.

Kurt smiled.

10

He could hear the ringing, wondering what it was. It seemed so far away. Then he realized it was the phone. King and Kayla gazed at him, as if to say, do something.

"Wilson here."

"Frank, sorry to call you so late. It's Bob. I just this minute got back to the hotel and received your message. You said call at any hour, so I knew it must be important. Are you all right?"

"I'm fine, but have a hell of problem, Bob." Frank went over the series of events, starting with Petersen's phone call. "It's nine hours since the accident, and still no word from Sharin."

"This is terrible, Frank. What can I do to help?"

"I believe every minute counts in this investigation. Sharin may be in danger. The longer it takes to find her, the more I fear for her safety. I want the maximum number of officers assigned to this case with the best possible effort from that team. I need your influence with the Commissioner to ensure we get their top people on this case, now."

"It may take some time, Frank. You must appreciate the Commissioner's office is one hectic arena of non-stop activity. I'll call him first thing in the morning and get back to you."

"Bob, we're talking about a human life here. Everything that's happened so far indicates Sharin is in trouble. You must impress upon them the urgency of this matter, and the need for immediate action."

"I have no doubt the police are on top of this, but agree with you, a push from higher-up will help. I want you to hang in there and trust the system," replied Bob.

"Dammit, I don't have *time* to trust the system, Bob. I want to know that top people are involved immediately. The Commissioner has already talked to the Lieutenant in charge and is convinced they are moving ahead satisfactorily. That's not good enough for me. He needs another push."

"How did you get the Commissioner involved?"

"An old friend of mine in the Ontario Provincial Police knew him and called on my behalf," said Frank. "You would have much more clout. I'm sure he's been awakened for emergencies before, so why not now?"

"You always were a bear when you wanted action, and you haven't changed," said Bob. "All right, I'll call him now and hope this doesn't turn him off. There's always a slight risk to that. However, we have a good relationship and I'm sure he'll appreciate where you're coming from on this."

"Thanks for seeing it that way, Bob. We'll need more pressure from his office." They hung up.

Frank went into the kitchen to make a pot of coffee. He looked around the well lit, spacious room. The kids were so happy with their new home.

There was a center island which acted as a full service unit. Frank pushed it around as he waited for the coffee to brew. It glided smoothly and effortlessly over the ceramic tile floor. The kitchen was huge. He guessed it must be at least twenty by twenty. He paced it off, just to see how accurate he was. Seven full strides, twenty-one feet, by, slightly more than six, say nineteen feet. About the size of the kitchen, dining area, and living room of the first apartment he and Judy rented, he mused.

The coffee was ready so he chose a large mug, filling it to the brim. The dogs watched his every move. They were so attentive and curious. Judy and he had been here for only two days, yet the dogs seemed to have accepted both of them. Kayla was a little standoffish, whereas King wanted constant attention. Frank had not been around dogs for many years, so not only was he enjoying their company, it was a badly needed source of comfort. They were a tie to Sharin.

The phone rang.

"Hi, Dad, any news?"

"Not really, Eric, but I have talked to two friends who will be enlisting the help of the Commissioner. Other than that, I'm afraid, nothing. Did you get checked in?"

"Yeah. I feel so helpless here. Are the police leveling with us?"

"I don't know for sure. We've just got to believe Sharin's okay."

"I know. You'll call right away if you hear anything."

"I will."

"I'll be leaving here at six tomorrow morning, getting into the Cities at seven-thirty. I'll take a taxi and should be home by nine."

"No, I'll meet you at the airport," said Frank. "Where are the keys to the Land Rover?"

"Are you sure? It's awfully late and you'll get only a couple of hours sleep."

"Nonsense, I won't have it any other way. We can go directly to St Cloud to see Petersen."

"Has that been arranged?"

"Not yet. I'll be talking to him soon, or first thing in the morning."

"Good. I really appreciate that, Dad. There's an extra set of keys in the kitchen. They're in the top drawer of the desk by the phone."

"Right. Now, as you said, let's see if we can manage a couple of hours rest. See you soon."

Frank had just hung up when the phone rang again. It was Petersen. "I assume you've had no word from Sharin or anyone."

"No, not a thing. Lieutenant, this is becoming more desperate. It's been nine hours since Sharin's disappearance. By now you must have a new plan of action."

"We do, Mr Wilson, however, I'm only at liberty to divulge so much. You'll have to trust me on this. Believe me, it's in everybody's best interest to proceed this way."

"I don't like being kept in the dark, Petersen. This is my daughter we're talking about."

"I understand, sir, and know this is not easy. I'll be able to give you more details after the forensic and traffic specialists have completed their work. Incidentally, I've been given the highest priority on this investigation. This came down from the Commissioner himself. You must be very persuasive or have a lot of well connected friends."

"I appreciate that, Lieutenant. I just don't like the fact there's still no news."

"Neither do I. We'll bring you up to speed tomorrow morning. I guess that's later this morning. Do you know when Mr Jensen is arriving?"

"Yes, I just finished talking to him. He'll be arriving here at seven-thirty and I'm going to meet him at the airport. We'll want to see you as soon as possible."

"With that arrival time, you could probably be in our St Cloud office by ten o'clock. Why don't we set it up that way? I'll be here regardless, but the earlier the better."

Suddenly, everything was dead quiet. There would be no more phone calls unless he heard from Sharin. The hall clock chimed two A.M. He would have to be up at five to meet Eric's flight.

11

Sharin heard the truck in the driveway. She had managed to stay awake but had nodded off occasionally. The sound of his footsteps echoed down the hall. The bedroom door opened and she shut her eyes quickly. She could feel him moving across the room. He sat down on the edge of the bed and she started. She stared at him in total fear.

"I'm going to remove the tape, but first I want you to know the rules. Do you understand?"

She nodded. What else could she do?

"I meant to kill you this afternoon, but obviously that didn't work. I'm not sure where this is going. After I remove the tape from your mouth, if you make any noise, you die instantly. Do you understand?"

Again Sharin nodded.

"This always hurts a little, but I'm sure you won't mind."

He worked a small piece of tape loose at her mouth and with one swift jerk, removed it. She took a deep breath.

"I'm going to remove all the tape now. Don't try anything foolish."

"I won't," she croaked. It didn't come out very well.

"I brought your dress, the one that was in the car. You may freshen up and change clothes if you wish. The bathroom is directly opposite this room. Leave the door ajar. I don't want you trying anything funny. If you do, you die. It's really immaterial to me." He flashed a slow, lazy smile.

Sharin slowly sat up, rubbing her ankles and wrists.

"I won't do anything silly."

She was slightly dizzy but felt she would be able to stand up. After a brief rest she made her way carefully across the room and into the bathroom. As instructed she left the door partly open and began washing her hands and face. She would have loved to take a bath, but wasn't going to undress with this nut around. She had to stall for time, to begin to think.

"I'd like to shampoo my hair. Is that okay?"

"Yeah, that's fine."

The sound of his voice made it seem as though he was in the same room.

It startled her. The fear returned. She forced herself to get busy. She inspected herself. No cuts, other than the one on her face, which appeared to be superficial and was dressed. The bruises would start tomorrow and from the several sore spots, she was going to have a few beauties.

Sharin had a good look at the room. There was one window above the bath tub, but it was quite small. She could probably get through but it would be a tight fit, and if she was in a hurry, it might delay her long enough to ruin an escape. In case she needed it as a last resort, she looked out to see how far off the ground they were. It was about a three or four foot drop. She decided to see if there was anything in the cabinet above the sink which could prove useful to her. It was encouraging to be planning and thinking.

During the several hours lying alone in bed, Sharin had tried to formulate her plan of survival. As tired as she was, the exercise was a must. Firstly, to stay awake, and secondly, if there was going to be any chance of getting away from this maniac, she had to be well prepared.

She had been able to work the tape a little looser on her wrists but not enough to free her hands. It would have to be cut. If there was a razor in the cabinet, it might be the first step to getting out of here.

She looked at the cabinet. It was metal with a simple latch. It might make a noise when being opened so she would have to be very careful. Where was he? The last time he had talked he seemed so close.

How to cover the sound of opening the cabinet? She could ask him for a hair dryer.

"Are you there?"

"Right here."

He must be standing right outside the door.

"Do you have a hair dryer?"

"No. Use a towel."

So much for that. She would have to chance it. The door was actually a mirror in a metal frame. She slipped the latch and using both hands, slowly opened the cabinet. Luckily there was no sound. There was the usual selection of deodorant, aspirin, bandaids, some cotton batten, two combs, hair spray, but no shaving items. However, there was a nail clipper. She took it out and gently closed the cabinet.

Sharin dropped the nail clipper inside her under-pants. She picked up the towel and continued drying herself. She glanced at the mirror. He was staring at her! How long had he been there? She kept drying her hair, but fumbled the towel and almost dropped it.

"Kind of difficult without a dryer," she said as nonchalantly as she could muster. There was no reaction.

"Don't be too much longer." He turned away.

Her heart was pounding. She finished drying her hair, and started to put on her dress. She was trembling. Her hands shook so much she only barely managed to get into the dress. There was no sign of her panty-hose or shoes. Sharin felt degraded and depressed, wearing this new dress for the first time in these conditions. However, the sheer terror of her situation made that seem insignificant. The mere actions of being up and about, washing her hair, and generally acting like a human being, helped produce a faint ray of hope. At least some courage began to surface.

He was standing in the hall when she came out of the bathroom. He took her by the arm, guiding her to the first door on the left, which turned out to be the kitchen. Directly opposite she could see the living room, with a large fireplace against the far wall.

The kitchen itself had a stove and fridge on one side, counter and sink on the other, and a small area at the far end with a table and four chairs. There was one window, again covered with drawn curtains. She could tell it was dark outside.

"Sit at the table. I have some soup for you."

It was plain tomato soup from a can, but it tasted like the finest bowl of soup she had enjoyed in ages. There were two slices of whole wheat bread on a side plate. She demolished it all.

He was drinking a beer, not saying very much.

"Like another bowl of soup?"

"Yes, please."

He poured her a second bowl and brought two more slices of bread. It didn't take long for it all to disappear. She felt much better with some of her strength returning, which was going to be badly needed.

"What time is it?"

"Nearly three o'clock," said Kurt, checking his watch.

"What's your name?" she asked.

He grunted. "It's Kurt."

"Are you going to tell me what is happening and why I'm here?"

Kurt stood up slowly and started cleaning up.

"How was the soup? Was that enough for now or would you like something else?"

She realized where he was coming from. Deflecting conversation when it suited him. If indeed he was a psycho, he was probably fantasizing about her and she would have to be careful to continue the game on his terms.

"I've had plenty to eat for now, thank you," she answered. "That really hit the spot."

"Well I guess that's it for tonight. I'm rather bushed. After all, it's been a long day. We'll talk tomorrow. Don't even think of trying anything. You wouldn't enjoy the consequences of any such action, although I might."

He led her to the bedroom and told her to lie down. He strapped her to the bed at the shoulders then used the tape to secure her arms and legs. Although her arms were bound together at the wrists, at least they were on top of the strap holding her to the bed. This would make it easier to cut the tape with the nail clipper.

"I'm going to leave the tape off your mouth. We're isolated here so no one will hear if you cry out. However, don't try it. I'm a very light sleeper and right next door."

He smiled, then left the room.

It was so depressing to be tied up again, however she had succeeded in completing step one, getting back to the bedroom with the nail clipper in her possession. She would have to wait for him to leave before attempting to cut herself free. It would serve no purpose to be rid of the tape with him still in the house. At least there was a ray of hope.

Sharin's thoughts turned to her baby, Eric, and her parents. Would she ever see them again? She had to believe. Hopefully sleep would come tonight.

12

The report from Lieutenant Callahan was on Jack's desk when he arrived Monday morning. He and Brett were old friends. They had joined the force together and were partners on patrol duty for three years in the Cities. However, Brett had developed a dislike for Minnesota winters and moved to L.A. They had kept in touch, so Jack was pleased to see his pal's name on the report.

It was now eight-thirty, six-thirty in L.A., a good time to reach Brett at home. He dialed his number. They caught up on each other and reviewed the notes on Jensen. The L.A. Detective had been impressed with Jensen and felt he would not have been involved in any foul play. Jack gave Brett a full rundown on the accident and findings to date. They promised to stay in touch.

Frank and Eric arrived at nine-thirty. Petersen greeted them and after the introductions, ordered coffee, gratefully accepted by both. Jack trusted Brett's judgement but would make his own conclusions about Jensen.

"I know how difficult this must be for you, but I want you to know all available resources are being employed to find Mrs Jensen. With your help, Mr Wilson, I've been authorized to exceed the budget and manpower normally used for this type of investigation. We have unlimited personnel and materials at our disposal."

Frank nodded. "Lieutenant, Sharin's been missing for too long. Just what is happening here?"

Petersen took the time to carefully review the investigation with them. He purposely held back his own thoughts and fears about a possible abduction or worse.

"The first results from traffic and forensics are due this morning. I'll be meeting with both officers right after talking to you. We've issued a state wide alert, providing full details of the accident as well as the picture of Mrs Jensen we received from you. We'll continue to up-date them with new findings. The news media has been advised with a missing person report.

Bulletins on radio and tv will be aired this morning, as well as reports in the local newspapers."

Eric leaned forward. "Lieutenant, last night you told my father-in-law there may have been another vehicle involved. Was this a hit and run?"

"We're reasonably certain there was contact with another vehicle but it's too early to determine how it was involved. More on that will be available to me later this morning. We're also running down hospitals, taxis, and local businesses, for any information that may help."

"Lieutenant, we haven't heard from Sharin since five o'clock yesterday. There's more to this than just a car accident," said Eric.

"Yes, that's true. However, at this moment I need the traffic and forensic reports before reaching any further conclusions. They're meeting with me right after our talk. We have the Jaguar in our compound and both teams of specialists have been over the car thoroughly. Additionally, all on-scene information has been photographed and detailed. This has been evaluated and will be presented this morning."

"Wait a minute," said Eric. "If there was another car involved, surely they would have stayed to help Sharin or at the least, reported the accident to the police, unless it was a hit and run. You're saying you haven't heard from anyone?"

"At this point we haven't."

"Then what the hell are we supposed to assume?"

"We'll know a lot more shortly. Look, I understand this is difficult, but you'll just have to hang in with us for a little longer. It appears your wife was not seriously injured in the accident itself. Although the exterior was badly damaged, the steel framing that supports the roof was intact, and thus the interior was protected. An extremely well made vehicle. No doubt that saved your wife."

"I get the feeling you're not telling us everything, Lieutenant," Frank persisted. "When do you start being totally candid?"

"I'll be in a much better position after the preliminary meeting with traffic and forensics. You'll have to trust me on this. I believe you were a highly ranked politician in Canada, Mr Wilson. Is that correct?"

"Yes. Why do you ask?"

"If an abduction has taken place, a request for a ransom would soon follow. Would anyone here know that Mrs Jensen is your daughter?"

"I guess that's a possibility, but doubt there would be any publicity about that here," said Frank.

"Mr Jensen, are you a wealthy man?"

"Not really. We're enjoying a comfortable life style, but that's all. So you're admitting this may be a kidnapping."

"It's certainly one possibility, but only one. Can you think of anyone who might want to harm your wife?" asked Jack. "Either from your work or social contacts?"

"None that I can think of."

"You run your own business. Any bad feelings amongst your employees? Any recent firings?"

Eric thought before answering. "Really, Lieutenant, we just don't have any enemies."

"How is your marriage? Any quarrels, serious arguments lately?"

"Look, I know you're only doing your job, but the answer is no. Like any couple, we've had a few disagreements, but ours is a solid marriage. It's been even better lately with the pregnancy and ..." Eric faltered.

"I don't mean to upset you, but there are several possibilities and we must look into all of them. You both could use some rest. Why don't you return home in case you hear any news about Mrs Jensen. It's important that you be available. I'll call you when I'm finished with the specialists."

Petersen saw Frank and Eric to the door, reassuring them he would be in touch soon.

Watson was waving at Petersen.

"Lieutenant, we have a homicide."

13

Petersen sent two homicide detectives to Crosslake to look into last night's murder. This could involve several detectives. He was going to run out of officers at this rate.

Special Agent David Folk of the Bureau of Criminal Apprehension, arrived at noon for their meeting. Patrolman Brooker from traffic, would be a little late. Jack had worked with David many times and highly respected this diminutive character, known for his talent and brains. He couldn't have been more than five foot six, one hundred and thirty pounds soaking wet, but he was a dynamo. David never seemed to run out of energy, nor waste any time. As a B.C.A. agent he had been assigned to the St Cloud Division for the last three years.

"You tell me you have a female driver, I tell you, you have a problem. Those footprints at the scene? It's a guy. The shoe size was twelve. He came down the hill, took your female driver, and carted her away. That's my conclusion. We have impressions by the Jaguar and at the road side. They're the same. The prints lead to the car and back up the hill. Here's the photos."

Jack examined them with David, who pointed out the different locations.

"Suppose this guy just happens by after the fact," said Jack. "He sees the wreck and as a good Samaritan goes to rescue her. She's already out of the car and gone for help, because we don't know when he gets there."

"So now you have a lady getting out of a damaged car, bleeding, and walking away. Where are her footprints? Is she so light she floats up the hill? There is nothing, *nada*, to indicate anyone else walked up and down this hill. We went over the area surrounding the car with a microscope. You have only one person, Jack, and that's this big guy."

"Okay. So he helps her out of the car and carries her to safety. Why is that a problem?" said Jack, knowing the answer before David replied. He just had to play it through.

"Right, only they don't call in, for what, eighteen hours now. So tell me, you think there off on a little tryst? Spare me, Jack."

"We still don't know this is the same guy who actually forced her off the road, if that's where we're going with this," Jack persisted.

"Traffic says there's another vehicle," said David. "I'll bet it's his. Brooker has tire impressions which don't match the Jaguar. He'll explain when he gets here. Where is he anyway?"

"He was running a little behind, but will be here soon. We know there's a second set of tire marks. Maybe there's a third vehicle. Then we'd have a hit and run, and a good guy."

"*Oy vey*," groaned David. "First we have a woman floating in space, now we have some fellow arriving on the scene, but we don't know how? You wait. Traffic will have proof of contact, and only one vehicle. I'm willing to bet those footsteps lead right to that vehicle."

"I didn't see any indication of tire impressions in your photos at road side."

"You didn't ask, or look close enough. See this last shot. Here are the footprints in the gravel and what do we have right next door? Now, that's from a tire that doesn't belong to the Jaguar. It's about thirty to forty feet behind the skid marks from the Jaguar, at the precise point it left the road. I say it's the other vehicle, the very one that pushed your missing lady off the road. Are we closer to putting this puzzle together, Mr Moriarty?"

Jack smiled. This was the usual banter between him and David. They respected each other and knew where they were coming from.

"I still want to see what traffic has to offer. Speak of the devil, here's Brooker himself."

Ed Brooker was as big as they come. Two hundred and sixty pounds were well proportioned over his six foot five inch frame. It was amusing seeing David and Ed together, as they each made the other seem even bigger and smaller than they actually were. Ed shook hands and apologized for being late. He was used to it. He was always late. What did his wife say? 'Ed will be late for his own funeral.'

He had completed his work from the scene, and on the Jaguar, which was now at their compound.

"The Jag was definitely hit from behind, several times. We're certain this caused the accident. The markings at road side clearly prove impact with the Jag, just several feet from where it flipped over and down the hill. We have fragments of rear lights at road side. They're from the Jag. There's an extra set of tire impressions at the point of collision and we're tracing them now."

"Any sign of other vehicles at the scene, Ed?" asked Jack.

"No. We have the Jag and one other."

David smiled and shrugged. "We had to be told?"

Ed looked puzzled.

"It's just 'Mr Figure It' bragging again," said Jack. "What else have you got, Ed?"

"The type of damage to the back of the Jag was fairly conclusive. It was struck by a vehicle with a grill like surface of considerable size. We originally thought it had to be a large truck with a squared off grill, or a bus. That doesn't match with the findings about the tires. It's probably a standard four wheel drive, van, or small truck. We've ruled out a van because it doesn't fit with the damage to the Jag. However, a pickup truck, or any vehicle with Bush Bars would be consistent with our findings."

"You said you were running the tires. Do you have any other ID's to help us."

"Yup. There's some paint smears. As you know, there's nothing better to help identify a vehicle. Those are being run now."

"When will we have some answers?" asked Jack.

"Later today. I'll get back to you soon. I understand there's some outside pressure on this one, Lieutenant. Am I right?"

"You are, but keep it to yourself. You know that's not for publication. We want that trace today. Do whatever it takes to ensure that, Ed."

"10-4, Lieutenant. You okay with this, David?" asked Brooker.

"Absolutely. You've just confirmed my own conclusions. Take a look at this photo. These footprints in the gravel are the same as those found by the Jaguar. See the tire impressions right next to that last set of prints? I say this is the same guy who pulled your missing person out of the car and then returned to his own vehicle, a truck or whatever it turns out to be."

"Certainly looks that way," said Brooker, making his way out of the office. "I'll be back to you this afternoon, Lieutenant."

"Thanks, Ed."

David looked at Petersen. "Where's the pressure coming from, Jack?"

"The missing person, a Mrs Jensen, is the daughter of a retired politician from Canada. Apparently he's well connected and had people contact Commissioner Boyle, who is now following the case. He's given me authority to use all the manpower and resources I need. I guess this has international over-tones and he wants it sewn up quickly."

"Sounds ripe for a kidnaping, but something is out of whack," said David.

"If it's an abduction, there's still time to hear from the suspect, David. It's not twenty-four hours yet, which fits the normal profile."

"True, Jack, but something else puzzles me. You have a guy in a truck who wants to nab this woman. Yet he smashes into the back of her car and sends her off the road down a steep hill. He's lucky she's alive. Why wouldn't he just cut her off and make her stop. He could then force her into his truck and be away."

"I don't know, David. Maybe he'd been drinking and screwed up by running into her. Maybe he's just a whacko who picked out a nice new Jaguar and decided to cream her. The fact is, we don't have enough yet to know. If another day goes by, we'll turn this over to homicide."

"Somehow, Jack, that wouldn't surprise me."

Jack's secretary, Tracy, was at the door.

"Detective Sean Murphy on the phone, Lieutenant. Do you want to take it? He's on line three."

"Yeah."

"Jack, I have to go. Call me if you need anything."

"Thanks, David. Talk to you later."

He picked up line three.

"Sean, what's happening?"

"I'm at Roy's Place, a small bar just south of Crosslake. We have a murder victim, Ginny Brewer. Young woman in her twenties. Think you should get up here, Lieutenant."

"What have you got so far?"

"There's a Sheriff Sven Larsen here who was with the husband when they found the body. He's got things under control. Wait till you see this guy, Jack. They say he's fifty, but looks like he could suit up for the Vikes at linebacker tomorrow. The husband's a real arrogant SOB and isn't too talkative. We also have some witnesses. One of them, Fred Pearce, showed up this afternoon for his usual midday snort, and found us here. Told us some stranger came in around closing time last night to have a few beers," said Sean.

"What time was that?" asked Jack.

"It was close to midnight. There was him, a married couple, Ginny, and this new guy. The couple, Albert and Jan, were first to go, then Fred, who left while the stranger was still at the bar. Said he was a big, emphasis on big, dude. He's been very cooperative, not like the husband."

"What about the other couple?" asked Jack.

"Someone's bringing them over right now. The Sheriff said he'd never seen anything as brutal. It isn't pretty, Jack. When will we see you?"

"I'll be there within the hour."

14

The late afternoon air had a bite to it. With the days getting shorter, you knew winter was not far away. Fall eventually reached a stage where the bright, crisp days began to cool to a point of no return. The temperature just kept dropping, a little more with each passing day, and inevitably the brilliant leaves would be gone with snow following soon after.

There were still a few Sundays left for touch football, but not many. Jack could manage only one sport at a time, what with his job and wife. He did his best to keep to a regular exercise routine, with a morning run of three to five miles at least five days a week. Coupled with occasional games of fastball in the summer, touch football in the fall, and swimming in the winter, he managed to stay fit.

Sean Murphy's car was parked in front of the bar beside the Sheriff's cruiser and a pickup truck. The crime scene tape was already in place. He found Sean with the local Sheriff and two other men in a heated discussion. Sean made the introductions to Sheriff Sven Larsen, Roy Brewer, the victim's husband, and Fred Pearce, their key witness.

The Sheriff was everything Sean had described, appearing much younger than his fifty years and built like a Mack truck. In fact Sven, who could pass for thirty, packed two hundred and twenty pounds of granite on his six-two frame. As Sean had said, you could easily imagine him at a Vikes training camp. He had been born in Sweden, but at the age of two, had emigrated to Minnesota with his family. He sported a full head of blond hair, attesting to his ancestry.

Jack offered his condolences to the husband, noting his belligerent attitude. Losing your wife tragically would understandably leave anyone despondent, but not necessarily contrary, as he was. Jack sensed it was more than likely the norm for this man.

"Is this the head guy who's supposed to solve this? How can a goddamned murder like this take place here? What the hell are you going to do about it?" Roy glared at Jack.

"Now hold on, Roy," the Sheriff interjected. "I know you're upset, but that attitude is not going to get us anywhere. The Lieutenant's here to help us. Besides it's his case."

"I know I shoulda been around more often, Sven, but a guy plays poker with the boys and his wife gets fucking killed? Is that supposed to happen?"

"Of course not, Roy. I don't think this was planned on your poker night. It looks like a random killing."

"Still, if I had been here..."

"I'd like to go over this, initially with you, Sheriff, and later with the witnesses," Jack said to move things along.

With that Roy huffily said he was going into town. Jack looked at Larsen who nodded.

"I know what you're thinking, Lieutenant, but he's clear. Roy was with me last night at a poker party. He had too much to drink so I drove him home. When we got here, he insisted I come in for a night cap. That's when we found Ginny."

"You know the drill, Sven, the husband's the first suspect, and this guy sure looks big and mean enough."

"He's all of that, Lieutenant, but in his own way he loved Ginny. Anyway we know he didn't do it for more than one reason. First of all he was with me. Secondly, wait till we give you the details. Now, Fred who was here last night, said there was a stranger who was still in the bar when he left."

"Sven, tell me what you found when you arrived," said Jack.

"I've never seen anything like this in my thirty years on the force. The door wasn't locked and the light was on, which Roy thought was unusual at three in the morning. We went to the bar to get a drink and Roy noticed the light in the office at the back was also on. Now, this was strange." Sven shifted his feet.

"We went back, and there was Ginny in a pool of blood. I had to grab Roy and turn him around. I forced him back to the bar. In addition to the blood there was money all over the floor, coins and bills. Her body, Lieutenant, had been hacked and stabbed, over and over again. There was a look of sheer terror and agony on her face. This is one cruel and sadistic bastard. If I ever get my hands on him..." Sven paused before continuing.

"Roy was going ballistic. He wanted to see Ginny. I can handle him, so I forced him outside into my cruiser. I realized we had contaminated the crime scene by walking back through the bar, but I just couldn't let Roy see her that way. I called the ambulance first, in case she had a chance, but I knew it was hopeless. The ambulance got here in twenty minutes. We had them use the back door, while my officer and I sealed off the area. They immediately called the coroner who pronounced her dead."

"What was the time of death?" asked Jack.

"Had to be after midnight. You know they can't be too definite about the time, but Fred had left before midnight, and we got here around three.".

"Did you send the body to our Forensics Unit in St Paul?"

"Yeah, once forensics was through their work."

"Sheriff, where was the poker game in relation to the bar?"

"We were at Stan Ball's house, a twenty minute drive west of here. We started with six guys, a little after nine o'clock. George Malin left around midnight, and the rest of us played till about two-thirty. We broke it off, then I drove Roy home."

"And Roy never left you for any period of time all night?" asked Jack.

The Sheriff shook his head. "Not only that, the same group of us, more or less, have had this game every Monday night for years. Nobody gets hurt too much so it's just a friendly get together. Most of the time it's at Stan's house because he likes it that way. No, Roy couldn't have done it, Lieutenant. It's not only me to back that up, but the other four guys with us, as well as Stan's wife. Besides, there's no way he could have done that to Ginny."

"You said a guy was in the bar late last night. Was anybody else around?"

"Yeah. Fred said Albert and Jan, came in for a beer around eleven-thirty. We have their report at the office. Then there was this newcomer who was at the bar when he left. We'll want to go easy with Fred. He knew Ginny all her life and is having a hard time with this. He came here everyday, not only for a beer, but to see Ginny. It's hard to tell, but he's close to eighty. Nobody seems to know his real age. Fred is a friend of everyone in town, but his special place was here."

Fred had been sitting in Sven's cruiser, appearing sad and rather sheepish. He was a kindly looking gentleman with a frail build. Jack went over to greet him and found he was amazingly strong with a steely, firm handshake. He certainly didn't look or act like an octogenarian.

"I'm sorry about your friend, Ginny. You may be able to help us a great deal with a description of the man at the bar last night. What can you tell me about him?"

He seemed on the verge of tears at the mention of her name, but he soon braced himself and collected his thoughts. When he spoke he had a high pitched voice that quavered, but his speech was precise and clear.

"This man came in pretty late last night. Must have been close to eleven. I know because Ginny usually sends me home around that time. He seemed very polite. He had a couple of beers, I think. Right after that, Albert and his wife came in and sat at one of the tables. Jan doesn't like sitting at the bar."

"What happened after that, Fred?"

"Well I think it was almost time for me to go, because Ginny said she'd flip a coin to see if I was to have one more beer. It was something we did all the time. Sometimes I win, sometimes I lose. This time I won, so she brought me another one. Then Albert and Jan got up to leave, and I noticed they talked to Ginny for a while at the door."

"Did you talk to the newcomer at the bar?"

"No. He sat at the far end from me and I just never got around to it. It seemed like he didn't want any company, other than talking to Ginny. You know what I mean."

"I think I do, Fred."

"Anyway, Ginny comes back and we continue talking. She tells me Jan was concerned about this new fellow, and wanted to know if they should stay till he left. She just laughed, saying there was nothing to worry about." Fred started to break down again.

Jack waited patiently and placed his hand on the old man's shoulder. He was virtually skin and bone and was shaking. Fred composed himself once again, apologizing. Jack assured him there was no need.

"Did you leave shortly after, Fred?"

"First, I finished my beer. Ginny said she had talked to this man a few times and he was charming and polite. She said Roy was due home soon anyway and there would be no problem, so I left."

"Fred, you could be a big help providing us with a description of this man. We have officers in Brainerd who can produce likenesses on a computer and we need your input. The sooner we do this the better. Would you go there now, to get this started?"

"I'll gladly take him down there for you, Lieutenant," said Sven.

Jack nodded. "What about the other couple, Sheriff? Could they describe him as well?"

"Their statements indicated neither of them got a good look at him.

They have a fair idea of his size, but no facial features. They also noticed his vehicle when they left. That's in the report."

"Sean, while forensics are finishing up why don't you review their statements and interview them again?"

"Will do, Lieutenant. I'll be back in a couple of hours."

"Thanks for your help, Sven. Have Brainerd send that composite to us ASAP. And thanks again, Fred. We'll be in touch."

Jack's beeper indicated he had a call.

"Watson here, Lieutenant. We've got our first break in the Jensen case. Seems a woman stopped at a local store just where the Waverley road starts. The store owner remembered her from this brand new foreign car. He's curious, so goes out to take a closer look at the car. As the woman drives away some guy across the road gets into a shiny Jeep with all kinds of 'stuff' around it, and drives off in the same direction."

"I'll be back within the hour," said Jack, his pulse quickening.

15

The phone call came at five in the morning, which was fine as his exercise routine always started early. It would be a pleasure to take care of William. He planned to be at his hotel around eight. There would be plenty of activity at that time, thus minimizing the chances of being noticed.

He would have to take two buses which would give him time to study the working fucks. Looking at the passing traffic and people watching were pet hobbies and this was a comfortable way of doing just that. He silently observed all the assholes on the bus.

The two young women opposite were a classic example. They thought they were so high and mighty in their tight fitting, little office clothes. He imagined doing them, mentally, then finishing them off while enjoying the look of fear in their eyes as he was slitting their fucking, pathetic throats.

Then there was the nerd in front of him with his baseball hat on backwards. He'd fix him. Just take his head and twist it right around while it was still on his neck. The hat would be on correctly but his head would be facing the wrong way. He chuckled.

The jerk who thought he was a big business executive, was the worst on the bus. He sat there with a brief case on his lap making notes with a Mont Blanc pen. He'd like to take his pen and shove it right up his ass. How would he like that, the stupid fuck?

The first ride took about twenty minutes, with a short wait for bus number two. The second trip was only ten minutes and he arrived within a block of the hotel.

As he expected there was a hustle in the lobby with all the stupid, working fucks going every which way. He took the elevator to the eleventh floor. A bellman passed him with a cart full of luggage. He waited till the bellman had entered the elevator, then knocked on the door. He thought William would still be in bed, and hoped he was alone. If not he would easily deal with both of them.

"Who is it?" a sleepy voice asked.

"It's just me. I have a gift for you."

"Oh, all right. Give me a minute," William muttered.

The door opened and William, clad only in a robe, greeted his visitor, admitting him to his room. It happened instantly. He drove his fist into William's solar plexus, doubling him over. He then grabbed his head and in one swift motion, calmly broke his neck. He lifted the limp body and flopped him on the bed. William was still breathing. He undid the robe and took out his knife, which was razor sharp. Slowly the slicing began, then he slit his throat from ear to ear. William's blood spilled freely over the white sheets.

He went into the bathroom and wiped down the knife, then left the room and rode the elevator to the lobby. He took a morning paper from the front desk, before casually strolling through the lobby out of the hotel, having taken less than ten minutes for the entire operation.

Walking on the busy sidewalk in morning rush hour, he realized it was time for breakfast. He didn't want to remain in the vicinity of the hotel so he decided to take the first bus and look for a restaurant in the area where he would transfer. The ten minute ride was boring as there were fewer passengers traveling away from the city at this time of day.

It took some time to find a place, but eventually he spotted a breakfast diner to his liking. He entered and ordered pancakes, sausages, and a pot of coffee. After the pleasant breakfast and a lingering read of the newspaper, he returned to the bus stop for the remainder of his trip home.

The ride was relaxing. Still fewer passengers but he was enjoying the passing scenery and continued his people watching, playing his imaginary games with those available. It was some time before he realized another passenger was continually staring at him. He paid little heed.

They arrived at his stop and he stood up to leave. As the doors opened and he left the bus, he noticed the same man was still looking at him. Why was his face familiar?

He had a three block walk to his house and was halfway there when it suddenly dawned on him. He remembered where he had seen the man who was on the bus. It was in the hotel this morning.

It was the bellman.

16

The hotel had seen better days. It was in a rough part of town, hardly a fashionable district. The homeless and street characters in the area spoke to the poor conditions of the neighborhood. One was marginally safe in this area in the daytime. You didn't even think of coming here after dark.

Callahan had received the call shortly after ten-thirty. One of the chamber maids had discovered the body of a white male awash in its own blood, in a room on the eleventh floor, and promptly threw up her breakfast. That should make the crime scene even more delightful.

He and Bob Dixon, his regular partner, arrived at the hotel with eight other officers, and were immediately escorted to the eleventh floor. The on-duty security officer had been on the job for only two weeks. He had not been through a homicide before and was understandably nervous and shaken. Apparently he was only fifty-four, but looked closer to seventy. Like the hotel he had seen better days. His heavy perspiration, which was rank, mixed with the odorous smell of death emanating from the room.

They had identified the victim from his wallet which had been left on the bed side dresser, along with his watch and an expensive looking ring. Obviously robbery was not a motive. His name was William Kyle of Clearwater, Minnesota. Brett made a note to contact Jack as Clearwater was near St Cloud.

The body had been cut in several places, including the neck. Not only was the bed drenched in blood, a copious quantity had dripped on the floor. The murderer had inflicted much more than death. It was bestial. Callahan had the officers seal off the room which was located at the end of the hall. He also ordered the three closest rooms and twenty feet of hallway designated as the crime scene, with the placing of the usual yellow tape.

"Have a look in the adjoining rooms while the rest of the officers seal off the hotel, and start a search in case our suspect is still around."

He was assured by security that no one had been in the room other than the chambermaid. She was now downstairs in an office with a nurse, who had just happened to be checking in at the time the body was found.

He and Dixon asked to be shown to the office to interview the chambermaid. Additionally they would want to talk to front desk personnel on duty, as well as all other hotel staff, any service people, and guests. Callahan asked for a list of all guests, either still registered or those who had recently checked out.

"The Manager may not like all this," the Security Guard ventured.

"Let's find the chamber maid," said Callahan, ignoring the remark. He had been through similar situations before with businesses in this district. In areas where homicides are not a rarity, management usually cooperates in the early going, wanting to help expedite the investigation and get back to everyday routine as quickly as possible. Being so new to the hotel, the security officer was probably not aware of that.

Brett Callahan was not a small man, with a muscular two hundred pounds on a five foot eleven frame, but he felt tiny compared to Millie, the chamber maid. She was, without a doubt, the largest female he had ever met. Millie, who was black, must have weighed three hundred and fifty pounds and was regarded by the entire hotel staff as the most thoughtful and jovial person amongst them. If there had been a Miss or Mister Congeniality award available, all agreed Millie would win hands down.

Today however, that sunny disposition had been extremely shaken with her witnessing of the ghastly homicide scene in the room. The nurse had done her best in attempting to calm Millie, who was just now beginning to regain some composure. Brett knew he would have to take this slowly. The security officer introduced everyone. The nurse acknowledged that Millie should be all right now and excused herself.

"I know how difficult this must be for you, Millie, but we have to ask you some questions and since time is crucial to us, we have to start now. Are you up to helping us?"

Millie nodded, gingerly taking another sip of tea. Her two hands engulfed the tea cup, making it look like a miniature from a kid's doll house.

She had arrived at the hotel shortly before her shift time of eight o'clock. After the usual joking and banter with some of the staff, Millie went to the staff room to change, then collected her trolley and took the service elevator to the eleventh floor, where she was starting.

It was her habit to begin in the middle of the floor and work towards the ends. Her list indicated which rooms were occupied or vacant. A cursory check of empty rooms was included in her duties. Those with 'Do Not

Disturb' signs were of course left till later and others were attended to as available. She didn't reach the end room till shortly after ten, when she entered and discovered the body. The carnage and amount of blood was something she had never seen before, and never wanted to again.

Under Brett's gentle urging Millie recounted her moves in the room, saying she only walked a couple of feet before embarrassingly vomiting, then leaving. She used the phone in the next room, which was vacant, to call security.

"So you didn't touch or move anything in the room, just turned and left."

"That's right, Detective. I wasn't in the room longer than but half a minute, and that was too long."

"No one else was in the room."

"Not that I saw. Lord, thank God for that. I sure wouldn't want to meet the person who could do something like that."

"Now Millie, you were on the eleventh floor for almost two hours before making the discovery. Did you see anyone else during that time?"

"Uh huh. I think there was only one couple – no there was also a man I saw just when I came out on the floor."

"Let's take them one at a time. Who did you see first?"

"Well, the service elevators are just off the hallway. When you come out the door, it's right opposite the bank of elevators used by the guests. Just as I came out there was a man getting on the elevator. I remember him well because he was so tall. Lordy, don't tell me...could that have been the murderer?"

"We don't that yet, Millie. Did you get a look at his face?"

"Only a quick glance. He had turned to push his floor button and then the doors started closing."

"Was that shortly after eight o'clock, maybe eight-fifteen or so?" asked Jack.

"No later than that. I'm on the job right on time most everyday."

"Tell me about the couple."

"That was about an hour later. I'm in and out of rooms you understand, so I don't see everybody coming and going off the floor. They were coming from the other end towards the elevators. I guess they were sixty or so. I know she was very tiny. I notice women like that. He was sort of average size."

"Millie, I want you to work with one of our artists to produce a likeness of the first man. It would have to be done at the station where they have access to our computers. We'll have an officer take you there now, if you're up to it."

"I'll surely try for you, but as I said it was only a quick peek. He was real tall though, that I remember well. I wonder if I'm going to get paid for today."

"I'll speak to the Manager on your behalf. Thanks, Millie. This will be a big help."

All officers were now in place and the investigation would take on its grinding routine. It was going to be a long day. Brett wanted a meeting with the manager to assure him they would do their best to be out of his hair as quickly as possible, but you never knew. While with the Manager, he also spoke to Millie's concern about her day's pay, seeing as they had commandeered her on police business, probably for the rest of the day. All he received was a noncommital shrug. Jerk, he thought.

Brett went back to the eleventh floor where they had taken over the room next door to the crime scene. A command post had been set up outside in one of their mobile units where they would conduct most of the interviews. An officer confirmed that the deceased's wallet and jewelry had been properly secured and identified. Everything had been dusted and printed, but they were still vacuuming the floor for hair samples. They would end up with far too many from a hotel room, but it was necessary. The sterile bags in the vacuum along with others would all go to the lab for testing.

He made a note to ask Jack to get to William's house and notify any next of kin of his death.

17

It was after seven when Jack reached the St Cloud division. He had picked up two cheeseburgers and treated himself to an order of fries and a milk shake. Another quick call to Jennifer explained he should be home in a couple of hours, but not in time for dinner.

He sat at his desk reviewing the Jensen case while polishing off the burgers. It had been over forty-eight hours since discovering the car and still no word from Sharin Jensen. He noted the media had been alerted about a missing person, as well as the police system. In their internal reports they had added, 'suspicious circumstances.' Crime stoppers had also been informed with a public appeal for any information relating to the accident.

Now they had their first break with an eye witness from a store on the Waverley road. The car description, including color, matched the Jensen vehicle, as well as the time of sighting, approximately three o'clock. That would fit with the accident, as Jack had found her car at five P.M. Additionally, the same witness had seen a white male get into a black Jeep and drive away immediately after the Jensen car.

Further questioning revealed the Jeep was equipped with off-road gear. David Folk's report indicated the damage inflicted on the Jaguar was not from another car, but some other vehicle like a bus or truck with a larger grill. He called David, reaching him at home.

"How do you manage to have it so easy?" asked Jack. "Sitting there watching television, while the rest of us are still at work."

That produced a mild grunt from David, who hardly ever watched television and had as demanding a schedule as Jack, which they both knew.

"What do you need this time, my master sleuth? I know, a detailed explanation of my latest report on the Jensen case, since none of you down there can understand anything without pictures."

"How did you know I was calling about the Jensen case, David? Maybe I was going to invite you to the Vikes next practice, or our final league game, or some other similar function you would salivate to attend."

David groaned. "You think I don't know about the witness from the store, including information not only about the Jensen vehicle, but perhaps some other trivial tidbit. Run it by me, Jack, my favorite detective, before I perish out of curiosity."

"You have me again. Does it ever become too boring for you, knowing everything in advance?"

"Sometimes, Jack, your naivete and honesty are too much for me. Please enlighten me on the news."

"This store owner sees a picture of Mrs Jensen and recognizes her. She stopped at his store Sunday afternoon to buy an ice cream cone. He remembers all of this because of her car. He was so impressed when she drove up in this brand new Jaguar, that after her purchase he went outside to have a closer look. She was already in the car and he thought it amusing to see her struggling with the seat belt while balancing the cone," said Jack. He finished the milk shake before continuing.

"The officer showed him pictures of Jaguars from a dealer's manual. He confirmed the car was a 1999 Jaguar S series, Mrs Jensen's car, as well as identifying the correct color. At the same time he had noticed a guy across the road getting into a black Jeep. His description includes details of all this gear on the Jeep, which turns out to be a complete off-road kit. That interested me because of your report. Now it's your turn to enlighten me, Einstein. Could a Jeep with that kind of gear cause the damage to our Jaguar?"

"Believe it or not, Jack, that was one of the scenarios I had imagined as we looked at the Jaguar in the compound. I knew it had to be a vehicle which firstly sat higher off the ground, and secondly did not have a conventional front end. With your eye witness, we'll be able to find out if there's a match. I'm glad he noticed the color. The paint smears will be the telling factor. I'll let you know tomorrow."

"This might be our lucky day," said Jack. "We also have a pretty good composite of the guy from our witness's description. If the vehicle is right, we'll have something to help ID the driver."

"Now, Jack, it's eight-thirty. You're still at headquarters. Tell me when you last had dinner with Jennifer."

"Thanks for that, David. I have the team meeting, we're turning this over to homicide, then I'm going home. Talk to you tomorrow. Shalom."

Jack had to call the Jensen home to up-date them. He surmised the involvement of homicide would not be well received.

Eric Jensen answered the phone and Jack briefed him on the case, leaving out the store owner's report. He would have to hold that until later.

"Why homicide?" asked Eric.

"We haven't heard from your wife for over forty-eight hours. At this point we have homicide assume the investigation because they have the resources and skills required for cases such as this. This will accelerate the activity and increase the manpower. Since I was at the scene originally, I'll be the case leader."

Jack heard a click on the telephone.

"Lieutenant, Wilson here on the other line. Any progress?"

"We now have the homicide division involved, as too much time has elapsed with no word from Mrs Jensen. Our first meeting will be in the next hour, with thirty-five officers on hand for a start."

"Do you have any information or leads yet?" demanded Frank.

"The findings from forensics and traffic are conclusive. There was another vehicle involved, as well as a male at the accident scene. We've circulated the photo of Mrs Jensen throughout the state police system, to the local press, and crime stoppers."

"Then Sharin has been taken or..." started Eric.

"Yes, and it does concern us that the abductor has not contacted any of you for a ransom. You are being completely open with me on that issue, aren't you?"

"The moment we hear anything, Lieutenant, you will know," said Frank.

Wilson was certainly taking charge here.

An officer caught Petersen's eye, telling him Callahan was on the other line.

"I appreciate your cooperation. We'll keep in touch. You'll have to excuse me. I have another call."

Jack picked up Callahan's incoming call.

18

Callahan was near exhaustion. They had interviewed for seven straight hours without so much as a coffee break. Time was so critical at the beginning of an investigation. He and his team knew each passing minute would make it more difficult to solve the crime. Thus far they hadn't uncovered any information to lead them to the killer.

He was just about to take a quick break, when Bob Dixon hurried into the room.

"Finally we have a lead, Lieutenant. One of the bellmen on duty last night was contacted. We were real lucky as he had just started four days off and was getting ready to leave with his wife. He has information on a guy that puts him near the scene of the crime and at the right time."

"When do we see him?"

"He's in a cruiser right now, on his way here. Probably take another ten minutes."

"Bob, get me a corned beef on rye will you – make that two. Have you had anything yet?"

"Yeah, I grabbed a snack a while back. I'm okay thanks. Be back in a minute with your sandwiches."

The sandwiches and George Ault, the bellman, arrived at the same time. Brett put them aside and started right away with the witness.

"Appreciate you coming in for this, especially since I understand you were on your way out of town," said Brett.

"I didn't have any choice. First days off I've had this month and you guys drag me in here like I'm a criminal. Christ, if my old lady had got off work early, you wouldn't have found me for three days."

"We'll get this over as quickly as possible, George. Start at the beginning and tell us everything you saw this morning."

"I've been working midnights lately, usually getting off at eight in the morning. Today, one of the guys was going to be a couple of hours late, so I volunteered to stay on till he got here. What the hell, the old lady wouldn't be home till four, so I figured I'd take two hours overtime. No sweat off my ass. We had only a three hour drive ahead of us and I could handle that easily with a short nap after work. You see, we were going to..."

"All right, George, let's get to the part we're interested in," interrupted Brett. "What did you see on the eleventh floor this morning?"

"Geez. The eleventh floor. Oh yeah. I had two trips up there a little before eight. I remember the time exactly because on the second one, when I saw this guy for the first time, it was just about eight. I know that because I was thinking, normally I'd be off by now."

"You say, you saw this guy more than once?" asked Brett.

"Yeah, I saw him on the bus on the way home."

"Let's go back to the first time," said Brett. "You say it was around eight. What happened?"

"I was taking a checkout from 1104, the couple had already gone down to the lobby, and I had a full cart of luggage. These people must have been here a month I figure, from the amount of crap they had. Anyway, I see this guy get out of the elevator and go down the hall towards the other end, where you found the body."

"How did you know where the murder took place?" asked Brett.

"When the Assistant Manager called me he said there was a killing in 1123. Look, I've been here a long time and I know where all the rooms are. 1123 is at the south end of the hall, and that's where this guy was heading."

Brett nodded. "Okay. Continue, George."

"When he got off the elevator I only had a quick side view of him. All I noticed was his size. He was big. When he saw me he kind of hesitated and turned around. That's when I had my first good look at his face. So when I saw him later on the bus, I knew it was the same guy."

"Let's stay with the eleventh floor for a minute," said Brett. For a guy who was anxious to leave on a trip, George was getting a little wordy, yet fortunately, not too impatient with the process.

"Well, when I reached the elevators there was one right there. The guy was just ambling along the hallway and I got on the elevator. I didn't think anything more of it. My replacement arrived a little earlier than expected, around nine, so I was off. I signed out and left. I take two busses to get home, and luckily just made the second, which was getting ready to pull away when I got there." George shifted in his chair.

"There's only a few riders at that time of the morning, and across the aisle, down about three or four seats, there he is. I didn't recognize him right away but each time I looked at him, I thought, I've seen this guy somewhere. I don't make it a practice to stare at people when I'm riding the bus, but I kept looking at him because it bothered me that I couldn't place him. Then I realized, it was at the hotel earlier in the morning."

"How did he appear to you, George? Was he nervous or behaving strangely in anyway?" asked Brett.

"No. He was real cool, looking kind of smug. He glanced at me a couple of times, but nothing unusual. He got off at Secord Street, about a mile from my place. I know all the stops on the line. Sort of a thing with me. Nothing else to do on the bus, so I've memorized the entire route."

"You've been a big help, George. We'll need a composite from you to help identify him, so I'll have an officer take you to that division. It shouldn't take too long, then we'll drive you home."

"Okay," said George. "Don't have a choice, do I?"

"You're doing us a great service which may help us catch this guy. We'll need the number of the bus you took, detailing exactly where he got off and the time. Include a description of his clothing and any distinguishing features.

Brett turned him over to Bob Dixon, then left to check on the rest of the investigation. While riding up to the eleventh floor he thought of William's Minnesota address, wondering where he had put his note. He better get to Jack right away so they could notify the victim's next of kin. It was only six-thirty here, making it eight-thirty in Minnesota.

19

Sharin heard the door close and knew he had gone out again. She had decided to go to work on the tape immediately the next time he left. As he had fed her twice during the day this probably was as strong as she would get. The longer she lay in bed, the weaker she would become.

She reached down to retrieve the nail clipper from her underwear. It was just beyond her finger tips, sitting below her rear. There wasn't much room to move with the strap holding her to the bed at the shoulders and her feet taped to the end of the bed. She had to raise her pelvis off the bed, then settle down again, sliding backwards in an effort to shift the clipper forward. On the fourth try she managed to get a tenuous grip on it. She waited a minute. Sharin was sweating from this effort alone, without even yet trying to cut the tape.

She slowly picked up the clipper, held it in position, and attempted her first cut. Holding it with both hands, she found she could maneuver the cutting end to the edge of the tape. She slid the clipper under the tape and closed it. It worked! She had succeeded in taking her first snip. Carefully repositioning the clipper, she tried again. It was successful. Pause. Then another. Pause. And another.

She found it necessary to hold her arms in the air to see where the cutting was taking place, which made the exercise extremely tiring. However, there was progress, maybe half an inch already. Continued work proved exhausting, but the small cuts were allowing a little play and some increased freedom of movement. She had to rest again.

Resuming her task, Sharin was anxious. Although she now had greater movement with her wrists, it was becoming more difficult to cut through the tape. As she progressed she encountered more resistance, because the tape was thicker. Obviously it had overlapped and now required extra effort.

It was painstaking work, cramping her fingers, but she was determined. The second layer of tape was slowing her progress and beginning to irritate her. She started to snatch at the tape, rather than using the slower, smooth cutting action she had mastered in the early going. She was about halfway through when an impatient hacking motion nipped her skin, causing an involuntary twitch. She dropped the clipper. It slid down the outside of her arm, bounced off her elbow and landed on the edge of the bed.

Sharin froze. What a time to be a klutz. Have to get under control and slow down. She stared at the clipper. It was perched precariously at the side of the bed. She willed it not to drop on the floor. Slowly she lowered her arms to the left, hoping to trap the clipper. Once secured, she could move it closer to her side, where it would be safe until she figured out how to pick it up again. It was just out of her reach, so she carefully eased her body a few inches to the left. The clipper started to slip over the side! She swung her arms down wildly and just managed stop it from falling.

She was afraid to move for a minute, holding on for dear life. Slowly she worked the clipper closer to her body for safety. Seconds later she grabbed it in her hands. She placed the clipper on her stomach, thoroughly relieved. She was panting from the exertion and fright.

How much time had been wasted? It felt like too much, but it was back to work regardless. Moving more carefully, she methodically snipped away until there was only a small strip of tape left. She let go of the clipper and yanked at the tape, trying to separate her wrists. It gave a little. Then a little more. Finally, she tore it apart. Her hands were free!

Sharin rubbed her wrists, massaging till the circulation returned to normal. It felt so good. Her spirits soared as she now knew there was a good chance of getting out. The shoulder strap presented the next challenge.

The strap was fastened along the top of her chest just below her armpits, with her arms on top. Her plan was to force the strap upwards with her arms so she could slide under. By moving her hands up under the strap, she was able to grasp it with her palms facing upwards, emulating a pushup position, only on her back instead of facing downwards. She would gather all her strength, then press against the strap, at the same time sliding her body down towards the end of the bed.

Her first effort failed. The strap did not budge. She rested and prepared herself. Pushing with all her available strength, Sharin thought she felt some give on the second try. She paused for a minute, then tried again. Nothing. This was proving far more difficult than she had imagined. She decided she must get out. She began violently pushing and moving at the same time, punishing herself in the process.

Driving herself to the limit and perspiring heavily, she finally managed to move. Suddenly she had her shoulders free, the strap was only at her neck. She turned her head, slid underneath, and was now able to sit up.

That left only her ankles. She was going to make it and get out of here. The tape could be peeled off, which would be much faster than cutting with the tiny clipper. She set to work, pulling and tugging, till gradually layer after layer were removed. When it was done she could hardly believe it. She found herself standing up, a free person, with no restraints. Slightly dizzy, she sat down quickly. Let's do this gradually, she told herself.

Not knowing how much time she had, she willed the dizziness to disappear, so she could get the hell out of the house. Where, she didn't know, but out. She was still wearing her new dress, but had no coat, shoes or socks. Well, too bad, she had to go.

As she left the room making her way to the front door, she stopped, stunned. Moving up the drive-way, which she could see through the kitchen window, were a car's headlights. It had to be him! How could she escape now?

This could be her only opportunity. She needed a weapon to attack him. There was no way to overpower him on her own. Then she remembered the fireplace. If there were utensils there, maybe she could surprise him and still get free. She turned into the living room, and found what she wanted, a solid, wrought iron poker.

The headlights went out. A car door opened and closed. His approaching footsteps were clearly audible.

Sharin waited behind the front door. Luckily, it swung in towards the living room, thereby shielding Sharin and giving her plenty of space to swing the poker. There would be only one chance. Her idea was to take a mighty baseball-like swipe at his head, hoping to at least stun him so she could run out the open door. She'd take her chances on whatever was out there. She knew he was over six feet and thus planned her aim carefully.

Her hands were wet. Time stood still. Where was he? She heard the key in the door. It opened and suddenly he was there. It was dark, but she swung. She connected, hearing a sickening sound of metal contacting skin and bone. He staggered forward, then started to go down. She didn't hesitate, running out through the open door.

It was cold. She ran. The driveway was long and winding. It couldn't be too far to the road. Not that it mattered. She was free. She ran. Never had she been more grateful for her daily running. Her strong legs pumped rhythmically and steadily. The driveway seemed to never end, but at last she reached the road. Turn left or right? She had no idea. There was a light to her left. She turned towards it, pouring on the speed.

What was that noise? It was him, behind her and gaining! That couldn't be. She could outrun him. She knew it. She pushed herself to a new level. He was getting closer. She could feel him, hear his breath. Christ, she had hit him with everything she had yet here he was, almost on top of her. This can't happen.

Sharin felt his hand on her shoulder. She swung her left arm wildly, connecting with flesh and bone. He flinched and let go. She ran faster. Something warm and sticky was on the back of her hand. It was blood. Must have done some damage with the poker. He hadn't given up as the sound of his feet on the pavement were again gaining on her.

What was the light she had seen? It had to be a house, hopefully with people inside. It seemed so close, yet so far. She began screaming for help. It wasn't easy, being winded from the running. He grabbed her again, spinning her to the ground. She scrambled to get away, kicking out at him, connecting again with his head. He winced but came on even stronger.

Suddenly there was a blinding light, coming right at them. It was a car. Not one car, but two. Immediately he was off her and sprinting across an open field. The cars screeched to a halt and two men bounded out. One came to Sharin, while the other headed after Kurt.

"Are you all right?"

"Where...where did you come from?" asked Sharin.

"It's a long story," said Lieutenant Jack Petersen.

20

Petersen eased Sharin into the cruiser, wrapping her in his top coat. She was shaking violently. He had recognized her immediately from the photograph he had been studying for the past three days.

"Did you get him? Am I going to be okay?"

"You're going to be fine. Did he run you off the road?"

"Yes. He said he would kill me."

"He held you somewhere? In one of these houses?"

Sharon nodded, then broke down. She was still crying when Jonsson returned.

"Lost the guy. He jumped down the embankment into the Mississippi River. Must have been a drop of twenty feet." He turned to Sharin. "Was that your husband Ma'am?"

"This is Mrs Jensen," said Jack.

"Not the missing Mrs Jensen?"

"Exactly."

"Then he's her abductor?" asked Jonsson. Jack nodded. They called in for help to surround the area.

"I'll wait for them, Lieutenant," said Jonsson. "You better get Mrs Jensen to a hospital."

"Take me home first. The General Hospital is only ten minutes from our house," said Sharin.

"That'll take maybe thirty, forty minutes," said Jack. "There's closer hospitals. You sure you'll be okay?"

"I'm a little sore but another half-hour isn't going to matter. My gynecologist practices at the General. I'll get Eric to have her meet us there. I'd like to call home."

Jack did a one-eighty and accelerated smoothly. He wasn't going to waste any time getting Sharin home. He dialed the number and handed her the phone.

When they answered, Sharin shouted, "Hi, it's me!"

Jack could hear the muffled responses, then listened to the wild outpouring of emotion between Sharin and her family as she brought them up to date. It went on for fifteen minutes.

"The police have me and we're on the way home. See if you can get a hold of Gwen and have her meet us at the General. See you soon. Love you all." She put the phone down and stared out the window. She started to cry.

"You've been through quite a lot in the last three days, to say the least."

"Guess I'm lucky to be alive. The crazy things that went through my mind when I was in there are hard to believe now."

"What did you think about?"

"All the normal things I suppose. How much I love my husband and how dear our marriage is. We're going to have a baby so I worried about my condition. Then there were the weird things. Like the thoughts of the shelter."

"The shelter?" asked Jack.

"Yeah. Eric and I work at one of the homeless projects every Tuesday in the Cities. Heh, that's today isn't it? Well, I was worried that my meals wouldn't get served if I didn't get out. Kind of crazy, no?"

"It was probably one way of keeping your sanity. Your family certainly was frantic. I talked to your husband and father regularly."

"How were you involved?" asked Sharin.

"I found your car. When we didn't hear from you, the investigation was turned over to homicide. That's where I work."

"Oh. I'm actually feeling a little warmer now. Thanks for your coat. Homicide? Probably what's needed for Kurt."

"That's his name?"

"That's about all I know about him. Other than I think he's a pyscho," said Sharin. The trembling started again.

"We'll be at your house soon," said Jack. He glanced at Sharin who was holding herself and shaking. "You okay?" She nodded. Minutes later they pulled into the Jensen driveway.

The family reunion was filled with emotion. Everyone was crying and talking at the same time, while two dogs kept barging in on all the hugs, wanting their master for themselves. Eric wouldn't let Sharin go. They held onto each other with Eric constantly running his hand through Sharin's hair. They were seated at the kitchen table as Judy had prepared some chili, thinking that her daughter would be starved. Sharin was doing her best to get some of it down, but not succeeding. She was more interested in holding Eric and vice versa.

They were all trying to review the events of the last three days while letting the reality sink in. Sharin couldn't believe she was home and safe. Neither could Eric or her parents. The last few hours seemed more like minutes.

"We should be thinking of getting you to the hospital," said Eric. "I did get Gwen at home and she can't wait to see you. She'll be at the General in the next half-hour. You sure you're okay?"

She leaned against Eric with her head on his shoulder. "It's just so good to be with you. I'm sort of numb now, but no serious pain or anything."

"How did you ever manage to escape?"

She related the details of the nail clipper, and the home run swing with the poker.

"You actually struck him, dear?" asked Judy.

"Yes, Mom," said Sharin. "He had threatened to kill me. I knew I had to get out of there."

"The nail clipper, that's incredible," said Eric. "Here we were, totally helpless and you find a way to free yourself. Who was this creep anyway?"

"I have no idea, but he was scary. I thought of all of you, over and over. You don't appreciate just how lucky you are to have such happiness," said Sharin. "You also don't realize how much will there is to survive. The finale was just as exciting, with the police arriving when they did."

"How did that happen?" asked Frank.

"That was just pure luck," said Jack. "A good friend of mine who works out of L.A. was investigating a homicide there. The victim's driver's license listed his address as Clearwater. He had called to have us go to the house to notify any next of kin. Since it was only a slight detour for me on my way home, I took the assignment. Turned out to be the house where your daughter was being held. I was certainly stunned when I recognized her."

"You should have seen the look on his face," said Sharin.

"I couldn't have been happier," said Jack. "Knowing you had been forced off the road, and most likely abducted was disturbing enough. On top of that, when your family hadn't received any ransom demands, we knew you were in a dangerous situation. You normally hear from the kidnapper within twenty-four hours."

"What happens now?" asked Eric.

"There are some questions I need to ask your wife. If you're up to it, Mrs Jensen, the sooner the better for all of us. We've secured the house where you were held. There's also a massive search underway for this guy. You said his name is Kurt?"

"Yes. I don't know his last name."

"Any information you give us right now might be the difference. While he's at large, you and your family will have round the clock protection, though it doesn't look like you need much help here with those two," said Jack, pointing to the shepherds.

Jack took the details from Sharin, then they agreed it was time to get to the hospital for a complete physical. Sharin's general condition seemed better than one might have expected, despite the bruising from the accident and weakness resulting from her captivity. However, they wanted to know that Sharin and the 'baby' were indeed unscathed.

The dogs never left Sharin's side. Jack was impressed with the two magnificent animals. In turn, both had taken to Jack immediately, proving they are able to sense good people. They seemed so friendly he had asked how protective they were.

"They're fine when someone has been welcomed," said Eric. "However, without the invitation, they challenge you. King would eat the tires off your car should you arrive unannounced. They're particularly wary if Sharin is alone. Last year we had a plumber in for some repairs. At one point while I had gone downstairs, he was making his way through the living room heading for the kitchen where Sharin was. The dogs went after him in a flash. Sharin was able to stop them. The poor plumber was unnerved, to say the least."

"They certainly look like a formidable team to me," said Jack.

The phone rang. Judy took the call, and with a puzzled look said, "It's for you, Sharin."

Sharin took the phone. She didn't say anything, dropped the phone and headed for the bathroom. Eric was right behind her. The sound of her retching and sobbing punctuated the stillness in the kitchen.

"What is it?" asked Eric.

"That was Kurt. He said it's not over yet."

21

It was one-thirty in the morning when Jack got home. Jennifer was asleep but had left him a note saying there was a casserole in the fridge which he could heat up if he hadn't eaten. He had missed every dinner with her this week, yet there was a meal waiting for him at this hour. He had better find a way to change.

He zapped the casserole, sliced some fresh Italian bread, and sat down to a feast. He figured it would be a good time to catch Brett and tell him the good news. His call was answered on the first ring.

"Brett, it's Jack. You're my savior buddy."

"I've known that for years. What did I do for you now?"

"Remember you gave me that address in Clearwater so we could advise any family members of William's death? Well I go out there with Jonsson and just as we're nearing the house we see a man wrestling with a woman on the road. Jonsson goes after the guy, who had jumped up and headed across an open field towards the river. I go to the woman, who's hurting, scared, and wearing only a dress – no coat or shoes. So I get her into the car cause it's getting a little chilly..."

"Getting chilly," interrupted Brett, "with snow on the ground and the temperature sinking below zero. Let's hear it for Minnesota."

"At least we don't have the West Coast phonies you inherit with your year round balmy weather. Anyway, Brett, turns out the woman is Mrs Jensen. Can you believe it?"

"I would if you told me who Mrs Jensen is."

"Brett, it's the case I've been on since Sunday. The woman in the car accident who's been missing."

"You're kidding. Congrats."

"It gets better. The guy who got away jumped into the Mississippi, down a twenty foot hill, if you can imagine. He'd held her in William's house. Kept her there for three days. So we got a full description from Mrs Jensen. We'll do the composites tomorrow, but so far he's a lot like the suspect who killed the bartender up near Brainerd last night. We have our guys all over the area looking for him. We've got to get him, because he called the Jensen house leaving a threatening message with her. Here she was all excited about being home, then this phone call knocked her for a loop."

"She sure it was the same guy?" asked Brett.

"Yeah. She'd heard enough of him to know. How's your case going?"

"I got a little lucky myself. Two witnesses, a maid and a bellman, saw some guy on the floor where William bought it. Looks like the timing fits the murder. Later, the bellman on his way home happens to get on a bus with the same guy. They're on the bus for about twenty minutes and the bellman recognizes him. Even knows the bus stop where the guy got off."

"What's he like?" asked Jack, opening a cold beer.

"The operative word here was 'big.' Over six feet with a hell of a build. Looks like the maid saw the same guy, as their descriptions are close. We're getting the composites done from both of the witnesses and I'm betting they're identical. We'll circulate them around the bus stop he used. I'd like to talk to this guy, run him down a bit. Must be a mean S.O.B. to cut up someone like that."

"What do you mean?" asked Jack.

"The upper body had been mutilated, cut several times. Christ, Jack, I don't know if I've ever seen so much blood at a crime scene."

"When you get the composites, fax them to me will you?"

"You'll get them tomorrow," said Brett.

"Anyway, at least you've got a lead which sounds right. What else is happening?"

"How about our Vikes? Looks like they're struggling a bit, but I'm sure they'll turn it around," said Brett. "If I come back for a visit, can you get any tickets?"

"For you, of course. Why don't you come this weekend? You can watch us in the fastball finals, then take in the Vikes game."

"Fastball in Minnesota in October. Jack, don't swing at any inside pitches. Your hands will drop off if you make contact. Or, are you now wearing special gloves for fall games?"

"You're such a card, Brett. How's your love life?"

"Non-existent with this job, you know that. But, the girl watching here is great. With this weather the girls don't have to wear those heavy winter parkas and stuff, so you see it all, e-v-e-r-y day. Talking about that, when was the last time you took Jennifer out?"

"Ouch! That's below the belt, Brett, but your point's well taken. I was just thinking about that earlier. I'm going to do something about paying more attention to Jennifer. She's too good to lose. Got to go, call coming in. Keep in touch and stay well." He hung up and took the other call.

"Lieutenant, it's Brooker. We've got another one."

22

Kurt had taken a leisurely drive on secondary roads working south from Clearwater, staying about twenty miles west of Minneapolis. He had no desire to go into a large city, preferring the quiet of rural Minnesota. Again he found a quaint bar with a few locals passing the night over beer and gossip. Nothing interesting materialized so he decided to call it an early night and return to the Clearwater house.

As he opened the front door he sensed something to his left and raised his arm in time to take some of the sting out of Sharin's blow. The poker had landed on the back of his hand and left cheek at the same time, momentarily stunning him. He had lost his balance and stumbled forward, giving Sharin the chance to bolt from the house, which infuriated him.

It took a few seconds before he had regained his balance and set off after her. He was a little dizzy initially and unable to produce any kind of speed. God, she could run. He was forced to pick up the pace to catch her. He had started to gain slowly, succeeded on reaching out to grab her, but failed to hold on as she swung her arm, and caught him on his injured and bleeding cheek. He had lost his grip on her but this only heightened his anger.

He closed the gap again, then lunged forward and tackled her, taking her to the pavement. He was holding her down, taking a minute to catch his breath, when headlights from some approaching cars blinded him. He didn't hesitate, jumped up and headed across an open field which he knew led to the river.

He was being chased and normally would have stopped to deal with his pursuer, but he had seen two of them, so he continued to the river. Without any thought he dove over the side, bounced once part way down the hill and entered the water. It was numbing cold but at least the asshole didn't follow him.

He reached the other side, ran up the far embankment, found a road, and waited. He would hitch hike, working things out as they happened. The first two cars didn't slow down, but the third stopped. Kurt didn't waste any time. The elderly driver was unable to ward off the vicious blow to his head. He was practically unconscious as Kurt pushed him out of the car to the side of the road. He might have left him there, but his anger over losing Sharin was too much. He inserted the knife just below the ear and sliced his carotid artery.

Kurt kept to side roads, working his way northeasterly, as the cops would be setting up roadblocks in no time. His head and fingers were throbbing. He had to have medical attention. As always, he had a contingency plan for emergencies such as this. A male nurse he had worked with in L.A. had retired two years ago, and returned to Minnesota to open a fishing camp in the Whitefish Lakes region. Last year he had sent Kurt a note, with pictures of his camp, the address, and an open invitation.

He took time to stop at a pay phone, calling Sharin to let her know he would be in touch. She had to pay for this. He called Phil, who said he would enjoy seeing his old friend again, then gave directions to his fishing camp. He made one other call, to L.A.

Kurt took care to stay off main roads, although it would take longer. Driving north towards Grand Rapids, he picked up a road heading west to an area north of Whitefish Lake, which left a short trip down to Phil's Fishing Camp. He needed some medical attention and warm clothes, as well as a story for Phil. There was more than an hour's drive to work this out. Thus far he had not encountered one police car, so his plan of staying on side roads, slow going as they were, was paying off.

Phil, who was a widower and living alone, had mentioned the fishing season was pretty well done, so not only would he welcome the company, he could use an extra hand in shutting things down. He was heading out to Florida for two weeks of sun, before getting ready for the snowmobilers. "You'll have to earn your room and board," he joked. Kurt would decide what to do with Phil after he was settled.

It was two in the morning when Kurt arrived. That was no problem, Phil had assured him. At the end of the busy fishing season, he was happy to relax with a beer or two, taking in late movies. Phil greeted his old working colleague, then asked what the hell he had been into.

"You look worse than some of those characters we used to admit to 'Emerg' in the middle of the night. What happened?" asked Phil.

"I was at a party on a boathouse, when this lovely started to come on to me. She was stunning. Also turned out to be very married. The husband caught us and was really pissed, not only with us, but from a lot of booze.

We were out on the deck and he picked up some piece of equipment, never figured out what it was, and nailed me. He hit me so hard, it knocked me overboard," Kurt said.

"There was only two or three feet of water, so I just waded to shore, got in my car and started driving. I remembered you had this place not too far from where I was, and knowing I needed some help, decided to call you. I didn't want to try to explain this to some hospital, so here I am."

"Well come on in. I'll have a look at that face, or what's left of it. You could use some dry clothes as well. I have a set of extra large lounging pyjamas which should fit you. Why don't you have a hot bath and change? Then I'll tend to you."

When Kurt was ready, Phil administered to his face and hand.

"You're pretty lucky. I don't know what the hell he hit you with, but it must have been solid. You have two broken fingers and maybe a fractured cheek bone. I can jury rig a splint for your hand, and clean your face up, but you need a doctor. Fortunately I'm allowed to keep medical supplies here for emergencies. I'll give you some Demerol to help for tonight, then take you to town tomorrow."

Phil prepared the syringe for an I.M. injection of the Demerol, then taped the fingers to two tongue depressors.

"That will have to do for now. How did this guy manage to surprise you?"

"I really don't know. One minute this gal's all over me, then she stiffened. All of a sudden this guy's swinging at my head with a rod or something. Guess I was lucky to get my hand up," said Kurt.

"Well, it probably saved your life, Kurt. If that blow had landed directly on your head, you wouldn't be talking to me now."

"Look, it's good of you to treat me like this," said Kurt. "Here I don't see you in a couple of years, then you have to play doctor to me. I really appreciate it."

"You need a good rest. The Demerol will take effect pretty soon, so you better get to bed. I don't want to have to carry you anywhere."

"Yeah, I know it'll help with the pain. I'd sure like to catch up with you so we'll do that in the morning."

"That's a good idea. It won't matter what time you get up, so we'll see you later."

"Thanks a lot, Phil. You're a real pal."

23

Phil knew Kurt was lying. He remembered a few incidents back in L.A. when Kurt was a little off the wall but it never seemed to be anything serious. He wouldn't have sent him this address had he thought otherwise. However, here he was, obviously in some kind of trouble. He had given him an extra dose of Demerol to ensure he would be out for a while. Phil would use the time to sort this out.

With some clever investing, he had managed to get enough money together to buy this fishing lodge in his home state. He had called it simply, Phil's Fishing Camp. With a last name like Lundquist, he preferred using his first name for the business. Easier to pronounce and remember.

He had always planned to come back here and work at his favorite pastime – fishing. Still healthy and strong at sixty-three, he was physically able to handle the requirements of running a fishing camp. Now in his third year, the business had prospered sufficiently to afford a few part-timers for some of the chores, while allowing him the opportunity to fish.

Four years ago he had lost his wife of thirty years to cancer. Without any children they had doted on each other. He thought of Sue constantly, and although lonely, had no interest in searching for another relationship. There was a constant stream of customers either fishing or snowmobiling, so this helped. With short breaks at the end of the fishing season and early in the spring, he usually took some time to travel. He had worked all his life for this and now it was a dream come true.

Kurt was sound asleep, so he decided to rummage through his clothes and car. Other than being wet and a little blood stained, the clothes didn't turn up anything out of the ordinary. He went outside and was instantly taken with the stillness and quiet of the early morning. There was no wind, thus the lake looked like polished glass. Perfect for skipping stones. The car was open.

He sat for a minute looking out on the lake, enjoying the early morning serenity. He rolled down the window to hear the occasional cricket or frog, then began searching the car. The glove compartment held some maps, pens, note paper, and the ownership. He turned on the interior light to read it, and was not surprised to learn the car was owned by someone else. Had Kurt borrowed the car, or stolen it?

He thought he heard a sound. It was so still and dark, it was unnerving. He jerked around quickly to look at the cabin, but nothing was there. The guy's out cold from the Demerol, so don't get jumpy. Phil was not undersized and in good shape, but he'd have a tough time handling Kurt. He decided to look in the back. There was nothing of note, so he leaned over to probe under the front seat. His hand found something strange. He couldn't quite grasp it, so he returned to the front.

Bending forward, he reached under the seat and found it again. He pulled it out carefully, and stared. Never had he seen such a knife. The haft was pure ivory, carved and shaped to exquisitely fit one's hand. The blade was five to six inches long and honed to a fine sharpness.

There was some foreign substance on the blade, which even in the dim of the car's dome light, Phil could recognize – dried blood. He had been slightly nervous and on guard before. Now the first sense of dread took over. His own car was in a shed at the back of the cabin, with the keys in the kitchen. There were a couple of outboards in the water but it might take some time to start one of them.

There was a thump on the roof of the car. Still bent over, he started so quickly he banged his head on the steering wheel. Nothing happened. The door to the cabin was still closed. Another thump. He jumped and spun around to look out the other side. Nothing. All was quiet again, eerily so. His heart rate was off the clock. Jesus, what to do?

He got out of the car. There on the roof were two pine cones. He started to breathe again.

Phil had heard about the murder in Crosslake, but surely it would be a stretch to connect Kurt with that. Still, that was only an hour south of his camp. He was certain Kurt was in some kind of trouble, but murder? This weapon was definitely not your average knife. It was unique and did have blood on it. Should he take the boat and get out of here?

Over the years Kurt had proved himself to be a charming and bright young man. He was a skilled nurse who took his work seriously. There were occasions when he appeared distant and preoccupied, rather distracted. Kurt had also attracted a lot of rumors about his behavior, but that was all, only rumors.

He heard another sound, this time from the cabin. Was a chair knocked over? A light went on in the kitchen.

Phil didn't hesitate. He headed for the dock.

24

At six-thirty Jack grabbed an Egg McMuffin and coffee at a drive through, arriving at the office shortly before seven. Brooker and two other officers were going over the latest murder with David Folk.

"Good morning gentlemen, and to you, David," said Jack as he sat down with his breakfast.

"Here comes Sherlock with his latest home cooked meal," said David, shaking his head. "When was the last time you had your cholesterol checked, handsome?"

"With my exercise routine, my LDL is well under the risk level, so I can afford to pig out occasionally. But thanks for your ongoing concern, David. What have you got, Ed?"

"At one-thirty A.M. a motorist sees a body on the side of the road. Location, Highway 24, two miles west of Highway 10. There's a lot of blood and he's sure the guy's dead. He calls in on his car phone. We're down there in fifteen minutes with an ambulance. Poor bugger's dead all right, with his throat slit. David can tell you more. The body went to the coroner and has since been taken to the lab in St Paul." Brooker leafed through his standard issue memo book.

"The witness sticks around for questioning. Good guy. He was on shift work till midnight. Works at a chemical manufacturing plant north of the Cities. Said he left work at twelve-thirty A.M. He lives in Fairhaven, so he had taken the exit to Highway 24. Everything checks out. A supervisor and two co-workers corroborated his story."

"Have we got the time of death, David?" asked Jack.

"Nine-thirty to eleven-thirty P.M. Absolutely no later."

"What have you got on the victim, Ed?"

"Al Lucas was a widower, living with an older aunt. She's really broken up. No sign of his car, so maybe the suspect took it. Anyway, we have an A.P.B. out on it. So far, no news."

"What did you find, David?"

David checked his notes. "The victim was a white male, sixty-six, in reasonably good health. He was struck on the top of his head, right side, most likely by a fist. Also suffered some bruising on his shoulders and back of the head. His throat was cut, precisely through the carotid artery by an extremely sharp knife."

"Through the carotid artery you say," said Jack. "We could draw a number of conclusions from that. Guy could have been a Navy Seal, a trained commando, or maybe a martial arts type."

"Not a bad thought, Jack. If none of those, he certainly has some knowledge of the human body. Either the knife wound was designed to ensure death, or it was luck. I don't believe in that kind of luck." David continued to check his notes.

"Something was bugging me about this knife wound. Then I remembered. It was the forensic pathologist's report on the female victim the other day. I looked it up and am positive the same knife was used in the two homicides."

Jack went to the local wall map. He located the site of last night's homicide, traced a line back across the Mississippi River, and discovered it intersected with the road where they had met up with Kurt and Mrs Jensen. Jonsson had seen Kurt jump into the river at a point which coincided with the location of the crime.

Jack knew it was the same guy. The kidnapper and the murderer. He could feel it. From everything Mrs Jensen said about Kurt, from David Folk's findings, and from the locale of the last homicide. From the black Jeep they had taken from William's to the description of the vehicle at Roy's the night Ginny was murdered. It all fit. He had a serial killer in his territory, who only last night had threatened to get to Mrs Jensen again.

"Bob, have you got the composites on the Crosslake homicide?" Jack asked.

"Yeah. We have two sets, Lieutenant. I put them in your 'in basket' late last night."

"Find out where Mrs Jensen is. I want to take these to her immediately."

Only two files below these composites was a fax from Brett Callahan. It was a computerized artist's sketch of the L.A. killer.

Jack intended to get through the rest of his files later.

25

Sharin was released from the hospital at noon on Wednesday. She had suffered a mild concussion but all was well with the pregnancy. Her feet were still tender and the assorted aches and bruises now only a minor issue, considering the good news about the baby.

Several times she had awakened during the night wondering where she was. On one occasion she had sat up screaming, believing she was still held captive in the house. The policeman assigned to her was in the room instantly.

"It's okay. You're safe now."

It had been a long night but now they were going home. Eric had both dogs in the Land Rover, who of course made a great fuss when their masters emerged from the hospital. They howled and each vied to outdo the other in attempting to get in the front seat with Sharin. Kisses and squeals of delight continued unabated till finally Eric started the car and told the dogs to 'get in the back and stay.'

They were both relieved to know there was no harm to the baby. Despite being a little weak and badly shaken, Sharin had come out of the ordeal remarkably well. At least physically. It would take much longer to heal the mental anguish suffered during the three days of hell, as well as the harrowing escape from Kurt. The phone call late last night only heightened her anxiety.

"I don't care what it takes, but I'm not leaving your side until they catch this maniac," said Eric.

"Thanks for that. I'm going to need you. Just when you think it's over, it starts again. I kept waking up last night. Didn't know where I was. I've never been so frightened. He's one hell of a scary guy, Eric."

"Between the police, me, and these guys, you're going to be fine."

Sharin placed her hand on his thigh and gazed out the window. A slight drizzle was starting on this drab overcast day. What a contrast to her return trip from the airport Sunday, when her life was rosy and the weather had reflected her mood. Now it was just the opposite. In spite of the good news from her doctor, she couldn't shake the feeling of gloom and dread, not unlike the weather.

"Eric, my sense of this is, he's a psycho. If I'm right, this will be even more dangerous for us."

"Why would that be?" asked Eric.

"Because he'll be unpredictable and consumed with getting to me. For whatever reason, he's obsessed with me. Psychos believe when they have chosen someone, they are their's alone. Nothing else matters."

"Why would he believe you're his?"

"He fantasizes that is the reality. It isn't, but in his mind it is. Then when I rejected him by escaping, he became furious with me. Now his obsession will be to destroy me." Sharin shuddered.

"We won't let him. The police are giving us twenty-four hour protection. Besides, he'd never get by King and Kayla."

"Yes, Eric. That's what I want to believe as well, but I know better. He'll find a way. If the police don't get him first, he'll get to me. We have to be ready for him."

"You don't even know if he was planning to..."

"Christ, Eric, where have you been the past three days? He came close to killing me on the Waverley road, then ties me up for three days, saying if I make a wrong move he'll kill me. You want more?"

"I'm sorry, honey. We've all been stressed out over this and I was trying to ease the pressure on both of us. I know it's wishful thinking."

The cell phone rang.

It was a hands-free model, so Eric pressed 'send' allowing Sharin and him to listen together.

"Hi," said Eric.

"Eric, it's Dad. Is Sharin with you?"

"Right here, Dad."

"What did the doctor say?" asked Frank.

"I'm fine, Dad. No harm to the baby. All I need is some rest."

"Great news. Get home soon, your mother has lunch ready for you."

"We'll try to do justice to that."

"Lieutenant Petersen called to say he's on his way over here with something important to discuss with you."

"Okay, Dad. We'll see you shortly."

They arrived within minutes of each other. The dogs remembered Jack and enthusiastically greeted him. They had wonderful dispositions with people they knew and trusted.

After a few preliminaries with Jack being updated on Sharin's condition, he briefed them on the recent homicides. "These may or may not be related to your case, but we have to be sure." Jack spared them the details of the two murders. It was tough enough to introduce these findings to an already terrified household.

"We had eye witnesses at the first homicide and have produced sketches on a suspect, which we want you to review."

Jack removed the composites and handed them to Sharin.

She was terrified, not wanting to see them, but knew she must.

It was over instantly. She dropped the pictures, not wanting to even touch them.

There was no doubt. It was him.

26

Kurt awakened suddenly. What was that noise? He was slightly groggy, but as usual began to think clearly immediately. The pain had lessened thanks to the Demerol, but he had seen better days. He thought he had heard a car door close, so decided to get up and take a look.

He didn't know the way too well and stumbled into a chair. He turned the kitchen light on, then heard a car door close again. That had to be his car. He crossed to the door, went out, and saw someone running towards the lake. It had to be Phil. Kurt didn't know what was going on but he wasn't about to wait. He took off after him, down the path which was narrow and twisting so he had difficulty keeping his balance.

The sound of someone trying to start an outboard reached him. Christ, he's trying to get away. Kurt reached the dock and sprinted towards the boat. The engine coughed and sputtered, then he saw the damn thing moving away from the dock. It was too late to catch him, but there was another boat. He leaped in and pulled on the starting rope. Nothing. He pulled out the choke and tried again. It caught. He undid the docking line and headed out on the lake.

Phil was out of sight but the sound of his outboard was like a beacon. Kurt held the throttle wide open and strained to catch sight of the other boat. The sound was getting closer, but still no sighting. It was cold. The night air stung his face, numbing the already tender cheek. The occasional spray of cold water lashed at his face. It felt like hundreds of tiny needles piercing his skin. He didn't care. The only thought was to catch Phil, who had become a traitor. How could he take off like this? Something had given him reason to flee. What?

Obviously Phil had been in the car. The damn knife was under the front seat. Without any time to clean it up, he had just left it there. Phil would know enough to recognize the telltale sign of blood, so had put two and two together and now was off to get help. No way. The sound of the other outboard was definitely getting closer.

The boat slapped against the water, the cold wind bit even more, but on he went. He thought there was the sign of a wake looming up. His eyes had grown accustomed to the dark, but it was a strain to keep searching for the other craft. It was a strange feeling. All the sounds were magnified on the water, and with only a sliver of a moon which offered little illumination, he was quite disoriented. He could hear, but hardly see, and had no idea of speed, only the sensation of moving. From the constant lapping of the water against his boat and the wind in his face, it felt like they were eclipsing all speed records.

It was even difficult to figure out where the shore was. There hadn't been a single light in view since leaving the dock. He continued to focus on the sound of Phil's motor, which was slowly getting nearer. There was his wake! He had him now. His boat was closing in rapidly. There was Phil, turning to look at him. Strange, he didn't seem concerned.

It happened without warning. Kurt's boat struck the rock at full speed. It lunged out of the water at a precarious angle, getting airborne for several seconds. The force of the impact drove Kurt forward. His foot caught and became jammed in the aluminum struts supporting the back seat.

The boat crashed back in the water at an angle, jarring its rider, who felt searing pain in his ankle as it scraped against the captive struts. Ice cold water began to pour in. Kurt tried in vain to get his leg free, but it wouldn't budge. He was having great difficulty moving his body against the rush of water, now up to his chest.

The boat was listing at a thirty degree angle and now half full of water. He grabbed the gunwale on the top side, trying to lift himself onto the hull that was still out of the water. He heaved with all his strength but couldn't move. His foot was held fast between the struts.

He pulled at his leg viciously. It didn't matter. He was locked to the boat. The water was now up to his neck. The boat began to slide more quickly now, dragging its lone passenger under. He kicked furiously at the strut with his other leg. He pulled and jerked with his trapped foot. There was little movement.

He saw a light. It had to be Phil. He cried out his name. Nothing. The boat and rider were sinking together. He took a deep breath and continued twisting and battling to free himself. How could a fucking boat take him down?

The boat and its captive were descending rapidly. The pressure increased in his ears. He couldn't clear them. The pain in his ear drums was excruciating. His head was going to explode. He saw stars. His ear drums shattered. He gulped for air. There was none. The cold Whitefish Lake water poured into his nose and mouth.

He felt his trapped ankle move slightly.

Everything went black.

27

Petersen actually slept in for the first time in ages. He was about to leave for the office when the call came through. It was Sven Larsen. They chatted briefly. Jack and he had got along well during their first meeting.

Sven was at a fishing camp where there had been a boating accident and drowning. One of the officers had called him to help with the inquiry. It was close to five in the morning, still dark, when he had arrived at the camp.

They took Phil's statement of the bizarre accident. A guy he used to work with in L.A., Kurt Schmidt, went down in a boat and neither he nor the boat had been recovered. Phil had recounted the events of the previous evening. Everything began to unravel very quickly. The car was traced and found to be owned by Al Lucas, the recent homicide victim just south of St Cloud. They confiscated the knife, knowing it had also been handled by Phil. Kurt's clothes were secured and taken. Phil happened to have a couple of pictures of Kurt, taken at the hospital where they both worked.

Sven recognized the likeness to the composites from the Crosslake homicide witnesses. Was Kurt involved in both homicides? It seemed unlikely that Phil would go all the way down to the St Cloud area, kill someone, steal a car, and drive back to his own camp. Granted he didn't have a corroborated alibi, since he was home alone watching television last night, but it didn't make much sense. He had then taped the interview and knew he had to call Jack.

"You have a picture of this guy?" asked Jack.

"Yeah. Apparently they used to work at the same hospital in L.A. Had a couple of shots taken of him at work. He's a dead ringer for the guy who killed Ginny."

"That would also make him the same guy who abducted the Jensen woman," said Jack. "What else did you find?"

"We've got a knife, a real dandy. Phil hadn't believed Kurt's story about how he was beaten up, so after a large dose of Demerol put him to sleep he had gone to look at the car. Found the knife and knew there was dried blood on it. That's when he decided to head out for help. He says Kurt had got up and he could see him in the kitchen. Phil couldn't get to his car keys, so the only way out was by boat. You know the rest."

"How did Kurt end up at Phil's camp?" asked Jack.

"When Phil retired, he moved back here to set up a fishing camp. He had sent postcards to a few of his co-workers, giving them open invitations to come fishing. Kurt Schmidt, that's his full name, called late last night, taking him up on it. We also have Kurt's clothes."

"How could that be?" said Jack. "I thought you said you couldn't find the body."

"Apparently Kurt arrived in damp clothes, so Phil had loaned him an outfit while he dried out. That's what Kurt was wearing when he went down."

"What are you doing about locating the boat and body?"

"We've got three dive teams arriving this afternoon. Phil knows the lake and even though it was dark, he has a good fix on where the boat went down."

"You sure Phil had nothing to do with this?" asked Jack.

"If you mean, putting Kurt away, I'm not sure. Boating accidents are kind of difficult to resolve. Not too much evidence out there. But he comes off as a square shooter. After all, he did call us as soon as he got back to the cabin. If he hadn't, we might never have known about this. As for Lucas, the deceased owner of the car, I can't see Phil being involved there, can you?"

"No, I agree," said Jack. "Everything points to Kurt on that one. We knew he had gone for a swim in the Mississippi, so that accounts for the wet clothes. He also needed transportation to get away and that's where Lucas came in. I appreciate you letting me know about this, Sven. I'll look for your tape of the interview as well as the other evidence. Call me the moment the divers find anything."

"All right, Jack. One of my officers will be leaving here shortly to deliver it to your office. Talk to you soon." They hung up.

Jack was on his way to the Jensen's to show Sharin the composites. He wondered if he should mention the apparent drowning. If it was Kurt that would cinch it. A sense of relief in knowing this might be over flowed through his tired body. He felt for this Jensen woman, who was still going through hell. Well, maybe it's coming to an end. As much as he wanted them to hear this news he decided to wait for Sven's final report.

After the brief stop at the Jensen's he continued on to his office. He called Brooker.

"Ed, there's a package coming from Sven Larsen, including a picture of Kurt. I'm sending a copy to Brett Callahan with a top priority. We'll have his office do a thorough check on this guy. I want to know everything about him – family, friends, hobbies, where he lived, the works. See that this picture is sent to all police services in the state. I want every last policeman in Minnesota to have a picture of this guy."

Jack started into his files in an attempt to get caught up. He wanted to close the case but knew he couldn't. They needed the body. Was it really over? Time to get to the paper work.

Jack sent updates to the Commissioner and Governor, pleased that results had been so quick in coming down. It never hurt to impress those in power. He started to sift through his files. Near the top was the fax from Brett and the composite of the suspect in the hotel murder. Incredible as it seemed, it was identical to Kurt. What had Brett said? This guy had cut his victim. In both of the cases here, the victim had been cut. Had Kurt returned to L.A. to kill William? If so, why?

Jack called David at the Forensic Unit.

"David Folk." He answered in his usual hurried manner, making his name sound like one word – Davidfolk.

"Do you ever do anything at a moderate pace? You can't even say your own name slowly."

"Good afternoon to you too, amazing Sherlock. What's up?"

"Another curious turn of events. As you know, I trade notes with Brett Callahan in L.A. on our respective cases. We've been doing this for years. His newest murder victim happened to own the house where Mrs Jensen was held."

"I know," said David. "It was his request that sent you out to Clearwater the other night, and lo and behold you find not only Mrs Jensen, but her captor, and now prime suspect in your latest two killings. Three crimes solved at once. Your brilliance in unraveling cases would make a fine Jewish mother very proud of you, Jack."

"Thanks again, David," said Jack. "To continue, Brett sent me a fax of composites done on his suspect, from two eye witnesses. Guess who they resemble?"

"Oh, I couldn't imagine. Perhaps, Krazy Kurt, himself?"

"The one and only. And there was a knife used in the L.A. homicide. Nastily, I might add."

"Ah, we now get to the main point of this phone call," said David. "My favorite super sleuth wants to know whether I can determine if the same knife was used in his two cases, as well as in L.A. Am I close, Detective Jack?"

"Yawn. Right on, David. Did I expect anything less?"

"The answer is, maybe. So I'm sure you'll have Brett send the post-mortem examinations here for me to review. I'll be pleased to spend my one day off going over this for you."

"Thanks, David. Incidentally, I'm about to order some gourmet burgers and home fries. Care to join me?"

"You just happened to catch me at a bad time, Jack. As much as I want to say 'no,' I'm going to say – 'no.' Bye for now."

Jack called Brett and caught him at his office.

"You're not going to believe this, Brett. Your guy is a dead ringer for my suspect. We might get lucky here. Me returning your favor by solving your case as well as mine."

"How do you figure?" asked Brett.

"We've got three murders, with some similarities. An extremely sharp knife was used, in two of the cases, unnecessarily. Your victim owned the house where my suspect was staying, at the least providing a connection with the two. The physical resemblance is too strong to ignore."

"Jack, I admit we have a good lead here, with this guy being at the scene at the right time, but so far, that's all. We know nothing about him yet. Don't have a motive. Hell, we're not even sure that he knew William Kyle. We haven't any other leads yet. Don't know his name, where he lives, and so on."

"If he's one and the same as my suspect, you'll have all those answers."

"Hold on, Jack. You say your guy had tried to kill this woman, then holds her in a house, which turns out to be William's. Why would he want to put William away, leaving his wallet and driver's license, so the police could track him right back to where he's holding a woman captive? This ain't sounding too good to me."

"Maybe he figured the system would take a while. Give him enough time to get back here, polish off Mrs Jensen, then split. Anyway, I'd like you to send me the autopsy. I want my forensic guy to have a look. See if the knife's the same one used in all three murders. No harm in that, is there?"

"Okay, Jack. I'll get it off to you when it's complete. You all right?"

"I'm fine. Just don't like the smell I've got with this one. Nobody wants a serial killer around. Our suspect got away from us, cut some guy's throat and stole his car. But the story gets better for the good guys. He ends up at a fishing camp owned by a friend of his and apparently drowns in a freak accident."

"How do you, 'apparently drown,' Jack?"

"Yeah, sounds weird I guess," said Jack. He then related the entire story as told by Sven.

"We're now waiting for the divers to find both body and boat. Then we'll put this to bed, maybe for both of us."

"Good luck and keep me posted," said Brett.

"Will do. Got another call. Ciao." He switched to the other line.

"Lieutenant, it's Sheriff Larsen on line two."

28

Sven had heard of Phil's fishing camp and was quite taken with the layout. The cabins and grounds were well kept with easy access to the dock and boats. There was the usual store, well stocked with fishing tackle, charts, and all manner of fishermen's needs. The same building housed the kitchen and eating facilities, which included counter service with eight stools as well as five tables, each seating four to six people.

Phil himself was a solid citizen and obviously a hard working guy who handled most of the numerous chores at his camp. The experience with Kurt had shaken him and now both men wanted to see the end of this affair. The divers were on their third dive, working down-current from the point where Kurt had entered the water.

Sven and Phil were huddled in the same boat Phil had used earlier in the morning in his attempted flight to get help. They were anchored beside the police boat, just off the rock which Kurt had struck. Phil had known the location of the rock and with Kurt gaining on him, had purposely set up the collision. He had merely wanted to slow Kurt down, allowing time to get to the authorities. He still didn't understand why Kurt hadn't got out of the sinking boat.

The temperature had steadily dropped to forty degrees by late afternoon. It was a penetrating, bone chilling cold that they felt, even through their lined parkas. The second thermos of coffee was almost gone. With no room in the boat to move around and generate any kind of body heat, both men were hoping for some positive results from the latest dive. They admired the divers working in these conditions. The visibility was poor late in the afternoon and although their dry suits kept them warm in the water, it was no picnic when they surfaced and had to endure the trip back to shore. Although their suits offered some protection it was actually colder out of the water, so precautions had to be taken. Extra blankets, along with the usual emergency equipment, were available.

The police had hired three teams of two divers each and Sven had been impressed with how quickly they had been organized. All were employed full time in other work, but were known to the police and available for various diving operations. Each dive lasted about an hour at depths ranging from thirty to forty feet. Surface rest time was mandatory to prevent excessive nitrogen build-up in the diver's blood stream. Fresh water diving differed from salt water and the dive tables were adjusted accordingly. Ten feet was added to the dive tables, so a thirty foot dive was profiled as forty feet, due to the higher nitrogen content. The other complication was colder temperatures and the risk of hypothermia.

Two teams were in the water while a third remained in the boat for emergencies. While diving, the teams were tethered to the boat and used a specific search pattern in their efforts to locate the body.

Phil was shocked to learn the details of the Crosslake homicide. "It's hard to believe I used to work with this guy, and harder to believe I just spent over twelve hours alone with him."

"You're lucky to be here," said Sven. "Good thing you decided to give him an extra dose of Demerol, although as it turned out, even that was barely enough. Why didn't he get out of the boat?"

"I don't know. When he hit the rock I looked around and turned the flashlight on him. I knew he wouldn't be able to chase me so I just wanted to make sure he was afloat while I got help. I noticed the boat was at a crazy angle and filling with water. He was lying down and trying to reach the upper side of his boat. He yelled at me and right after, both Kurt and the boat disappeared."

"Funny that he was conscious and still didn't get out," replied Sven. "Anyway, we should know soon enough, I hope. Don't envy those divers, working in these conditions. You ever try Scuba?"

"Nah. I like boating and fishing," said Phil. "But I've never been too keen on getting into the water. Not afraid – just don't care for it. You think Kurt also killed the guy in the car?"

"After talking to Jack Petersen, the homicide detective on this case, we're pretty sure. They found the victim with his throat cut. With his car here, there's no doubt now."

"I keep thinking back to our L.A. days. Kurt was very professional on the job and extremely bright, but he was a bit of a loner. I don't remember him having a lot of friends, but unfortunately as it turns out, I was one of them."

The third dive was due to end soon with both men anxious for some good news. After seeing Ginny's mutilated body, Sven couldn't help but hope that this sadistic maniac hadn't survived the boating accident. It was not his nature to harbor such thoughts, but Ginny's brutal slaying had left him with no sympathy for her killer. For the first time in his career, he wondered if he would be able to trust himself if he ever met up with Kurt.

That should be academic now. There was a marker on the surface. Something had been found. The procedure was to tie a marker to the found item, identifying it for future access.

They saw the bubbles first, then the emergence of the first two divers. The second team surfaced minutes later and soon all were aboard the special police craft. The divers signaled they were headed back to shore.

It took less than ten minutes to get back to Phil's camp, but it seemed much longer. The suspense leading up to the divers's findings, coupled with the long, cold wait, was almost too much. The divers unloaded their gear and made their way to Phil's store and restaurant. They were cold and tired.

Sven and Phil let them be for the moment as they secured their own boat. Phil had called in his cook to be on hand for the day and she had steak and eggs on the grill in no time. Everyone dug in and the divers began their report.

Yes, they had found the boat. Only the boat.

29

Fred Pearce had trouble getting up, which was unusual for him. He was not going to enjoy today. The funeral service was set for eleven this morning. Being a widower with no children, the most important person in his life had been Ginny. He had known her since birth, and after her fourth birthday, had been unofficially declared her self-appointed God Father.

Fred had been present at every important day in Ginny's life. He hadn't missed a birthday, school graduation, Easter, Thanksgiving, or Christmas celebration in all her young life. As Ginny's father had passed away prior to her marriage, Fred was chosen to give her away. It was a proud moment. Now, he was going to bury her.

He managed a single piece of toast with his coffee, then showered and dressed. There was one dark suit, navy blue, in his closet, and he chose a shirt, tie, and shoes which should match. He wasn't very good at coordinating colors, nor was he in the mood to care about such details. He set out for the fifteen minute walk to the church, not bothering to lock any of the doors to his small home, and not aware his every move was being closely monitored.

Fred arrived at the church at twenty to eleven, where he met Ginny's Mom. They sat together, removed from Roy, who had never been too popular with either. Sven Larsen, the county Sheriff, set an imposing figure alongside Roy and some of his poker buddies. The town had heard the rumors about a drowning incident over at Whitefish Lake, and knew Sven was involved in the investigation. It was believed that Ginny's killer might be at the bottom of the lake, which was a consoling thought to most.

The small church was packed with standing room only at the back. Ginny was well known. Practically the entire town had turned out to pay their respects.

The congregation adjourned to the cemetery behind the church for the internment. Low, brooding clouds scudded along the hillside, darkening the sky and reflecting the somber mood of the mourners. Nasty weather was on its way, but certainly not on the minds of those at the funeral. Following the burial, all gathered in the church basement for refreshments, to huddle and commiserate with each other over this senseless tragedy.

Fred and Ginny's Mom received most of the attention and condolences, even more than Roy. Fred and Sven Larsen were also beleaguered with questions. Did the man drown at Phil's camp? Was he really Ginny's murderer? Was he the only suspect? Where did he come from? Why did he kill Ginny? What did he look like?

They all meant well, but it was becoming too much for Fred. Sven did his best to run interference for him, knowing how much the old man was suffering. Parents should never have to bury their children and everyone knew Ginny had been very much like a daughter to Fred.

Fortunately Albert and Jan, the only other people to have seen the killer and thus were also being questioned, came by and guided Fred off to a corner where they could have some peace. Fred gratefully accepted their company and the three quietly traded stories and memories of Ginny.

It was shortly after three when people began leaving. Sven's wife, Ingrid, had prepared dinner for Fred, Ginny's Mom, whose only relative was a sister living in Sarasota and unable to make the trip, and Albert and Jan. Sven drove them to his house for their private evening.

Roy had been invited but had opted to be with his poker group, with the intention of drinking himself into oblivion. He kept repeating how badly he had treated Ginny, making her work all those long hours while he was off with the boys. If only he had spent more time with her, this would never have happened. He would carry this guilt with him for the rest of his life.

Ingrid Larsen served a delightful baked ham, scalloped potatoes, garden fresh vegetables, and home made butter tarts for dessert. The small group did their best, but with their hearts not in it, failed to do justice to her cooking. The Larsens were gracious hosts and Fred was thankful for the company and quiet intimacy of close friends. Although it was only seven o'clock he felt it time to leave.

Sven wanted to drive him home, but Fred was adamant that he needed the walk. After all it was only ten minutes or so. The ominous sky warned that the weather would soon worsen, but other than a brisk wind, there was little to deter Fred from leaving on his own. He offered his thanks and bade them all good night.

It was colder than he had thought, so he huddled in his suit jacket, pulling the lapels together in an effort to keep the wind out. Not that he really minded. He was content to wage his small battle against the impending storm, striding forward at a steady pace into the wind. He was so lost in thought, he almost missed turning down his street. It would have been better if he had.

He was barely inside the house when he removed the jacket and loosened his tie. Fred hadn't worn a tie since Ginny's birthday dinner in August. A single tear rolled down his cheek. Life would never be the same again. He debated on having a cold beer or just sitting in the living room to collect his thoughts. He decided on the latter.

Abruptly the storm whipped up, with sleet lashing the front windows and wind forces so strong they rocked the entire house. The stillness inside, coupled with the ferocity of the weather outside, presented an eerie contrast. The trees across the street practically bent to the ground with the gale-like winds. Flying debris scurried along the lawns.

Despite the turmoil, Fred was quite calm. Then a hand clamped tightly on his mouth and pinned him against the back of the chair. He pulled on the arm restraining him but couldn't budge it. Terror seized him. He saw a glint of steel. The attacker's arm flashed by, driving the knife deep into Fred's stomach. The pain was unbearable. The knife was removed and it thudded in again. Fred died of a massive heart attack before the third wound. The stabbing continued with unabated viciousness.

The killer calmly wiped the knife clean and left the small home. He strolled to his vehicle, parked just two houses away, and drove slowly through the town.

No one saw him leave. The streets were deserted.

30

Jack was on his way out to Pete's, his favorite hamburger place, when Watson signaled there was an incoming call. He took it at the front desk.

"Petersen here."

"Jack, it's Sven. We've got another one. Fred Pearce was murdered last night. Stabbed to death. You better come up. I'll be in my office."

"Be there in an hour." Jack hung up and briefed Watson. He picked up a burger and shake at a drive through, Pete's would have to wait for another day, and drove north to Crosslake. You just don't eat Pete's hamburgers in a car. They're gourmet burgers, with the best sauces anywhere in the nation. Not only is it an injustice to eat them while driving, they're too messy.

The beat goes on. Did that maniac survive the boating accident? Is he now taking up where he left off? He called Watson and ordered more protection for the Jensens. He wouldn't tell them about the new murder – not yet.

On arrival, Jack was immediately taken into Sven's office. The Sheriff was angry. Jack was sure that if Sven ever laid his hands on this killer, he would simply crush him to death, much like a boa squeezes the life from its prey before devouring it.

"Thanks for coming," said Sven. "I'll take you to Fred's house."

Sven briefed Jack on Fred's homicide. His speech was abrupt, and as he talked his face flushed. He was more than upset. This latest killing, with its brutality, seemed too much, even for an officer of the law like Sven.

"It wasn't enough for this bastard to take Fred's life," said Sven. "He used him as a pin cushion. Over twenty stab wounds. Most in the stomach. Fred died of a heart attack before most of the wounding. The coroner could tell from the pre-mortem and post-mortem wounds. Sick son of a bitch." Sven sped around a sharp left turn, tires squealing.

"Fred was at our house last night. We had a few people over after Ginny's funeral. I offered to drive him home. He wouldn't hear of it."

Sven's grip on the steering wheel was so tight, Jack thought it would snap in two.

"Don't let me catch him, Jack. You'd have to arrest me."

Jack knew this was temporary anger. Sven was too good an officer to allow his emotions to control his actions. At least he hoped that was the case, especially for Sven. They arrived at Fred's house. The entire lot was cordoned off with several officers and specialists on the scene.

"We're canvassing the street," said Sven. "One neighbor saw a car that was new to her. Not owned by anyone around here. She said it was there for a few hours from late afternoon on. She remembers looking out shortly after the storm started and it was gone."

"She able to ID the car for you?" asked Jack.

"We're working on that now. She's pretty observant. Spends a lot of time checking out the neighborhood."

"If you had the same storm we did, it must have played hell with any outside evidence," said Jack.

"There's nothing left. We had rain and sleet for several hours. We'll have to see what forensics gives us from inside the house. Jack, it has to be Kurt. He'd have no trouble tracking Fred down. And Fred had seen him at the bar the night Ginny was killed. So did Jan and Albert. I've got an officer over there now but there's a limit to how long we can supply that service. We just don't have enough staff for round the clock protection."

"Sven, I read your report on the boating accident at Phil's. Do you figure Kurt had any chance of surviving? I mean, the guy's had a severe whack on the head, he's dosed up with extra Demerol, and Phil sees him go down with the boat."

"Remember, it was dark and Phil couldn't understand why Kurt hadn't just surfaced. He thought maybe the guy had been knocked out, but then he was sure he had seen him grabbing at the side of the boat as it went down."

"Didn't Phil stick around for a while, checking for any signs of Kurt?" asked Jack.

"Yeah. The lake was calm that night, so Phil should have been able to see him in the water, but he didn't. Maybe you better talk to Phil yourself, Jack. Heh, we better let him know about this. If it is Kurt, Phil's in danger as well."

"Good idea, Sven, I'm going up to Phil's camp. Do we drive or go by boat?"

"We've got a boat going with more air tanks for the divers. It'll take about half an hour."

"That's fine," said Jack.

Sven got Phil's number from the office and dialed him on his cell phone. The cook answered, and explained that Phil was out on the lake with the dive team. Sven left word that Lieutenant Petersen was on his way.

The trip to Whitefish Lake took forty minutes on clear water and along a shore line dotted with magnificent splashes of color. The multi-colored fall leaves, mixed with evergreens and silver birches, provided a breath taking backdrop against the deep blue water. Jack thoroughly enjoyed the water and its sports, but never seemed to find the time to enjoy either. It was another topic on his mind lately – organizing time for Jennifer and recreation.

As they entered Whitefish Lake, Jack wondered where Kurt was. He had to be the prime suspect in Fred's murder. There was not only motive and means, but also the resemblance to the other homicides. However, if Kurt was at the bottom of this lake, a new investigation would begin. Jack didn't relish either alternative.

Despite the chill from the fall air, Jack was comfortable in the cabin of the sleek police craft. He spent the remainder of the trip chatting with the boat's captain, a young officer with nine year's experience, who was at home on the water and a big Vikes fan. He was quite disturbed over the recent homicides in Crosslake, the first in his career.

When they reached Phil's camp, the divers and Phil were in the main building, having a quick meal prior to the next dive. So far, no trace of Kurt. After Jack was introduced Phil asked him if he'd eaten. Jack inquired about the hamburgers and was assured they were the best in the state. He ordered two.

Between bites of what Jack admitted was a great hamburger, Phil reviewed the accident and diving activities.

"I'm sure he went down with the boat," said Phil. "I circled the area for several minutes before leaving to call the police. It was dark, but the visibility was good, and I'd be damn surprised if he'd surfaced and I hadn't seen him."

"If he did somehow survive, Phil, he's likely to come back here. For your own safety I'd rather you move somewhere till we find him. Is there someone you can stay with?"

"Yeah, that's not a problem. The divers have two more goes this afternoon before packing it in. If nothing turns up, I'll go into town. We're about ready now. You going to join us?"

Jack said he would, complimented the cook on the delicious burgers, and headed out with Phil. They boarded the two boats, Phil with Jack, and headed out to the dive site.

Jack wanted a review of the entire visit with Kurt. There was still a killer at large and he needed every bit of information available for the files. The divers entered the water and the two men went through Kurt's visit and accident. It took the better part of an hour before Jack was satisfied. It seemed incongruous, discussing this murderer on a quiet peaceful lake, surrounded by beauty and nature.

The divers reappeared, shaking their heads. Sadly, nothing yet. They would take another mandatory surface break before continuing. Jack said he had to leave, wished them good luck, and received assurances from Phil that he would move into town unless they found Kurt's body.

It was dusk as the boat sliced its way through the water. There was a slight ripple on its surface which caused a quiet lapping against the hull. It was hypnotic. Coupled with the gentle rocking motion, Jack could have nodded off had his mind not been racing with the twists and turns of this case.

If Kurt has somehow survived, there is a depraved killer on the loose, responsible for three murders in this state and probably one in California, all in the last week. How many others? The other scenario is, the guy did drown. Then someone else brutalized poor Fred. Jack didn't like one any more than the other.

Maybe David had the info from Brett and had reached some conclusions. He'd call him from the car to arrange a meeting with the inimitable scientist at his office. It would be after six when they got back to Crosslake, close to eight by the time he reached St Cloud.

No dinner at home tonight.

31

They rounded a turn in the trail and were startled by the noise. The dogs flew off in the direction of the disturbance. Sharin started to run, frantically calling after them. She found them, camped at the base of a tree, as a harried porcupine climbed its way to safety, luckily for all. A confrontation between dog and porcupine invariably results in a mouthful of nasty quills for the dog, and their subsequent removal by the vet.

It was unnerving, but it had been her decision to take this walk alone. Sharin had suggested that life had to be resumed, and the sooner the better. They had received a call from Jack Petersen who gave them a brief update including the news of the drowning. There was a diving operation underway to find the body. Although it couldn't be assumed Kurt was gone, there was a ray of hope.

Therefore Eric had been cajoled into going to the office for half a day, and her parents were off to the Minneapolis Mall. She knew police officers were nearby, but at least they managed to provide their protection in an unobtrusive way, allowing Sharin a relatively private stroll through their wooded lot. They had insisted on her carrying a special whistle, just in case.

One side of her said she was nuts to do this, but she was determined to try. Despite being half scared to death, she willed herself to go on.

The fifty acre parcel offered an abundance of wildlife, including squirrels, chipmunks, fox, porcupines, racoons, and deer, as well as a wide variety of bird life. An old logging trail cut through their land, providing a pleasant path to meander along while enjoying nature. Sighting deer was the highlight of their ventures. Sharin marveled at these graceful animals who were absolutely fearless of the dogs.

More than once deer had materialized on the path. The dogs had roared off after them, only to return minutes later with their tongues hanging out. On each occasion the deer had nonchalantly turned and effortlessly bounded off into the brush. The dogs had no chance of overtaking the graceful animals.

It was midmorning with the temperature hovering near forty. The bright sun made for a perfect day to be out. She had the feeling someone was watching her. It had to be the police. What was happening up at that lake? Did Kurt really drown? That would put an end to this and allow them to get on with our lives.

Sharin continued deeper into the woods. Today she was keeping to the logging trail, whereas normally she preferred to wander through the heavy brush. It was a more intriguing walk when you were off the groomed path. However, she had promised Eric and the police to stay on the trail, where she could easily be found if the need arose. They reached the end of their property and turned to go back to the house.

King froze. He stared further into the woods. His hackles rose. A low growl started deep in his throat. Kayla picked up the scent and both their heads tilted high as they sniffed the air. A breeze had picked up. The trees groaned as they swayed. Leaves rustled, birds chirped, and crows cawed. Only the forest was talking. Sharin did not see or hear anything other than nature itself. She was still concerned.

Had she come too far? Maybe it had been too soon to attempt this trek alone. She wouldn't use the whistle unless it was absolutely necessary. She quietly told the dogs to come, and began walking. Kayla came immediately but King hesitated, continuing to stare in the same direction. He started barking, Kayla joined in. Sharin called him again. Reluctantly, he came to Sharin's side and the three began making their way back along the trail to the house. King still continued to look back. Sharin picked up the pace.

Again King stopped, this time staring straight ahead. Kayla joined him. Two men came rushing around a corner towards Sharin. The dogs lunged. Sharin said, "No, stay." It was the two policemen.

"We heard barking. Are you okay?" the first officer asked.

"I'm fine," said Sharin. "The dogs acted strangely a minute ago, but I didn't see or hear anything unusual. I admit, it gave me a start."

"Maybe we should go back, Ma'am. These are not the best conditions for us."

"That maniac is controlling our lives," said Sharin as she kicked a loose branch away in frustration.

"We'll get him for you if he isn't already gone. I'm betting he's at the bottom of the lake. From what I read on the report, there's no way he survived," said the first officer.

They were both so young. God, she was only thirty-two, yet these guys looked like boys. The one who did all the talking had a full crop of red hair, while the other who sported a finely trimmed moustache, appeared shy, but very serious about his job. Fine with her.

"I hope you're right. That would end all of this. I keep thinking it's not going to get to me, but it does. I was scared back there. I'm not used to that."

"Don't know anyone who is, Ma'am. You're holding up real well," said Red.

"It may appear that way, but I'm not. I'm frustrated, angry, and scared. Odds are he's a psycho, which troubles me even more," said Sharin.

"Yeah, I know what you mean. They're the worst kind," continued Red. "But you're well protected. I've never seen so many officers assigned to a case. Understand your father had something to do with that."

"Probably. Dad can be real persistent and he does know a lot of people. You begin to wonder if it's ever going to end."

"Oh, we'll get him Ma'am. No doubt about that. Lieutenant Petersen, he's the best there is. Been in his division for three years now. He's the finest. Yes sir, Ma'am. Just the best. That right, Jim?"

"Yup," said moustache. He nodded enthusiastically and smiled.

"Jim doesn't say much, Ma'am, but he's my favorite partner."

"He's Jim. What's your name?" asked Sharin.

"Ted, Ma'am. Ted Knott. Guys always kidding me about that little poem. 'Knott and Shott fought a duel. Knott was shot, and Shott was not. Was better to be Shott than Knott.'"

Sharin giggled. He had succeeded in lightening the situation, but at the same time remained serious and focused on his duties. The shift of officers changed regularly and this was the first time Sharin had actually met her protectors. It was comforting. Despite their youth they appeared alert and capable.

The house was now in sight as was Eric's car in the driveway. They turned up the path leading to the house and Eric emerged through the patio doors. The dogs raced to greet him.

"Couldn't stay at the office any longer?" asked Sharin.

"Everything is fine there. I wanted to be back here," said Eric. He greeted Sharin with a hug and nodded to the officers. "She been behaving?"

"More or less, sir," said Ted. "We did have a little incident back there, but nothing developed."

"Just what was this little incident?"

"Oh, the dogs started barking when we were at the fence line," said Sharin. "I didn't see or hear anything. We were about to return anyway."

"The woods are not a good place to be until we know Kurt is gone, permanently," said Eric with his arm around his wife. "You talk me into going to the office, then you take off for a stroll in the woods. Not again without police approval. Do we have a deal?"

"Yeah. I know you're right. Thanks for caring."

"We sort of suggested that, sir," said Ted. "Maybe we'll hear from the divers today."

"Were there any messages, Eric?"

"No. Let's call Detective Petersen and get an update."

The Jensens and their dogs went inside while the officers took up their posts.

At the tree line, a sumac tree shifted slightly, though there was no wind.

32

Jack actually slept in again. The second time in a week. His morning run was in ideal conditions, cool and sunny. By eight-thirty he had showered and tucked in a healthy breakfast, consisting of a bowl of hot cereal with fruit. Breakfast had been alone as Jennifer attended university classes every Saturday and had to leave the house by seven.

He arrived in plenty of time for the ten A.M. meeting with the investigation team, giving him an opportunity to review the situation. There was a map with pins and notations of the activity thus far. The area was growing, as was the number of staff assigned to the case. A black pin with a date attached indicated the homicides to date. White pins showed pertinent events, also dated.

Jack stared at the map.

White pin – Sun. Oct. 10th: Jensen's Jaguar found – Waverley Road. Missing person report filed.

Black pin – Sun. Oct. 10th: Ginny Brewer murdered – Crosslake.

White pin – Tues. Oct. 12th: Jensen found – Kurt escapes – Clearwater.

Black pin – Tues. Oct. 12th: Al Lucas murdered – Clearwater – car stolen.

White pin – Wed. Oct. 13th: Kurt missing – Whitefish Lake – diving begins.

Black pin – Thurs. Oct. 14th: Fred Pearce murdered – Crosslake.

At the bottom of the map another notation:

Black pin – Tues. Oct. 12th: William Kyle murdered – L.A.

Four homicides in five days. Murders of Ginny and Lucas, definitely connected. Those of Fred and William, not so clear. William known by Kurt, but no obvious motive. Did have time to fly to L.A. and back, but seems questionable. Kurt certainly had the motive to kill Fred – but what if he did drown in Whitefish Lake? According to Phil, that accident occurred Wednesday morning at four. Fred was killed late Thursday afternoon. That would mean another killer.

Summary. Four murders. One, two, or three killers. All victims connected to Kurt. Time for David Folk. Jack knew he was expected for the morning meeting. He went to the door of his office.

"Has David Folk arrived yet?" asked Jack.

"I think that's his car now, Lieutenant."

"Send him in right away. I want to talk to him before the meeting."

Jack returned to the map and his notes. David arrived a few minutes later.

"Ah, good morning, Shylock. I mean, Sherlock. What's up?" asked David.

"At least you're consistent. Consistently bad. Things are getting a little muddled here. Do you have anything from the autopsies that will help me?"

"You want comparisons on all four homicides?"

Jack nodded.

"I'll need to talk to the unit in L.A. to clear up a couple of issues, but here's what I have now. There's at least two knives, maybe three. Forensically speaking, all four murders could have been performed by the same person. On the other hand, it's possible there's more than one killer, but not more than two."

"Let's do the knives first, David. By victim, please."

"The knife you sent me from up north, let's call it number one, is the murder weapon in both Ginny's case and Lucas's. We know it couldn't have been used on Fred, not only from my findings, but because we had the darn thing at the time of his death. Was number one used in William's murder? Maybe, maybe not. Need more info. So make number two the weapon in Fred's case. Ditto for William? Don't know yet." David put down his notes.

"Here's the recap. Ginny and Lucas by number one. William by number one, two, or three. Fred by number two or three."

"Okay. What about the suspect?" asked Jack.

"Again, forensically there may be only one killer. DNA testing proves Kurt definitely killed Ginny. We had blood samples from William's house where Mrs Jensen nailed him with the poker. Additionally Ginny had managed to cut him with the letter opener so we had more blood from the bar. No doubt, it was Kurt. We're still waiting for evidence from the L.A. hotel and Fred Pearce's house. There wasn't any blood or other fluids but we do have hair samples. So far no match."

"What else?" asked Jack.

"Another factor suggesting one killer is that the strength used inflicting wounds in three of the cases is consistent. The penetration of both stabbing and slicing actions is practically identical. Although not conclusive, the evidence strongly suggests one person. Multiple weapons of course means nothing. One killer could have a room full of knives. One knife is simpler, as it most likely would implicate only one suspect."

"David, go over all of this at the morning meeting, along with a recap of the other evidence from the different crime scenes."

Watson hurried into Petersen's office.

"Lieutenant, telephone. It's the Commissioner."

"See you in the meeting, David." Jack picked up the call.

"Good morning, Commissioner."

"Jack, what the hell is going on out there? This morning's headline is screaming about another murder in Crosslake. You just had one there the other day. Along with Clearwater, that's three in a week. Are they connected?"

"They may be, Commissioner. I don't want to jinx us, but we're very close to clearing up most of the mystery surrounding these cases."

"Brief me."

Jack went over his notes, Folk's report, and the diving expedition on Whitefish Lake. "Obviously, finding Kurt's body will take care of several issues, but leave the last homicide open."

"I don't like either scenario. How's your manpower holding up?"

"We have thirty-eight officers on the case now, sir. I'll wait till we hear from Whitefish Lake. We'll be okay till then."

"Have you heard from the Governor lately?" asked the Commissioner.

"No, sir."

"Maybe he's still away. Better for you and me if he is. What about Frank Wilson?"

"I talk to the family regularly but haven't discussed the latest from Crosslake. I'll call them right after this morning's meeting," replied Jack.

"I know you have a fine record, Jack. Don't let this one spoil it. We're going to start getting a lot of heat. Keep me posted."

"Will do, sir." He hung up.

That's all he needed right now. A few politicians breathing down his neck. Well, it goes with the territory. Jack picked up his case file and went into the meeting. An hour later he returned to his office where the message light was blinking. There were calls from the Jensens, Jennifer, the Commissioner again, two newspapers, a tv reporter, and three radio stations. He was about to start sorting out the order when Watson came in.

"Sheriff Larsen on the phone, Lieutenant."

"Good morning, Sven. Any news?"

"I'm not sure if this is what we wanted, Jack. They're ready to cancel the diving operation. No body. They say three days is it. It's possible a body could turn up yet, but they can't justify any more time. Of course it's your call, but that's their recommendation."

"Do they realize how that hampers our investigation? Do we assume Kurt's alive, and keep looking for him as the lone killer? And if we're wrong, some other maniac slips through?"

"I read you, Jack. The divers say that with the current down there, he could be anywhere. The odds just got slimmer and slimmer as each day passed. If he did drown, they say he'll float and you'll find him sooner that way than they will."

"I guess I understand. It's just that doing nothing doesn't feel right. Let me think about it."

"It's your decision, Jack. You have the authority to continue if you want."

"Let me talk to the Dive Master," said Jack.

Fifteen minutes later Jack was convinced of the futility of extending the operation. He briefed Sven before ending the call.

Is that bastard still out there? Fred's death certainly made it look that way.

33

The Jensens and Wilsons were huddled in front of the television set late Saturday afternoon, watching a special news break. They didn't want to believe what was happening. A large group of reporters had cornered Senator Bob Johnston as he was entering his office. He was adamantly denying any connection between the Clearwater and Crosslake murders.

"What about the Jensen abduction? We're told the same guy responsible for that is also the prime suspect in these murders. Any truth to that?" asked a reporter.

"Lieutenant Jack Petersen is handling this investigation, and he is one of the country's best. Not just the best in this state, but in the entire nation. Commissioner Boyle assures me we have the best team possible assigned to this case."

"Then you're saying this is big," said another reporter.

"We're merely being cautious and not taking any chances. The people of Minnesota deserve the best protection and they're getting just that."

"Are you saying there's no serial killer here?" asked the first reporter.

"I've just returned from Atlanta and am seeing the Commissioner within the hour. I'll know more after that meeting."

With that, Johnston was escorted away from the persistent reporters and the interview was over.

The coverage droned on with assurances that Commissioner Boyle and Lieutenant Petersen would be contacted and further updates would soon be aired.

Frank Wilson was the first to break the silence. "Why hasn't Petersen returned our calls? Surely he realizes our concern with this latest murder."

"You're right, Dad," said Eric. "Who was Fred Pearce, anyway? Do we have any idea?"

"Obviously Jack would know that," said Sharin. "Surely he'll call soon."

"I hope sooner than later," said Eric.

"Of course, sooner than later," snapped Sharin.

"I think I'll make some tea," said Judy Wilson. "Anybody interested?"

All three nodded. An uneasy silence ensued.

"Sorry, honey." Sharin went to her husband and hugged him. "Christ, that was stupid."

Eric put his arm around her and gently stroked her hair. "This is really taking its toll, isn't it? So far Petersen has kept us up to the minute with this case. What's his problem now?"

"My guess is, he's not only being pressured by the Commissioner and the Senator, but now the media is hounding him," said Frank.

"I know where I've seen that name before," said Sharin. "Fred Pearce was one of the eye witnesses at the first Crosslake murder. Remember, the girl in the bar. There was Fred and another couple. They both saw Kurt there the night she was killed."

"That's right," said Frank. "But wasn't he killed sometime Thursday?"

Sharin and Eric nodded. Judy brought the tea and some home made cookies. She began serving everyone.

"But Kurt apparently drowned," said Sharin. "At least he went missing on ..."

"Yes," said Eric. "Early Wednesday morning."

"Which would mean only one thing," said Sharin. The trembling started again. The mere thought that the monster was still alive was terrifying. "Is this ever going to end?" Eric held her tightly.

Judy started crying, seeing her daughter distraught again. Frank took over.

"Now, we're only guessing here. Yes, if he killed Fred, he did survive. But we don't know that for sure."

Sharin hadn't touched her tea. "Dad," she began slowly, "this man was an eye witness. Kurt knew that. He'd track him down, wouldn't he?"

"It certainly looks that way," said Frank. "We do need to hear from Petersen."

"I think I'll help get dinner. Okay, Mom?" Sharin wasn't in the least hungry, but had to do something.

The phone rang and Sharin took the call. She indicated it was Petersen, then listened closely. She hung up and heaved a deep sigh.

"Are you all right, dear?" asked Judy.

"I guess so. Here's the latest. The divers were unable to find Kurt's body, so that leaves them up in the air. If he did drown, a body will show up soon."

"If we thought this situation was bizarre last Sunday, it's not any better now is it?" asked Eric. "You survived the first part of this, honey, now we'll make sure you're okay till they work this out."

"It's the not knowing, isn't it? Is he still alive? There's something I'm trying to remember that may help. It happened when Kurt had me in that house. I just can't recall what it was."

"You've got enough to deal with. Let Petersen and his team solve this. Somehow we've got to do what he said. Stay alert and be careful," said Frank.

"It's going to bug me till I remember," said Sharin.

"The fact that Petersen still wants the police here shows his concern. I feel better with them around," said Eric.

Sharin went to the kitchen with Judy to prepare dinner. The first incident occurred when she accidentally bumped into her mother with two saucepans in her hands. One of the lids clattered to the floor. In short order she managed to knock over the sugar bowl, nudge a carton of milk off a shelf in the refrigerator, and drop a tray of ice cubes.

"I know I'm a klutz, Mom, but this is ridiculous," said Sharin. She burst into tears.

Judy held her daughter. "I wish I could do more for you. Make this madman disappear."

"Thanks, Mom. If only I could get a decent night's sleep. I keep waking up with a start, thinking he's in the house. The bastard's never out of my mind."

"I'm sure we're safe here with all this protection, policemen, dogs..."

"I know you're right, Mom, but somehow, it just doesn't stop the fear. It won't till they get him."

Eventually dinner was ready. Eric surprised Sharin with a well chilled Montrachet, her favorite white wine. During her pregnancy Sharin drank little alcohol, so she limited herself to half a glass of the fine wine. Judy insisted on doing the dishes and Frank said he would help. Sharin and Eric said goodnight and retired to their bedroom.

They had not made love since the ordeal, what with Sharin's recuperating from the accident and captivity, and the general tension in the house with Kurt still on the loose. Eric was quite mellow having had most of the wine, but was a patient and gentle lover. They had always been so compatible in their love making, and it was a welcome relief for Sharin to finally relax and let herself go.

"I almost forgot how good this was," said Sharin. She bit his ear and hung on tightly.

"I knew you'd come around. I'm just too irresistible," said Eric.

Sharin bit harder.

"Ouch," he said.

"You know you can't live without this body, even in its present state." She bit him again.

"Okay, okay. You're right. But you bite me once more and I'll jump on your bones again."

"You couldn't be ready for me yet. You're just bragging." She playfully nibbled again, then slid her hand down to hold him. Eric was aroused instantly.

"Well maybe with a little coaxing, you could be talked into this," said Sharin.

This time there was more urgency and passion to their love making. She realized how much she had missed Eric, while all the tension of the past week seemed to flow from her. They felt they could go on forever. Their orgasms were seconds apart, then they stayed together, each unwilling to let the other go.

"Imagine being so wrapped up with that maniac that I could leave you alone for a week."

"You sure made me forget all about what's been happening," said Eric.

"Likewise. You're still a great lover."

"Thanks. I've really missed you," said Eric.

Another bite. Another ouch. Another long hug.

Sharin cried. Eric comforted her. They had managed to push the monster aside and out of their lives, at least for the moment. They clung together, then eventually sleep came.

Sharin awoke with a start. The evening returned. It had been wonderful. Eric was a joy. Yet the monster was still out there. Nothing seemed to ease the tension or stop the gnawing fear.

How much longer could she go on like this? Her doctor had prescribed a sleeping pill but so far she had refused to take one. It was as if she had to remain alert and thus forgo an uninterrupted sleep. She admired Eric for the resilience he had shown throughout. Although he wasn't awakened every time she was, he also had been deprived of regular rest.

King came to her side, put his chin on the bed and eyed her concernedly. It was incredible the way the dogs showed emotion. Could he possibly understand she was worried? They could certainly sense fear. She stroked his massive head, thankful for such comfort. Kayla nudged her way in not wanting to miss out on the petting.

It helped pass the moment. How much longer before this is over? Hopefully they'll find him soon. Sleep gradually returned.

34

Phil admitted he was concerned that they did not find Kurt's body. It was hard to believe he could have survived, but if so there would be trouble. It had been a scary experience, housing someone who turned out to be a killer, and may still be alive.

The diving crew had determined there was little sense in carrying on, and after consulting with Lieutenant Petersen, had canceled the operation. They returned to the camp and the crews began cleaning up, preparing to leave. Phil's cook had stayed on to prepare lunches for the group while Phil served a round of beer.

The conversation got around to fishing and football. Could the Vikes go all the way this year? They all replayed the missed field goal in last year's final, which had allowed the Falcons to come back and tie, then eventually win in overtime. What a bummer! Especially after a fifteen and one season. Can Randall do it again? Like most fans, when your team looks like a Super Bowl contender, anticipation runs high every Sunday.

Phil was more interested in fishing and he soon had two of the team trading notes on various techniques, while the others continued to discuss quarterbacks, receivers, and defenses. He had soulmates, who both agreed that ultra lite rods and four pound test were the way to angle for walleye. You get a challenge with any decent sized fish, and of course there's nothing better on the table than fresh walleye.

The conversation continued for an hour before breaking up, with the divers and police officers heading back to Crosslake. One of the officers was assigned to stay with Phil. They helped the cook clean up before she headed home. It was suddenly very quiet and still. With all the commotion and activity over the past three days, coupled with the tension of waiting for results, the peace was welcome.

He thought a dinner would be in order, and called two neighbors, asking them to join him and the officer for a fish fry. Both couples would be delighted, saying they would arrive around seven, with dessert. The freezer had more than enough walleye to feed the party of six, but Phil decided to take a boat out and try for a fresh catch. It was nearing five o'clock and dusk, a good time for walleye. He certainly knew where they were. The officer said he had had enough of the lake for today, and would rather stay put and mind the store.

Phil took a warm jacket, a thermos of coffee, and his trusty ultra lite. The boat eased away from the dock and headed for one of his favorite spots. Less than half a mile from the camp there is a shelf, straddling thirty feet of clear water with a gravel bottom, some forty yards off a small peninsula. Perfect for the fish. He'd anchor for a while, and if nothing developed, would drift fish along the shelf.

Phil started casting, throwing the lure out, letting it settle to the bottom, then bringing it back slowly against the current. The sun was just off the horizon, peeking through the trees, reflecting sharply on the still water. The quiet of dusk settled on the lone fisherman and his lake. Only the occasional, gentle sound of the reel gathering in the line permeated the golden silence. His dream come true.

He would not allow the thoughts of his harrowing escape from Kurt spoil this night. He did think of Sue, of the joys during their marriage. She'd be happy for Phil. He knew that. Another cast, still no bites. He opened the thermos and poured a mug of hot coffee, which he cradled between his legs as he continued casting. The warmth felt good. It was chilly now, but not numbing.

It was perfectly still and gently quiet. One would have thought the world had stopped. Above him a cloudless sky with no airplanes in sight. The birds were still. There was no sound of cars or trucks. No other boats on the water. He put the reel on silent, as if disturbing the tranquillity of this night was sinful. Eventually he stopped reeling in.

He must have dozed off momentarily because the sudden tugging on his line startled him. Yes, there was a fish swimming with his lure. He set the hook, and gently reeled in the catch. The cobwebs cleared as his mind was getting in gear to land the fish. He fumbled for the net, brought the line closer to the boat with the tip high, and scooped up a handsome walleye. Must be three pounds. What a start. As often happens with walleye, he was into a school. Within fifteen minutes he had five more, averaging about two pounds each. Plenty for his dinner party.

The anchor was gathered in, the fish stored safely, and the return trip underway. The boat ran slowly, with the fisherman savoring the evening and natural beauty surrounding him. As if too soon, the camp appeared and he headed for the dock.

Phil tied up the boat, took the catch to the fileting table, and as it was now dark, turned on the one light they used for cleaning fish at the end of the day. It was only a forty watt bulb, but it served the purpose. He took out his Rapala knife and began working on the catch. Walleye were so easy to fillet. You ended up with a tasty serving that was free of bones.

There was a thump on the dock, shocking him out of his day dreaming. It was surprising that the disturbance was so frightening. He looked around. Nothing. Probably just the boat. There was a bit of breeze in the air. The quiet was now punctuated with sporadic interruptions. Water lapping the shore was noticeable. The melodic sound of an occasional loon echoed across the water.

Back to work. Company's coming and dinner has to be ready. He was on the fifth fish now, one more to go and he'd be done. The dock shifted. He turned again to check behind him. Nothing. Why hadn't he got a dog? Sue had said, 'When I'm gone, you move back to Minnesota, open a fishing camp, and surround yourself with a bunch of dogs.'

Anyway, there's no reason to be manic about this. He did wonder where the policeman was. It had just been a bad week with lingering thoughts of what might have been. He picked up the last fish. How was he going to prepare these tonight? Just plain and simple. A little batter and fry them. Serve with a soya, lemon, and onion sauce. God, he could taste them now. Add some boiled, new potatoes, with extra butter, and what more could you ask for?

Phil felt a sudden rush of air. The blade struck him high on the forehead. It coursed down the side of his face. He recoiled in pain. The Rapala dropped on the dock. He clutched at his face. The killer struck swiftly. The knife plunged deep into Phil's chest, again and again. He slumped forward, onto his fileting table. The killer continued stabbing his victim in the back, long after he was dead.

Phil's dream had ended.

35

Sven was at home when he received the call. His office reported two more homicides, one of their officers and Phil. Two neighbors had found Phil, stabbed to death on his dock. They had found the dead officer in the restaurant. An ambulance had been called.

Sven immediately sent out an A.P.B. with photos of Kurt as a possible suspect. He alerted the State Troopers. Stop every vehicle and check for this man. Next he called the National Guard to help comb the area for their suspect. Then he reached the K-9 unit and directed them to Phil's camp. He would enlist all the help he could, advising everybody that a police officer was one of the victims. Sven ordered a police boat to be readied, along with a team to help him at the crime scene. He called Jack who was still at his office.

"Petersen here."

"Jack, it's Sven. We've got two more murders, an officer and Phil."

"Christ almighty. Who was the officer, Sven?"

"Patrolman Brian Wertz. Young, single kid, twenty-four."

"Didn't we have two officers on duty up there?" asked Jack.

"Phil said he didn't need anybody," Sven replied. "We insisted on leaving one officer with him."

"Dammit, Sven, we can't operate that way. We'll decide who needs what, okay?"

"I know, Jack. We thought one was enough. I've made sure Al and Jan are still covered."

"What have you got going so far?"

"I've notified the Troopers, National Guard, and K-9 unit, but we could use more help. We've also sealed off water access and the road into the camp. We're stopping every vehicle in the area. We sent out a photo of Kurt with the A.P.B. We could use more, Jack."

"I'll requisition two helicopters and additional officers. Call me after you get there, Sven. I'll be here."

"Understand you're getting some pressure."

"Yeah. The media's having a field day and it will really heat up with another homicide in your area. As well, the Commissioner and one of our Senators are following the case. They all want answers. I'll wait for your call."

Sven hung up and left for the marina, where the boat and staff were waiting. Once again they headed out to Phil's camp. The boat sliced through the night, the bow slapping the water, as there was a slight chop on the lake. It was crystal clear. The stars glittered and danced in the blue-black sky. The outline of the pristine forest's trees was barely visible.

With all this natural beauty in the world, why did we have to harbor such a vile creature as the person who had committed this spate of murders? Ginny, Fred, and now, Phil and one of our men, who were all decent folks, didn't deserve to die. Sven had never experienced multiple killings in all his years as Sheriff. Now he'd had four in less than a week.

They eased into Phil's dock. The neighbors were still there and had left all the lights on. The medics had pronounced Phil and the officer dead. They were ready to take the bodies back to the coroner in Crosslake. Sven didn't want anything touched until forensics had finished. The dock was covered in blood. What kind of bastard does something like this?

Sven went up to the house where the four neighbors were showing their shock and grief. They each went through an accounting of the evening. Phil had called around four-thirty, saying he was having a fish fry. They were to arrive at seven, which they did. Nobody saw or heard anything or anyone. They found the officer in the restaurant, then the men went down to the docks, as they could see a light. That's where they found Phil. Since then they had remained in Phil's house. Both neighbors lived about a quarter of a mile away, towards the main road, but neither had seen any vehicle or person on the drive over.

Sven thanked them for waiting and began looking around. Nothing had been disturbed or vandalized. The specialists who had worked Ginny and Fred's cases were here. It was becoming too familiar.

In less than a week, he had become somewhat of an expert on murder scenes. That had never been one of his goals. One of the officers he had recruited from Brainerd had been murdered. The decisions weighed heavily on Sven. What manner of lunatic had been foisted on him? He and Jack would have to find the answers, soon.

It was time to call Jack. They reviewed the details of the murders. This time there were no witnesses. Hopefully forensics would come up with some clues. Meanwhile they went over the list of people they felt should be protected.

Sven stayed till the Specialists were finished. They pulled out at ten o'clock in the police boats, heading back to Crosslake. The loss of another citizen and friend was difficult enough, but add to that the murder of a fellow officer, and the desire to solve the case just went up several notches.

36

Jack was at his desk before seven. A fried egg sandwich was wedged between a cup of coffee and a pile of file folders. Last night he had managed to get out of the office for thirty minutes. He had made straight for Pete's, where he feasted on the double burger special with extra sauce. Finally, one gourmet meal this week.

Jack now had Kurt's picture everywhere. It was in municipal police stations, sheriff's offices, as well as tv networks, daily and weekly newspapers, bulletin boards in shopping centers, libraries, schools, office buildings, post offices, bus stops, train stations, drug stores, food stores, hospitals, walk-in clinics, hotels, motels, and anywhere else he could possibly use. The downside to all this exposure was the total awareness of the community and subsequent focus on the police departments. What were the police doing?

It was a trade-off he had to take. Somebody had to spot this maniac before he killed again. All the information from B.C.A. agents and forensic studies from the different crime scenes hadn't been able to prove there was a lone killer, or deny the possibility of more than one.

The press were having a field day with the latest news. Now that a police officer had been killed, the public outcry would intensify. There were calls from all the expected sources. The Commissioner and Senator Johnston were first on the list. He had talked briefly with the Jensens last night, but that was prior to the latest homicides. Frank Wilson had called minutes ago, and Jack had made himself unavailable. He just wasn't ready for Wilson at this time of the morning. He wasn't sure if he would ever be ready for him.

The team was meeting at nine, so he had a couple of hours to sort through the latest reports. He updated his chart.

White pin – Sat. Oct. 16th: Diving operation canceled. No trace of Kurt.

Black pin – Sat. Oct. 16th: Phil and Patrolman Wertz murdered at Phil's camp.

Kurt brutally murders Ginny, then kills a man for his car. Had full intentions of doing away with Phil and Sharin. If still alive is prime suspect. Did he kill William? If not, who did? Is that important? He made a note to call Brett.

Now there's three more homicides, two of them vicious. In every case, a knife was used. Jack felt he needed a lucky break. Where would it come from? He also knew, you made your own breaks. He continued sifting through the reports.

David Folk was meeting with the coroner to discuss the latest autopsies. He'd be in later and Jack looked forward to his input. Of course his friend would want a summary of his food intake this week and details of his social life with Jennifer. When close scrutiny reveals him lacking in both areas, the lecture would start.

Jack was feeling the effects of the strain of the investigation. With only four hours of sleep a night for the past week and the mounting pressure, he needed results. He continued reviewing the case file, with his wall chart detailing all the events in chronological order in full view.

The first two homicides in Crosslake, Sunday, and Clearwater, Tuesday night, had been solved. They had a positive ID on the suspect, Kurt, and the weapon. Kurt had also abducted the Jensen woman. Held her at William's house. That house was secured, and the B.C.A. agents had been through. He made a note to review those findings with David.

William's homicide in L.A. was Tuesday morning. Could it have been Kurt? Jack made another note to check with Brett. Also to check airlines for a male passenger – traveling alone? Earliest departure from L.A., nine-thirty A.M., with latest arrival in Minneapolis, eight-thirty P.M.

He looked at the file on Kurt. They had prints and pictures. Pictures of Kurt! Brett had an eye witness who had spent some time on a bus with their prime suspect. The composites from two witnesses had a strong resemblance to Kurt. Maybe they had prints from the hotel room. Jack had the prints and photos of Kurt sent off to Brett. If there's a match, that could solve Brett's case. They'll have everything but motive. That's still a puzzle.

Phil and police officer murdered Saturday. Is it Kurt again? What if Kurt does turn up in the lake, dead since Wednesday? Then who? A close friend? Highly unusual for a psycho to have a close friend in on such activities. A lover, male or female, seeking revenge? A relative? Father, mother, brother, or sister? Most likely suspect is male, due to the force of knife wounds, but not necessarily. A copycat? Certainly the press had reported the use of a knife in all the homicides.

"Dr Watson checking in, Sherlock," said David Folk.

Jack started at the sudden intrusion. He grunted and motioned David inside. Together they reviewed the file and his current notes.

"Where is it, David? What am I missing? If Kurt's still alive, we know where we're going. If not, we have a second killer. Who's the most likely? Lover, friend, somebody close, or none of the above? Just a weirdo getting in on the act?"

"Don't concern yourself with that right now," said David. "I think there are other areas to be explored first. I like your idea of comparing the William case with these. Let's tie that up quickly, because if Kurt killed William, you still have only one suspect. However, if he didn't, the second suspect would be a strong candidate for these last three homicides, if Kurt did drown last Wednesday.

"Because the MO's are similar," said Jack.

"Yes, Super Sleuth. That, and the connection to Kurt. You know I don't believe in coincidence."

"But we're back to motive again. Why would Kurt eliminate William, or have someone else do the job? There he is, holed up neatly, with Mrs Jensen. Once William is dead, here come the authorities. Whoever killed him didn't even try to hide the corpse. David, Kurt had to know him, didn't he?"

"Oh yes, Kurt knew William. I can't see him holding a hostage in a vacant house, not knowing who the owners are or when they're going to return. He must have made prior arrangements with him for the house."

"So why kill William?" asked Jack.

"Maybe he had decided it was time to relocate Mrs Jensen. He doesn't want any trace to the house, so he gets rid of William, comes back and moves. If she hadn't freed herself, he might have had time to sedate her and drive away. We'd be none the wiser."

"Then why didn't he remove the guy's ID?" asked Jack.

"Who knows? He was rushed or he panicked and forgot."

"Kurt isn't in that picture, and you know it," said Jack.

"You're right. So Kurt didn't do it, which might be better for you."

"Only if it's a friend of Kurt's, or someone connected to him. In that case your second theory would hold up and that person would be a likely candidate for the new homicides here. But what if William's murder is totally unrelated to Kurt?" asked Jack.

"I've already answered that. Don't even consider coincidental events like that. Kurt's a killer, holed up with a hostage in William's house. William gets it. They're connected – period."

Jack nodded.

"Back to the original scenario," said David. "Go over the notes from your visit with Phil. I think you should also get back to Mrs Jensen and review her stay with Kurt. After all, she was in that house with him for three days. There must be something we can glean from that."

"Okay, David. I like all of that. Now, if there is a second suspect, what's your take on an outsider? I don't think we can rule that out. With all the publicity this case has received, it's not a stretch for some nut to find Fred and Phil."

"All of which is true. It's also highly unlikely, as you well know. It has about the same chance as you taking Jennifer out to dinner tonight. Care to discuss that, maestro?"

"I think the meeting is about to start and I've got to make a couple of calls. See you in there."

Jack called the Jensen home and Sharin answered. He told her they needed to review the entire time she had spent in William's house.

"I want you to prepare a journal, detailing all the events during your stay. Don't omit anything. Take your time. Set it up day-by-day, it may be easier to put together that way. Will you start right away?"

"I don't relish the thought of reliving those days, but if it will help, I'll do my best," replied Sharin. "We've heard of the new murders. He's not going away, is he?"

"We may be getting closer. I've got our regular meeting now, so work on that and I'll be back to you soon."

He hung up, reflecting on what he had just said. Are we getting closer? Well, no harm in trying to boost their morale. He had increased the size of the protection unit assigned to their home, so at least they were safe. Did he have everybody covered? He'd go over that with David. Maybe they'd have lunch after the meeting.

37

The killer read every word of the report in the Sunday paper. He was always well prepared and had a photographic memory. Normally he would commit information like this to memory but he decided to set up a diary.

He had been forced into a new plan and they would pay. All of them. He began going over the list. It was so easy, remembering the details. It reminded him of a game he used to play with his best friend. They'd start with a number comprising ten digits. Each would write their number down and pass it to the other. You were allowed two minutes to memorize it, then the numbers were returned. At any moment during the next week, you could challenge and ask for your number. Get it right you win. He usually had a slight edge. If they couldn't stump each other, they'd increase the number of digits. Eventually they got to fifteen. He still won most of the time.

There was a new list now. He began recording the names, addresses, phone numbers, place of work, and family details. Everything he needed. He discarded Fred and Phil. No need for them anymore.

Sven Larsen's on the list now. Big time. Put him there along with that Petersen fuck. Both these guy's married too. Won't forget that. Have to add in the other witnesses, Al and Jan. He was enjoying setting up his private notes. A beer would go well now and there just happened to be a case in the fridge. He opened two at once to save time going back and forth.

The chronicling continued. Then there's Sharin, the one who started all this. The little bitch has a husband and her parents are here, which is really convenient. He added a few more names before pausing to reflect on who would be first. This could be the fun part. He spent more than an hour shuffling the names around until he was satisfied. The timetable might be altered, but for now it looked good to him.

The woman should be home soon and he would welcome a change of pace. They were so easy to pick out. He had found her in a bar. She was quite plain, but well endowed, lonely, and loved the attention she was getting. He was the perfect answer for her. She'd serve his purpose for a while, then he'd decide what to do with her.

With the glasses, moustache, and dyed hair, his appearance had been altered dramatically. There was little resemblance to those stupid composites they kept publishing.

He slipped the list into his wallet, opened two more beers, and sat back to patiently wait for his paramour to come home. He had found himself very angry in the last two killings. There would be more control from now on, which he would need in order to accomplish his task. This was going to take time and organizational skills, and he had plenty of both.

He heard the key in the door and rose to help her enter. She had two large bags of groceries, which he immediately took and unloaded in the kitchen. He appeared to be so thoughtful and caring. Together they packed the food away in the fridge, freezer, or cupboards, whichever applied, and within ten minutes, were undressed and making love. An hour, and two orgasms for her later, she was sleeping and he was sipping another beer.

If he kept her contented, he would have a nice arrangement. A quiet place to stay, a handy diversion, and time to plan and carry out his quest. She was a loner, which suited him fine. Everything was in place.

Maybe he'd just start with Sharin. Forget the other fucks. No, they all had something to do with this. Why did they have to interfere anyway? He'd just stick to his plan, methodically setting the record straight. Some might be a challenge, with all the protection they're setting up. It wouldn't matter. Might even make it more interesting.

Linda stirred. Yes, she was kind of dowdy, but with her great body and craving for sex, it was a wonder she was available. You just never know. He had met her Saturday night, after doing Phil and that cop, who got in the way. He had chosen a quiet, little bar to celebrate, feeling very good about himself and the night's events. It was easy turning on the charm for this one.

He could tell by the look in her eye, she wanted more. "Why don't I make us some supper?" asked the killer. "Then we'll continue fucking."

Linda giggled. She seemed to enjoy his crudeness. Sometimes he talked like that. If that turned her on, all the better. If not, he could care less. He brought her a beer, told her to stay put, then went to the kitchen. He enjoyed cooking and in no time had their meals on the table. They both dug in with gusto, their little romp having created healthy appetites.

She insisted on doing the dishes, so he cracked another beer and waited for her in bed. When would he start? Perhaps he should ease off for a while.

There was no hurry now. Let the mood take over and dictate the schedule. That would give him time to plan the executions. They were after all just that, executions.

Linda came into the room with two glasses of brandy and peeled off her housecoat. She began fondling him and soon their playing resumed. It was merely a diversion for him. Let tomorrow decide what would happen. He'd know when the time was right.

38

It was Monday morning, eight days after the case had begun. Jack was going directly to the Jensen's as Sharin had recorded, in detail, events from the accident to her escape. She thought some of it might be helpful.

He arrived shortly after nine and was relieved to discover the Wilsons were off to the Minnesota Mall again, while Eric was working in the den. He felt they would get through Sharin's information much quicker without an audience. There were two officers on the property, and of course the dogs.

Sharin had fresh coffee and home made muffins on hand, as they sat at the kitchen table to review her notes. The muffins were delicious and Jack realized he was reaching for a second, even before they had started their discussion. He was a little embarrassed, but Sharin grinned and told him to please help himself. He guessed there hadn't been too many grins lately.

"I decided to begin this by going back to the accident itself, hoping it would help refresh my memory," said Sharin.

Jack nodded. "Good idea," he said.

"I've recorded, as best I could, all our conversations, verbatim. I don't know if there's anything that will be helpful, but here it is anyway. However, there was something that kept nagging at me, some incident during my time in that house that I felt might be helpful to you."

Jack reached for another muffin.

"Go on," he said.

"As I thought about Sunday and the accident, from blacking out to coming awake in the house, something I had been trying to remember, came to mind. When I first woke up, he was talking in another room. I knew it was a telephone conversation, because there were no responses, only his voice. I'm sure this happened several times. My point is, suppose it was the same person each time. If so, could he be responsible for any of these murders? Whoever it is, was surely connected to Kurt. Couldn't those calls be traced?"

"Absolutely," said Jack. "We'll start running phone records immediately. Do you have any sense of how long he may have been there, prior to taking you captive?"

Sharin checked her notes. "Nothing came out of our conversations to indicate that. And of course, once I was free, I didn't have time to stick around for a look."

"I'm sure you didn't," said Jack. "Our guess is that William had been on holidays, and let Kurt have his place for a while. We'll trace calls for a two week period prior to your arrival, and through last Tuesday. If necessary we'll go back even further."

They went over the rest of her notes carefully, but there was nothing more to assist the investigation. The phone records though, might provide a valuable lead. Jack had inhaled five muffins during their chat, and while apologizing, admitted they were just too good to resist. Sharin said Eric was anxious to talk to him, and while Jack agreed, he said it would have to be brief. He asked to use the phone while she was getting Eric.

Jack instructed one of the officers to get a warrant to obtain the phone records for William's house, then left a message for David that he would be in the office within the hour.

Eric was highly agitated and admittedly, frightened. Jack spent fifteen minutes assuring them that the maximum protection was in place. They were due for a break. Rest assured, this guy will make a mistake.

Jack thanked Sharin, saying the phone records would be traced as soon as they had the warrant. He left wondering just how much he had succeeded in lightening their load. Probably very little. They certainly seemed a devoted couple. The more he saw of Eric and Sharin, he realized how much each cared for the other. He'd have to find more time for Jennifer.

They had forty officers on the case now. Forensics had been devoting extra time everyday for him. And what had it got them? It seemed as if they were at a standstill.

They were fortunate to have solved the Jensen abduction and two murders so quickly. Maybe three murders, if you count William's, but that was still unknown. Then everything started going badly. Is there a second killer? If so, they're definitely connected to Kurt. At this moment they were still looking for Kurt, but could that backfire?

He reached the outskirts of St Cloud at noon. Time to pick up a couple of burgers on his way in. Maybe he'd get an extra one, in case David could be persuaded to join him. He was thankful for David. Not only did the little scientist know his stuff, he was creative and up-beat.

David was waiting in his office when Jack arrived.

"A feast fit for a king," said Jack. "All the extra trimmings are in these cartons. Help yourself."

David grimaced, but took a burger and doctored it with mayonnaise, pickles, lettuce, and tomato. After carefully examining the finished product, he had to admit, it looked quite edible.

"*B'tay a von*," said David.

"And to you," said Jack. They settled into their lunch, with Jack briefing him on his visit with Sharin. David confirmed he had received the info on William's homicide.

"We know there has to be a connection with Kurt," said David. "That relationship must also be a strong one. From two of the homicides, Fred and Phil, there was evidence of extreme anger, not only from the depth of the stabbing, but the numerous wounds."

"Wasn't there similar, excessive wounding in two others cases, Ginny's and William's?" asked Jack.

"Yes, Jack. William's killing bore some resemblance, but entirely different circumstances in Ginny's case. The latter was calculated and torturous, the work of a sick man, not an angry one."

"Does your info give us anything on this guy?" asked Jack.

"Interesting you should say guy. Why not a woman, Jack?"

"No particular reason. Just that the crimes have been so violent and the evidence of unusual strength."

"My sense is you're probably right, but for different reasons. The knife wounds could have been inflicted by a female, an especially strong woman mind you, but a woman nonetheless. However, in Phil's murder, I believe the suspect was most likely male. The initial strike landed high on his forehead, coming from a great height. Phil was a tall man, and from the evidence, whoever delivered that blow had to be well over six feet."

"So the odds favor a male," said Jack.

"Exactly. Now, if we could match the results from DNA testing, hair samples, or finger prints from the different crime scenes, it would help establish a link between the homicides and who was responsible for which crime. You know Kurt killed Ginny and Al Lucas, and we assume that one individual is responsible for the last three – Fred, Phil, and the police officer. From ID's and the bellman's info, it appears Kurt also killed William. We've got Kurt's prints. They were all over William's house, at the bar where Ginny worked, Lucas's car, and Phil's cabin. As well we have hair and DNA evidence."

"What have you got from the other scenes?" asked Jack.

"At Fred's house, we have a set of prints, not identified at this point. Unfortunately no DNA there, but we do have hair. In the other homicides at Phil's camp and the hotel, where there's been so much traffic, it will take longer to run all the evidence. At this point, we've been unable to match Kurt with anything found in William's room. We're still cross-checking the others."

"That won't prove he wasn't there," said Jack. "I'm anxious to hear about the bellman's reaction to the photos of Kurt. I'm sure Brett is as well."

"I have a funny feeling about that, Jack, but unfortunately that's all it is, a feeling."

"Well I hope you untangle your feeling and turn it into a conclusion. We're getting stampeded here. Talking about that, I have to be in the Commissioner's office in an hour."

"You still getting political pressure, thanks to Frank Wilson?" asked David.

"Yeah, it's partly due to him. He did start the ball rolling by calling the Commissioner and Senator Johnston, but with the rash of homicides, especially the police officer, they would have been on to us anyway."

"At least you handle that well, Jack. Talking about handling matters, how's Jennifer?"

"Ouch. I've been thinking a lot about that lately. Maybe after this case is over, we'll take a trip, get away for a few weeks. I know she deserves better."

"Sounds good to me. Make sure you do just that," said David.

"Thanks. Keep slugging away, will you?"

Jack gathered his reports and headed for the Commissioner's office.

39

After Linda left for work, the killer had gone back to bed for a few hours. He didn't know about her, but he needed some more sleep. It was close to noon when he arose and decided to make himself a hearty brunch, needing the fortification for what may lie ahead. He devoured a three egg omelet, loaded with cheese, mushrooms, bacon, and chives, along with six slices of whole wheat toast. This was washed down with two cold beers and he was now ready for action.

He reviewed his list. Where to start? Her name jumped off the page, making an easy decision for him. Linda walked to work everyday, and had left her car keys in case he wanted to take a ride during the day. How convenient.

It was easy finding the small town, an hour north of Minneapolis, but it took almost as long to locate the street. Not wanting to ask anybody directions, he just kept driving around in search of her house. The town was full of stupid fucks, meandering aimlessly about. Some were huddled at the local store, their conversation probably nothing but gossip, while others tried to appear busy in assorted ways. None succeeded, to his mind.

A few were raking leaves, trying to keep their stupid little yards neat. Didn't they know more leaves were yet to fall? And besides, who cared? There were even a few mothers pushing their baby buggies along, to show off their new kids. Who gave a fuck? The world's so screwed up. Well, he'd show them. Let's rearrange a few things and a few lives.

He cruised past the house, checking things out. It was in a secluded area on the outskirts of town, surrounded by woods. Was that an unmarked police car coming down the street? What the hell. It stopped right in front of her house, and two guys came out, while the two new ones went inside. Christ, it's a shift change. She's got police protection. Well nothing like a challenge, but not today.

He drove straight out of town, picked up Highway 10 heading south, and felt like flooring it. That wouldn't do. Getting caught without a driver's license could jeopardize the entire operation. There must be some way to overcome his disappointment. An hour later, on the outskirts of Minneapolis, his anger had not abated. Not being able to do that little bitch was rankling him more and more.

The killer parked the car at a meter, and headed for Lake Street and Chicago Avenue, where there was lots of action. Maybe something could brighten up his day yet. The amount of pedestrian traffic surprised him, pleasantly.

Spotting the hookers was easy. It always was, no matter what city or state, they were all the same. Despite the fall chill, the street walkers were clad in the usual tight mini skirts or shorts, barely covering their assets. Abbreviated tops revealing all sorts of cleavage, high, leather boots, and generously applied makeup, completed their ensembles. It was enticing. What little surprise could he bring to one of these tarts?

A few beers was too tempting to pass up, even though it meant extra exposure in this part of town. Now that a plan had been hatched to make up for his earlier disappointment, it didn't matter. The anticipation of the new event overruled any logic. After wandering around, he noticed several bars enjoying a rather brisk trade, including a bunch of shady looking characters and plenty of hookers. Perfect. He chose the busiest on the street.

The killer lost himself in the busy goings on and proceeded to put away several beers. It reminded him of similar times in Los Angeles, when he'd occasionally have a couple in the afternoon. The number of drinkers always astounded him. The same situation here. It's four o'clock Monday afternoon and these joints are crawling with boozers.

A tall hooker sashayed into the bar as if she owned the place. She went straight to the bar, eased her soft, round ass on a stool and ordered a drink. Probably one of those fake drinks. The girls get to ply their trade in the bar, and in return have prospective clients buy them a couple of expensive cocktails while they're making the arrangement. Only the cocktails are fake, with no booze. The bartender benefits and everybody's happy. Fuckers.

He was feeling no pain at this point, but was still angry. The tall one was looking around. Their eyes met and he beckoned her to join him. She flashed a lascivious grin, picked up her drink and sidled over to his table. He rose to pull out a chair for her, which she gracefully accepted. As she eased onto the proffered seat, he felt her hand slide along the inside of his thigh.

"Such a big guy," she said. "You big everywhere, honey?"

"Just average, gorgeous. What're you drinking?"

"Ah, the modest type. I love it. I'll have a daiquiri, beautiful."

The killer signaled the waiter for a beer and a daiquiri, then turned on the charm. He chatted amiably, praising her good looks, great body, and dazzling personality. Told her he had been in the bar all afternoon and nothing even close to her had come in. She lapped it up and asked for another drink. It would be a pleasure. He waited for her to talk business. How old was she? Maybe twenty, no more.

"Well, what's your pleasure? You name it, it's yours."

"Nothing too quick," said the killer. "I'd like an hour with you."

"That's gonna cost, honey. A quickie's a hundred, you know."

"Yeah, I figured. You'll be worth it, I'm sure."

"It'll be three hundred for the hour, and that's a deal, only 'cause I like you."

"Sounds all right. You got a place?"

"No," she said. "There's plenty of rooms around here. Get 'em by the hour, or whatever we want."

"I'd rather go to your place, gorgeous."

"Sorry, honey. Have to stay close by."

"I can't register for a room. Gotta wife you know. Have to be careful."

"Look, give me thirty bucks. I'll register, give you the number and meet you in the room. Give me another hundred in case you get cold feet and leave me there."

"Okay. Where's this place?"

"Just down the block."

They walked to the hotel and the killer waited outside while the hooker got the room. She gave him the room number and disappeared into the hotel. He waited a few minutes, checking out the entrance and elevators. There was only one clerk at the desk, and as soon as he was occupied, he slipped by reception and took the stairs. One flight down was a parking garage with an exit back onto the street. He liked that.

The room was on the fourth floor and she was sitting on the bed wearing only her high boots. He'd like to take his time with this one, but he couldn't risk that. He took off his jacket and shirt. She smiled.

His left arm shot out and grabbed her by the throat, forcing her back on the bed. She couldn't make a sound. Her eyes showed surprise, shock, and fear. The vice-like grip held her fast against the bed and cut off all breath.

He drove his knee into her chest, restricting all movement. Then he took out the knife. She bucked and kicked furiously, her eyes now wide with terror. He liked that. Her nails raked his arms, drawing blood. His smile faded. He began carving and slicing. It continued long after her life had slipped away.

He calmly removed the long hair wig, moustache, and glasses, putting them in his jacket pockets. After washing up, he donned his shirt and jacket, took the stairs to the basement and let himself out onto the street. Nobody noticed.

Time to go home to Linda.

40

Jack returned to his office for an early evening meeting with the team. The Commissioner had been curt but fair. He was under a lot of pressure. The public had little or no patience with this. Five homicides within a week, in an area bounded by Clearwater and Crosslake, was preposterous. It was simple, find the killer and apprehend him – quickly.

He had time to review the phone records from William's house, call Brett, then after the meeting, maybe get home for dinner. The calls were revealing. Every night, from September 26th to October 11th, there was an incoming call from Los Angeles. They all originated from pay phones, with the time and actual numbers listed. The locations were identified, and Brett would be able to plot them for him.

There was a total of sixteen calls, from four different numbers. Eight calls from one number, six from another, and single calls from two others. He had the information faxed to Brett, to prepare a grid of the four pay phones and determine if their locations could be helpful.

The meeting had just started when Watson apologized for interrupting, but told Jack he had better take this call.

Jack took it in his office. "Petersen here."

"Lieutenant, this is Detective Francis Mulholland from Minneapolis. We've got a homicide here. Looks a lot like the case you're working on. Young hooker, strangled and cut up badly."

"Where are you, Francis?" asked Jack.

"At the Excelsior Hotel on Chicago Avenue. The ambulance is here, and the coroner's on his way. She's dead. Forensics and other B.C.A. special agents just arrived. Manager's a bit of a dick, but that's expected here. You coming in?"

"Yeah, I'll be there in an hour. Thanks for the call, Francis." Jack hung up, told Brooker to get a car – they were off to Minneapolis. He then called Jennifer with the all too familiar news.

They reached the hotel within the hour. Brooker was very good at getting somewhere fast when he had to, which for him was often. The crime scene tape was in place and the curious who had stopped to gawk, were crowding the street. An officer was clearing them away as best he could. Jack and Brooker showed their ID's and entered the hotel. If the lobby was any indication of the rest of the place, this wasn't your five star category, or any star for that matter. They were escorted to the fourth floor and introduced to Detective Mulholland.

Francis Mulholland was as florid as a ripe tomato. He had an unruly mop of short, curly, red hair and seemed to have freckles for freckles. If there was a classic example of a bantam rooster, this was it. He appeared to be everywhere at once. But the man was organized and efficient. They had set up a command post in an adjoining room, had a van in the basement parking garage with all the equipment for interviews, which were well underway, and the B.C.A. agents were at it next door.

"I'd seen the reports on your recent homicides, and this looked like the same guy. I've seen some bad ones, but nothing like this," said Francis.

"The body still here?" asked Jack.

"Yeah. Forensics is still working the room. Probably be another hour or so before we have the coroner release her."

"Ed, when the coroner signs off make sure David Folk knows about this one. I want him in on the autopsy," said Jack.

"10-4, Lieutenant."

"What's the time of death, Francis?"

"Coroner says late afternoon, early evening.

"What have you got from the hotel?" asked Jack.

"We had to lean on the Manager a bit. He finally admitted the girls use this place quite a bit. They work the street or local bars. This one was a regular, who usually hung out at Harry's, a couple of minutes from here. We've got two men there now. One of the bartenders saw her leave with a guy around five-thirty. They had a few drinks together, so we have a good make on him. They're doing a composite with him now."

"We've got some pictures here," said Jack. "I'd like to have this guy look at them. He's still here?"

"Either downstairs or back at the bar," said Francis. "I told him to stick around till you got here." He sent an officer to get the witness.

"Anybody in the hotel see anything?" asked Jack.

"The front desk clerk says the girl paid for the room, but he didn't see the john. Time checks out with the bartender, around five-thirty. Other than that, nothing."

"Who found the body?"

"The front desk guy had it checked out. He said she took the room for an hour, and normally they're out before the booked time. By seven, almost an hour and a half later, and no girl, he called the room. Nobody answered, so he sent up a bellman. Guy freaked out. He's a part-timer. Says he's quitting."

"I'd like to talk to the bellman, bartender, and desk clerk," said Jack. "Any good burgers around here?"

"Just two blocks away, best in town. What do you want?"

"I'll take two cheese burgers with lettuce and mayo," said Jack. "I'll do the interviews in the van, after I take a look at the room."

An officer appeared at the door, handing Francis an envelope. "Here's the composite we got from the barman."

Jack peered over Mulholland's shoulder as he pulled out the computer likeness of the man in the bar. There was something about the face, but overall, little resemblance to Kurt. And where was the battered cheek Phil talked about?

"Doesn't look much like Kurt," said Jack. "You'll want to circulate this around the hotel. See if anyone recognizes this guy."

Forensics were finished so Jack went next door to the murder room. Not too dissimilar to Ginny's death scene. Is it Kurt again? This one has no connection to the other victims or to him. The john in the bar is the likely suspect, but he doesn't look like Kurt. Has he been here? It's only a couple of hours since the crime. Jack wondered if he stayed long enough, would he smell him, feel him?

He spent the next two hours with the three witnesses, recorded their stories, then went over the case with Francis, who said he'd send out all the reports from the Identification Units and forensics. By the time he left with Brooker, it was after midnight.

There wasn't much conversation, with each lost in their own thoughts about the case. Jack thought about the witnesses, especially the bartender who described the john. He couldn't match him with Kurt's photo, but did say there was some kind of resemblance. Said the guy was well built and big. Fits Kurt, as well as how many others? Said he was charming and polite. Another fit. Again with how many others? The MO of the homicide fits. David doesn't believe in coincidence. Hmm.

The burgers were pretty good. Never have had a bad one. They weren't Pete's, but still pretty darn good. He wondered when he'd find more time to be with Jennifer. When he was on a case like this, the hours were endless. Admittedly they weren't all like this, but maybe life was too short to be so occupied with one's work that your private life was sadly neglected. She had been so understanding over the years. Yes, there was her work which she really enjoyed, her volunteer work at the hostel for troubled women, and the university courses were a challenge, but they had little quality time together. She deserved more from him. David and Brett were right on with their constant gibes about his lack of attention towards Jennifer. He would find a way to show his love and appreciation for her.

Jack eventually dozed off.

41

From Thursday on things were finally falling together for Brett. With the picture sent by Jack, he and his partner, Bob Dixon, had gone to the hospital where Phil worked. They met Alice Bell, his supervisor. She confirmed it was Kurt Schmidt, employed as a nurse and currently on three week's vacation, returning tomorrow morning, October 19th. He wasn't due back till Tuesday, as Columbus day had occurred during his holidays, thus the extra day off. His last day worked was Friday, September 24th.

Brett briefed the supervisor on Kurt's wanted status. "We need as much information as possible on this guy. We'll need to look at his employment file."

"They're kept in the personnel department. It's on the second floor. I think you'll need a warrant or something to see the file. Those departments are always fussy about things like that," said Alice.

Brett had anticipated this and had picked up a court order prior to coming to the hospital. "We understand. Dix, take the search warrant down there and get a copy of his file. I'll meet you at the front entrance. What can you tell me about Schmidt?" asked Brett.

"He was quite bright, efficient on the job, very punctual, and for the most part, dependable. He did appear to be a loner, hardly socializing with any of the staff here."

"Do you know if he was married?"

"I don't. His records indicate he was single. I really didn't talk to him that often. When I did, it was purely business. He seemed to want it that way," said Alice.

"Was there anyone here close to him who might be able to help us?"

"Not that I know. As I said he was a loner who volunteered little about himself. It was all work for him."

"Did you ever have any trouble with him? Incidents with staff or patients?"

"You'd have to check his records for that. I'm really not at liberty to say."

"Then, there probably was the odd spot of trouble, Alice. Is that what you mean?"

"Please, Lieutenant, it'd be much better if you just consulted his employment record. If there is anything untoward, it'll be there, I assure you."

"Okay, Alice. If you hear of anything regarding this guy, contact the police immediately. He's dangerous."

He left his phone number. She was shocked but got the message.

Their next stop was George the bellman, and Millie. The hotel Manager wasn't too keen on having George off duty for long, so asked them to make it quick. It was Millie's day off. Brett was going to ask him if Millie had been paid for the day when she was being questioned, but thought better of it. He had her home address so he'd send someone around to follow up with the ID on Kurt. George arrived shortly and they were given one of the offices for their meeting.

"At least this is on company time, not mine," said George.

"Right, George. There's several photos here and I want you to go through them to see if there's anyone you recognize. Take your time."

"This got anything to do with the murder here last week?"

"Just look at the pictures, George."

George started through the file. "How many you got here?"

"Not too many," said Brett.

"You know this may be on company time, but I'm losing my tips."

"You really don't mind helping, do you, George?" said Dixon. "You're a fine solid citizen, sacrificing all to help the police catch a murderer. Get on with it, before he comes back here, cuts off your balls, and sews them in your mouth." Dixon made a face, mimicking a squirrel with its cheeks full.

George winced and set about the task quickly. About half way through, he picked out a picture, studied it, then pushed it over to Brett. It was Kurt.

"That's him. Except for the nose, I'd swear that's the guy."

"What's with the nose?"

"I'm not sure, but it's just not quite right. Other than that, it's him. Hell, I was right across from him, only ten feet away, for twenty minutes. I know."

"Thanks, George," said Brett. "Stay alert around here. He probably doesn't know where you live, so if he comes back looking for you, it would be here. You see or hear anything, let us know."

"Do I get some kind of protection?"

"If we felt you were in danger, yes. However, that's not the case. He's in Minnesota right now, so you'll be all right."

They left, thanked the Manager, and headed for the suburb where they had traced the phone calls. The circulating of Kurt's picture, and the location of one of the pay phones, had landed two witnesses. One was in a variety store near the pay phone, the other, a neighbor. The neighbor had put them on to the realtor who handled the renting of the house where Kurt lived. Appointments were set up with the store clerk, neighbor, and realtor, the latter's office only a few minutes from the store.

They met Marie Coster at the store, situated in a small strip mall. She was stunning. You would think she had just came off a movie set. She stood a good five feet seven inches, with long, sleek blonde hair flowing to her shoulders. Her shapely body featured show girl legs, which were highly visible as she was wearing the shortest mini skirt Brett had ever seen. Marie had a regular daytime job, but worked here part-time, mostly at night. She identified Kurt from the picture, as the man who made several calls from the pay phone in the last two weeks.

"You see the phone is right outside, at the corner of the parking lot. It's not very busy late at night so I'm usually sitting here at the cash register, facing the phone booth."

"The lighting isn't great there. How can you be sure this is the same guy?" asked Brett.

Marie shifted her body and gazed at Brett.

"Look, he came in here two or three times to buy things. He's awfully big, so when he was over there at the phone booth, it wasn't difficult to know who it was."

"How did you find him as a person?" asked Brett.

"Wadda ya mean by that?" asked Marie, accompanied by another sultry shift and winsome look.

"Well, Marie, was he rude or polite, talkative or quiet, smiling or sullen? Anything you can remember about him that may help us."

"He was a little abrupt, I guess. Not necessarily rude, but he sure didn't go out of his way to be nice either. Most men who come here are quite friendly towards me. He wasn't."

There was a hint of a pout. They both knew she didn't appreciate the fact the guy hadn't hit on her.

Dixon took over.

"Look young lady, I don't give a fiddler's fuck what this guy thought of you. We want to know exactly how he acted and what he looked like. Now let's get on with it."

"Christ, I'm just trying to help and you come on like that." She looked to Brett for some solace.

"We've been on this case for a while, Marie," said Brett. "It gets a little testy sometimes. Just do the best you can."

"Like I said, he was big. He had strong, athletic movements, well controlled. He didn't waste any time either. Just got what he wanted, paid for it, and left."

"And you're sure this is the same guy in the picture," said Brett.

"You know, the first time I looked at it, I was sure it was him. Now, there seems to be something different, but I don't know what it is."

"Try hard now. This could be important."

"You see a guy a couple of times, only for a few minutes, you can't remember everything." She stared at the picture. "I don't know. I really don't. It's too much like him not to be. I'm sorry. That's all I can tell you."

"I'm going to leave the picture with you, Marie. If you think of anything at all, just call us." Brett handed her his card. "And thanks."

They drove out of the lot, heading to the realtor's office. Hector Shiraz was a real salesman. Good looking with a huge grin and firm handshake. They got right down to business, handing over several photos. He picked him out immediately. No doubt, an exact likeness of Kurt Schmidt.

"Signed a two year lease last July. Here's the papers. I've had no contact with him since the deal, as his rent checks go directly to the owner. The guy apparently never misses, otherwise I'd hear about it."

"Where was he working?" asked Dixon.

"Let's see, it should be right here. Yeah, he's a nurse. Works at the Franklin Hospital. Had no problem with his salary."

"Married or single?" asked Brett.

"Uh, single."

"What about references?"

"We don't need that for this type of lease. Just his employment info. That's all we care about," said Shiraz.

"You hear anything about this guy, let us know, quick," said Dixon.

"He in some kind of trouble?" asked Shiraz.

"Just kidnaping and murder for starters. Bad and dangerous. Better let the owner of the house know. Has he ever met his tenant?"

"Doubt it. He owns a lot of these with some other guys. They just get the rent while we manage the places for them."

"And you haven't seen this guy for what, three months?" asked Dixon.

"He never called to complain about anything. As long as the rent was paid there was no need to see him."

"We have a warrant to search the house for evidence. You have a problem with that?" asked Brett.

"I don't but I better clear it with the owners. I'll call them right now if you like."

Brett nodded. Shiraz reached the owner, explained the situation, and got the okay.

"He asked that I go with you."

"That's fine," said Brett. "We'll have to call in a forensic team to go over the house, which could take a couple of hours. They'll be here in about thirty minutes."

"Okay. I'll meet you there in half an hour with the key."

The forensic team had been alerted and were ready to leave. Brett and Dixon drove to Kurt's house. Their next appointment was with the neighbor who lived across the street and two doors down. Mrs Bustria, an elderly widow, had been born in the Philippines but had moved to the Los Angeles area because six of her seven children had migrated here. She obviously doted on her family and was immensely proud of her fourteen grandchildren. Pictures of all families strewed the living room walls and furniture.

The officers politely refused her offer of tea, explaining they were on a tight schedule. Brett showed her the picture of Kurt.

"Mrs Bustria, you recognized this man as your neighbor?"

"Yes. He lives just over there," she said pointing to a small bungalow across the street.

"When did you last see him?"

"Last week, Tuesday or Wednesday, I think. Not since."

"How often do you see him?"

"Many times I see him in the morning. You see, I get up early every day, and he likes to run then."

"Are you positive this is the same person?"

"Yes. You see, I met him once in a store, months ago. It was just after he had moved in. We literally bumped into each other. He was so big. I'm so little. He almost knocked me over. He was very nice and actually held my shoulders to make sure I didn't fall. He was strong but gentle. I will never forget his face and eyes. He seemed to stare right through me. That was the only time I've ever seen him up close. But when I see him running, I'm sure it's this man."

"Do you see him every day?" asked Brett.

"Not always, but several days. I don't always look outside when I get up. Many times I'm talking on the telephone to my family. I have many here."

She had the sweetest smile which became even broader at the mention of her children. Her English was excellent although she had a slight accent. It seemed she had a little difficulty with the letter 'f.' When she said, 'family', he thought it sounded like, 'pamily.'

"And the only times you've seen him are when he goes for his morning run?"

"I think so. I don't go out too much. But my children come here often, with their children." Again the infectious smile.

"Now, please think carefully Mrs Bustria. You say the last time you saw this man was Tuesday or Wednesday last week. What about before that? Did you see him running any other day?"

"Well not for quite a while. You see, I was staying with Marietta's children this month. She's my youngest daughter, and while they were on a holiday I moved to their house and looked after the children. I liked that very much."

"When were you there, Mrs Bustria?"

"I have that on my calendar." She went to the kitchen and returned with her notes.

"I left here Sunday, September 26th, and came back this past Sunday."

"So you were away for those two weeks."

"Yes, sir. And I loved it. Taking care of my grandchildren is very special for me."

"Back to Mr Schmidt, do you know if has any friends in the neighborhood?"

"I don't know, sir. You see, I keep to myself mostly. I'm sorry."

"You've been very helpful, Mrs Bustria. If you think of anything or see this man, call us immediately. Here are our phone numbers."

"He's in trouble, this man?" asked Mrs Bustria.

"We believe he is, but you don't have to worry about him. He's in Minnesota now. Thank you for your time."

They left to join the forensic team which had just arrived. Brett briefed them on the case and stressed the urgency. Multiple killings, including a police officer were at issue here. They needed this info yesterday. The team understood. Shiraz came by with the house keys.

"Thanks for your help," said Brett. "As I said, these guys will need about two hours."

"I figured. My cell phone's here, so I can make calls."

"Well remember, call us immediately if you get any word about him," said Brett.

"Yeah, sure. Heh, you guys ever need to rent or buy over here, give me a call. Here's some cards."

They thanked him and headed back to the office. Brett had made up his mind, he was going to Minnesota. Hopefully they'd get some useful evidence from Kurt's house. It was all circumstantial, but given the guy's track record, it was a safe bet he was the suspect in William's homicide.

"That Shiraz was a smooth type, wasn't he? A little too slick for me," said Dixon.

"Yeah, me too," said Brett. "What's going on with these witnesses and the photo? Shiraz says it's our guy, yet the others have a problem with it. They're not sure."

"I've been thinking about that. The realtor hasn't seen Kurt since last July, while the others met him recently. What's with the nose thing? It was the nose that bothered George."

"But the nurse at the hospital didn't have that problem, Dix. She matched Kurt with the photo right away."

"True. Something's screwy."

They returned to headquarters and Brett made arrangements to leave the following day. He'd need the rest of the afternoon to tie up a few matters, longer actually, but he had no choice. There was a report from the officer interviewing Millie. She thought there was some resemblance but couldn't be positive. After all she had only a quick look at him.

He called Jack, but learned he was in Minneapolis, investigating another homicide, which could be linked to his current case. Brett said he would forward his flight itinerary within the hour, and asked that Jack call him at home tonight.

He wondered if there were any suitable clothes in his wardrobe to handle the change in weather he was about to experience.

Hopefully they would solve this case before winter hit.

42

Jack was pleased that Brett was coming east. Not only was he a good friend, they needed all the help they could get on this case. He agreed to meet him at the airport if nothing cropped up, and insisted he stay at the house with him and Jennifer.

He arrived at the office for the regular morning meeting in time to review his file. He added the new entry:

Black pin – Mon. Oct. 18th: Hooker murdered – Minneapolis. Connection?

With all the publicity the case was getting, he couldn't believe they didn't have a solid lead yet. The replies and sightings were numerous, but so far all bogus.

Hospitals and medical clinics had been checked, but none had recognized Kurt, or treated anyone like him for facial injuries. He knew that somebody, somewhere, had to make him. The guy can't just disappear off the face of the earth. He reviewed the list of people who were in danger and ensured their protection was in place.

He called the Commissioner. There didn't appear to be a connection with the latest murder in Minneapolis, however it was being followed by a local homicide detective. He explained the possible link with the L.A. killing, and Brett's upcoming trip to Minnesota. The Commissioner reminded him of the gravity of the case and the bad press they were all getting. The Senator wanted a daily report. End it soon, he had been admonished.

Jack's next call was to Sven.

"What's the story on the hooker's murder, Jack?" asked Sven. "Is there any chance it's our guy again?"

"Don't know yet," replied Jack. "A bartender saw the girl with a john just before she was done in. Physical description matched Kurt, but his composite didn't. They went to a nearby hotel, but so far, no one there saw the guy. The MO's the same, but that's it. How are you making out?"

"We haven't found an owner for those fresh prints from Fred's house. They come from a big hand and an equally big guy, but they don't match Kurt's. I know that doesn't prove he wasn't there, but who belongs to these new prints? Fred didn't have many visitors in his house, and the only large men who knew him well, are Roy and me. The prints don't match either one of us."

"What about hair?" asked Jack. "We have plenty of Kurt's from William's house. You must have some from Phil's place as well."

"Yeah, we have some from Fred's," said Sven. "I'll make sure they compare what they have with Kurt's."

"A detective friend of mine from L.A. is coming in today. He's the guy working on William's murder. He showed Kurt's picture to their witnesses and got a positive ID. We catch this guy, we solve several murders."

"I don't know how this asshole stays out of sight. There's not a policeman in this state who hasn't seen his picture, as well as all the other sites where you've had it posted. Is there a citizen here who hasn't seen his ugly mug?"

"I doubt it," said Jack. "Someone has to spot him, hopefully soon. Keep at it, and Sven, be careful." He hung up just as an excited David entered his office.

"So the plot sickens," said David. "Does the Minneapolis hooker belong in our picture, or not?"

"Possibly not, yet I'm sure you have just as many theories for one side of the argument as the other. You have something up your sleeve, am I right?"

"It may surprise you to know I have more reason to believe it is the same case, than it isn't," said David. "As a matter of fact, I believe I know. Firstly, the attack and killing are a carbon copy of all the others. As well, the bartender's description of the john's physique was too much like Kurt to be ignored. The composite was off, but it bothered me. Then a great piece of luck."

"There's never been any luck involved when you're on a case, David," said Jack. "At least that's what you've been telling me for years. Continue."

"I'd been looking at the various hair samples from the hotel room. There was enough variety to put on a fashion show. A few strands didn't have the regular features of human hair. I recognized the pieces as coming from a postiche or wig. That's when I began playing with the bartender's composite. When I shortened the hair, it started to look a little like our man. Then with the glasses and moustache gone – bingo. Care to look at the finished product, Jack?" David handed the altered composite to Jack.

"It certainly is close. Is it really him?" asked Jack.

"These composites are never exact. With all the other info from this scene though, it's too much like him, not to be. Your friend Callahan is coming in today isn't he?"

"Is there any detail about this operation that escapes you, David?"

"You know better than to ask, Jack. What have they come up with on Kurt? They must have quite a file on him by now. We're going to need all the help we can get."

"You're right on both counts. I'm leaving soon to meet him at the airport. Care to come along?"

"I'd enjoy that but it would mean lunch with you. I'll pass," said David.

"Miss my chance to show you and Brett the best burgers in the country?"

"Don't know how I can resist, but I will. I'm off to the lab. Say hello to Brett. We met once. See if he remembers."

"As if anyone could forget," said Jack. "Thanks for the good work on this one, David. Appreciate it. By the way, what's the difference between a postiche and a wig?"

"Kind of like the difference between a yarmulka and a hat – coverage, Jack. Ciao."

Jack called the Jensens and got the answering machine. He immediately called the unit on duty at their house. Everything there was fine, but Mrs Jensen had gone to the Minneapolis Mall with her parents. They had left first thing in the morning, though nobody liked the idea. Her husband was driven to work by a co-worker and Sharin had taken the Land Rover. She was adamant on getting out, so one unit had gone with her to the mall.

This made him nervous. The Jensen woman definitely had a mind of her own. He hoped it wouldn't cost her one day.

His secretary confirmed Brett's flight was arriving ten minutes early and it was time for him to leave for the airport. He took the stairs to the basement where the vehicles were parked. The thought of seeing Brett again and working the case together was exhilarating. The souped up police vehicle roared up the ramp, made a screeching left turn and headed for the highway.

Why did he have a sense of foreboding about the Jensen family traipsing around in public? His route would take him right past the mall. Traffic was fairly light at this time of day and he was making good time. The entrances to the mall were coming up. He passed the first one, and the second, but by the third he had made up his mind. He wheeled across two lanes and swung into the off ramp. He called the unit, who turned out to be Ted Knott and Jim Ferris, and located their parking spot.

He found the Jensen's Land Rover at the end of an aisle, so he parked illegally in the space beside it. As he entered the mall he called Ted again. They were in Section A, second level, heading westerly. That was more than three sections ahead of his position. The volume of people was amazing for a Tuesday afternoon, or at least he thought it was.

He updated Watson. Told him to have someone else pick up Brett. This could take some time.

Jack was working his way towards the family when his portable rang. It was Ted.

"Jack, it's him. He's here in the mall."

43

Sharin was delighted to get out again. She felt secure with her favorite team of Ted and Jim. Frank wasn't as interested in shopping as Judy and Sharin were, but he was most impressed with the mall and looked forward to their third visit in as many days. The place seemed endless.

Sharin was getting a big kick out of her Mom as they walked into store after store. They even made a couple of purchases. After two hours Frank insisted they all stop for coffee and check the map of the mall to plan their next foray. The officers, dressed in plain clothes, kept their distance but always had the family in view.

They picked up three café lattes along with three carrot muffins. There was an open food court area where they found a table and sat down to enjoy their treats.

"The car dealer called yesterday, Dad," said Sharin. "They got the Jaguar back from the police compound. The insurance company agreed it was totaled. They won't have a new one in that color for me till December, but they're going to give me the use of a demo model at a very reasonable rate."

"Well that sounds fair. You certainly have a great car. Probably saved your life," said Frank. "I didn't know cars had all those safety devices."

"Like what, dear?" asked Judy.

"You tell your mother, Sharin. You know more about it than I do."

"It seems the Jaguar is fitted with a special solenoid, Mom. It automatically shuts off the engine and fuel pump when the car is in an accident. This reduces the chances of fire or an explosion. No doubt it was the main reason nothing happened."

"Sounds very impressive," said Judy.

"Also the frame is constructed with three steel spars supporting the roof, which prevent it from collapsing. So when I rolled down the hill, I wasn't crushed."

"Thank God for that," said Judy. "I still can't believe someone actually tried to kill you. They will catch him, won't they, Frank?"

"They've certainly put together a sizeable team of detectives to work the case. Don't think we could ask for more, but they better find him soon."

"You know I have moments like this when I'm confident enough to straight up challenge him, whoever he is," said Sharin. "I know that's not realistic. Most of the time I'm just plain scared. Mainly it's the not knowing. Is he alive? If not, who is responsible for these latest killings?"

There was an awkward pause. Then Sharin turned the mood around as she was so capable of doing.

"Mom, this carrot muffin is so fresh – it's still warm! Almost as good as your own, but not quite."

Sharin took a big bite, savoring the experience. She gave her Mom a wide grin and wink.

"Heh, the coffee's pretty good too, eh?"

Smiles all around. It had been a while since Sharin had used that Canadian expression.

"Okay, enough of this," said Judy. "Let's get back to shopping. I do want to see some glassware, and I think we should find a golf store or two for your father."

"Now you're talking," said Frank.

They finished their coffee and headed for a sporting goods store, which happened to be in the same section as a Bowrings. Sharin and her mother would look at glasses and leave Frank to his own shopping. They'd meet in thirty minutes between the two stores.

With Sharin's approval, Judy picked out a set of wine glasses by Orefors as a house present. She ordered twelve each, red and white, and arranged to have them delivered to the Jensen's home. Sharin said they were perfect. Eric would love them. She saw how excited her Mom was.

They slowly strolled down the aisle, window shopping as they worked their way towards the store where they had left Frank.

"Is the mall always this busy?" asked Judy.

"We don't come here that often, but it does seem there's always a good crowd. This is only what...a Tuesday? Impressive isn't it?"

They were surprised to discover Frank was still shopping. Sharin glanced in the direction of the store where her father had been shopping. Suddenly her mother fell against her. She looked back. For a brief second her eyes met with...was it him? Her mother was collapsing. Sharin tried to hold her up. There was something warm and sticky on her hand. It was blood! Sharin screamed.

Ted and Jim came running. They saw the blood.

"It's him. Blond hair, black jacket. Going that way, down those stairs," said Sharin.

Jim darted off in his direction. Ted called security, stating a medical emergency. Told them to get a doctor or medic on the scene immediately. He identified the section of the mall.

Hearing the scream Frank had bolted out of the store. Sharin knelt beside her mother, who was now lying on the floor. The wound was bleeding profusely through Judy's blouse.

"What the hell," said Frank.

"Dad, turn Mom on her side and give me a handkerchief."

Sharin pulled up her mother's blouse to expose the wound. She rolled the handkerchief into a ball and held it firmly to stem the flow of blood.

"Mom, are you okay?"

"I'm not sure. It hurts, though."

Judy was very pale. The medics arrived and began treating the wound. They said she'd be okay. A stretcher would be there shortly.

Sharin trembled with hurt and fear.

44

Jack was sprinting towards the area Ted had described in his first message alerting the emergency. Minutes later Ted called back saying he was with the family. Jim was pursuing the suspect, believed to be Kurt. They had taken a flight of stairs down to the first level and were now running easterly.

Jack stopped a security guard, quickly told him where the chase started, who was involved, and where it was headed.

"Follow me," said the guard.

Jack kept the line open to Ted, barking orders on his portable. "Have them close off the mall. Shut down all vehicular exits. Get the locals in here fast. We need as many officers as possible."

The security guy was fast and good. They'd have to be lucky, there were so many ways to go.

"Around the next corner, three sections straight ahead, that's where those stairs are. He should be headed this way," he shouted back at Jack.

They slowed and started looking, each taking a side of the wide aisle. Announcements were being aired, explaining the emergency. They described the suspect. Tall, blond hair, black leather jacket. No sign of Jim or Kurt.

Jack called Jim. No answer. Up ahead, someone was shouting at the guard. He was motioning down another aisle.

"They went down here. Big guy, blond hair, followed by a smaller guy, running like hell."

People were parting and looking at the chase. They must be close. Still Jack couldn't spot Jim or Kurt. They plunged on in the direction of the chaos. Nothing. They rounded a corner, it was like a dead end.

Jack's phone rang. It was Jim, out of breath.

"Lieutenant, I lost him."

"Where are you?"

"Went through an 'employees only' entrance. There's a long hallway here. Took the first door. Looks like a staff locker room. It's weird, hardly a soul here."

"Be careful, we'll be right there." Jack relayed the info to the guard, who immediately knew where to go.

"He can get outside from that room," said the guard. "It exits to the employee's parking lot."

They were in the locker room in less than a minute, moving fast.

"Where's the exit?"

"This way," said the guard.

"Jim, where are you?" asked Jack.

"Still following him. Two guys just saw him go through. Said he was headed for the exit."

"That's where we're going."

There were a few employees at their lockers, all ducking out of the way. They had seen the big, blond guy, running fast. They caught up to Jim just as he was opening the exit door. The three burst through the door and quickly scanned the parking lot. Nothing.

"How many exits out of the parking lot?" asked Jack.

"Only one," said the guard. "You can see it from here. It's about fifty yards away. Get up on this railing. There it is. There's some cars headed there now."

"Stop them. Tell the attendant to stop them!"

Jack and Jim started running towards the gate, while the guard was dialing the parking attendant. Two cars went through. Then a third. The guard was waving frantically as the phone rang for the attendant. He could see him chatting with somebody in one of the cars. Answer that phone, damn it! The attendant let the car leave, then he answered.

"Rear gate, Charlie here."

"Charlie, it's Mays from security."

"Hi, Willie. What's up?"

"Don't let any more cars through. There's two police officers headed your way right now. You should be able to see them."

"I don't see anyone...oh yeah, I've got them," said the parking attendant. "What the hell's going on?"

"They'll explain. I'll be right there."

Jack and Jim reached the attendant, who had lowered the gate. He was elderly. The name 'Charlie' was on his uniform. There were now four cars in the lineup, with more coming.

"Nobody leaves without their car being checked," said Jack. "We'll start the process until some backup arrives. I'm Lieutenant Petersen. This is Patrolman Ferris."

He briefed Charlie on what they were looking for. Ferris was scanning the cars, looking for any sign of Kurt. Horns started honking. Jack ignored them. He was looking at the attendant.

"What's wrong, Charlie?" asked Jack.

"I think he may have been in that last car."

"What do you mean?"

"Well, when Sam Hurst went through, there was a big guy with him, like you just described. He had blond hair and was wearing a black leather jacket. Sam said he was a friend. I didn't know there was a problem, so I let him through."

More horns blaring. Jack took out a picture of Kurt and showed it to Charlie.

"Yeah, it looks a lot like him. Different hair though and..." said Charlie.

"And what?" asked Jack.

"I don't know. I guess it could be this guy. He definitely had blond hair and a black jacket."

"Christ," said Jack. "Jim get State Troopers in this area alerted. Tell me about the car. Make, color. You have a plate number?"

"It's one of those Japanese cars, Toyota, something. It's white and fairly new. Don't know his plate number, but we can get that for you."

"Two-door, four-door?"

"Two, I think."

"Don't think. We have a killer in that car. Hurst is in serious trouble. Tell me anything you can about the car. Ski rack? Dents? Anything."

"Yeah. Whole lot of stickers on the back window. You know, those souvenir things with names of places you've been."

"Jim, get the plate number from the guard here and give the Troopers all that info. What routes can he take out of here, Charlie?" asked Jack.

"That's Brant Street. Goes north to #394, or south to – who knows?"

"Jesus. Well, at least let the Troopers know this is where he started from."

More horns honking and people shouting. Jack told Charlie to let them go through.

"Charlie I need more info on Sam Hurst. Get personnel on the phone for me. Jim, you better get back to Mrs Jensen and the Wilsons."

Charlie called administration, explained who Jack was and gave him the phone. Minutes later he called his office with the information and had them trace the car registration.

"Get on this quickly and get it to the State Trooper's dispatch. They've been alerted but could use more info on the car. Advise them the driver is in a hostage situation. We'll need the tactical guys. Put out an A.P.B. on the vehicle. As soon as you have Hurst's address, send four detectives over there to stake out his house. No uniforms. Fully alert them on what's going on. I'll be back in thirty minutes."

"Charlie, did you get a good look at Sam's passenger?"

"Yeah. When I was talking to Sam."

"We'll want to get you to our nearest unit to do a composite of him."

"I'm not off duty till five today," said Charlie.

"I'll get it cleared through your supervisor and arrange a replacement. This has to be done immediately. We'll have a cruiser take you there and back."

Jack thanked the attendant and asked for directions to his car. The guard said he would gladly show him the way.

"Who's the head of security here?" asked Jack.

"Doug Stinson. You need him?"

"Does he have the authority to get Charlie out of here quickly."

"Yeah. He's in charge of all those guys."

"Good. Have him take care of that right away. Do you have video surveillance cameras in the mall?"

"Yeah, practically everywhere."

"They must have footage of our suspect running in the mall. Have him send us the tapes that cover the escape. This guy uses a lot of disguises so it would help us to have a look at him now. If he has a problem releasing the tapes have him call me. We could get a warrant. Make sure he knows we need them immediately."

"After I drop you off I'll get over there and have it done right away. Where do we send the stuff?"

"Here's a card with the address and the numbers, phone, fax, etc. Send it by courier, fastest service possible. Never did get your name," said Jack.

"Willie Mays," he said. "My Dad was a Giant fan and his favorite player was number '24.' I guess he hoped I'd be a ball player."

"I'll say this Willie, you move like your namesake. You did a good job back there. I'm going to send a report to your boss. You gave us the best chance of getting him."

"Is this the guy I've been reading about? Killed some people up north?"

"The very one. He's as bad as they come. Been after him for over a week now. We'll get the bastard."

When they got to Jack's car the Land Rover was gone. He thanked Willie and called Ted.

"I heard you just missed him," said Ted.

"Yeah. Maybe by one car. Let's hope we get lucky with one of the State Troopers. How's Mrs Wilson?"

"She's going to be okay, but they had to take her to a hospital. We're following Mrs Jensen on their way to the Minneapolis General."

"Call me from the hospital with an update. I'll also want to talk to Mrs Jensen." He hung up.

Brett was in the office when Jack arrived. They greeted each other warmly, but Jack was still upset.

"Understand you almost had him," said Brett.

"He was the last car to get through the gate. We tried to get the attendant to stop all vehicles but couldn't reach him in time. He's most likely holding the driver hostage. I doubt he'd have a friend working there."

"Let's get over to this guy's house. I'd like to be there if anything goes down," said Brett.

"Thought you might want to do that. Where's your gear?"

"Just have the one bag. It's out front."

Jack left word to have Ted call him in the car. He and Brett headed out. Hurst lived north of the Cities, about an hour south of St Cloud. A call to Jennifer let her know he and Brett would be late.

"How many dinners have you had with Jennifer since this case started?"

"None," said Jack. "I promised her we're taking a trip as soon as this is over."

"Good. No snow yet. I'm surprised."

"Give me a break It's only October, Brett."

"This guy's a piece of work isn't he. I understand your victims have been cut pretty badly too," said Brett.

"Everybody on this case agrees. Nobody's seen victims this bad. Sharin said he was one cool customer. She figures he's a psycho."

"She the one he held in William's house?"

"The very one. Was that the exit for #610?"

"Yeah. How would she know he's a psycho?"

"She was a nurse and worked in a psychiatric ward for three years in Canada."

Jack took the next exit. His phone rang.

"Petersen here."

"Lieutenant, it's Ted. Mrs Wilson's okay. Knife wound is deep but no serious damage. They're getting ready to leave now."

"Is Mrs Jensen there?" asked Jack.

"Yeah. Just a second."

"Hello," said Sharin.

"Mrs Jensen, I'm really sorry about your mother. Understand she's going to be all right."

"Sure, Jack. With a three inch hole in her back, she's just fine. How do you stop this creep?"

"We're going to tighten up security at your place and I suggest you stay put until this is over."

"That includes my parents, I guess."

"And your husband. That's our recommendation."

"I'll let everyone know. My father is absolutely furious."

"I understand. We'll be in touch. And again, I'm sorry. Give my best to Mrs Wilson please." They hung up.

"Is her father the one who got the Commissioner and Senator involved?" asked Brett.

"He's the guy. There's one of our cars now."

They stopped to talk with the detectives. Nothing had happened. Hurst's wife was home. They had two officers inside with her. The house was on a corner lot, with the second car down the other street, on the north side. Hurst would have to go by one of the cars to get there.

"We'll set up in the next block. Stay alert."

Jack drove past the house, down the next block. He turned around so they now faced the other car, two blocks east. Jack and Brett went over the case. Two hours later they got onto their favorite topic, the Vikes. The offence and defense had been thoroughly analyzed, the schedule carefully studied. Their chances of going all the way soundly debated. Things were not as optimistic this year.

His phone rang. Jack and Brett listened to the report. They had found the car. The driver had been stabbed in the heart.

Death had been instantaneous.

45

The killer had not enjoyed his afternoon. First the botched attempt on the mother. He knew his thrust had not been fatal. Then the narrow escape from the police, which would have been disgraceful had they actually caught him. Imagine being taken by that asshole, Petersen. Fortunately that sucker was just getting into his car and took him to safety. Too bad he couldn't live to tell the tale.

He'd directed the driver to within a mile of Linda's and after finishing him off, had a relaxing walk home. At least one thing had gone right today. After a long shower, he put on a fresh shirt and casual slacks, opened a beer, and waited for his nightly diversion. Three days had gone by and he hadn't accomplished one of his goals. Everybody on his list was still alive.

Time to take a look at his make-up kit. With all those composites and pictures out there, he'd have to make some adjustments. Certainly, after today's fiasco, the blond hair would have to be changed. That would be easy. With make-up, facial adjustments, various wigs and hair pieces, and a wardrobe to alter body size, he could create several new looks for his coming adventures.

He remembered Linda was going to be late tonight. She was meeting her nephew for dinner. Maybe he should try a new look right now and take a ride up north. It had been a wise decision to take a bus to the mall and leave Linda's car here. Within an hour he had changed dramatically and was heading north on Highway 169. He had to move the seat back to make room for his new look. The pants were a fifty inch waist to accommodate the padding, which made him look like a three hundred pound man.

The first stop would be Roy's Place. Maybe Al and Jan would be there. It would take about two hours to get there. He would be good and thirsty by then. This last minute decision might be the perfect answer to a rather disappointing day.

It was just after nine o'clock when he pulled up at Roy's Place. It was totally deserted. No lights or cars, or any sign of life at all. Jesus, two hours of driving for nothing. Wonder where those two fucks live? Can't very well start asking directions. He was contemplating breaking into the place just to have a beer but thought that wasn't such a good idea.

A pickup truck came down the road, slowed and turned into a spot beside his car.

"Looking for a drink, mister?" asked the driver.

"Actually, I just wanted one beer. I'm trying to find the road to Brainerd," said the killer.

"Well, this bar is closed for a while. There's a few back in Crosslake, but that's the opposite direction from where you want to go."

He recognized the driver. It was Al! And his wife was with him. What a bonus. He was going back to his car for the knife when another car pulled up and stopped on the side of the road. There were two men inside.

He changed his mind. "I'm more interested in getting to Brainerd."

Al gave the directions and told him to follow them for two blocks to Highway 25. They were turning north and he would have to go south. He got in the car and started following Al and Jan. The other car pulled out and slowly tracked behind. They were obviously cops. He had no choice now. When they reached the highway he turned south.

What a wasted opportunity. This day was getting worse instead of better. He decided to stay on Highway 25, which wasn't the main highway, but preferable right now as his anger had reached a dangerous level. He had to relax and get under control.

With all these cops around the plan may have to change. After all, the only one he really had to get was the Jensen woman. Maybe that would be better. He'd concentrate on her and not waste his time with the others. He passed through the little towns of Pierz, Genola, and Buckman. Ten-thirty and they were all asleep. Little Rock was next. Little Rock, Arkansas? He must have been really motoring. Despite himself, he laughed out loud. He pulled off the highway to change back into the extra clothes he had brought along. The oversized pants and shirt were stowed in the trunk.

Maybe he'd be in a better mood by the time he got to Linda's. That's what he needed. He pulled into the driveway at twelve-thirty. There was a light on in the upstairs bedroom. Maybe she had waited up for him.

She had. It was another two hours before they fell asleep.

46

Timothy Holland was not the type of person who worried easily. He worked at a low key job with the municipal government in urban planning. Despite holding a degree in economics, he had accepted a position in the city offices which required only high school education. At twenty-six, he knew there was time to work his way up slowly and make use of the degree later. The lack of responsibility and challenge suited his lifestyle at the present time.

Being a bachelor in the Cities offered some carefree living and the abundance of good looking, single girls kept him on the go. While not yet earning the big dollar, there was enough to allow a decent living and dating money. Most of his budget was taken up by the latter.

The dinner last night had given him reason for concern. Linda Strong was his favorite aunt, who he tried to see at least once a month. They both came from small families and most of their relatives lived in Rochester. She was his mother's younger sister, who had divorced three years ago from a childless marriage. During this time the two had become close. At forty-two, she viewed him as her younger brother, although on some occasions she thought of him as the son she had never had. Their regular meetings included anything from lunch or dinner to full evenings out on the town.

They met at the Sofitel, one of their favorites, and his aunt chose to eat in the main dining room as she was feeling special. The hotel offers three choices for dining. Very casual in the bistro, smart casual in the cafe, and formal dining in the Cafe Royale. Linda had chosen the latter as this would be her treat tonight.

The restaurant specializes in French cuisine, which they decided would be their choice. With the help of the waiter they started with the vichyssoise and a half bottle of Chablis premier Cru. For the main course they selected the rack of lamb, medium rare, parisienne potatoes, stewed tomatoes, and buttered carrots. This was complemented by a 1995 Chateau Pontet Canet, a full bodied, smooth Bordeaux.

Following a light salad, typically French to have the salad after the main course, the waiter brought a decadent chocolate torte. It was over coffee that Linda's reason for celebrating surfaced. She was so full of enthusiasm over her new friend, the words tripped out of her mouth non-stop for the next few minutes.

This wonderful man had come into her life unannounced and was now living with her. He was charming, bright, and ruggedly handsome. He had literally swept her off her feet. Life was full again.

"Where did you meet him, Linda?"

"Now I don't want you to be upset, but I met him in a bar."

"When did this happen?" asked Timothy.

"Sunday night. I didn't feel like eating at home, so I went down to Tony's. They have a decent buffet and the Vikes game was on, so I decided to eat there and watch the game. He was sitting at the next table and we started talking during the game. He was really totally charming and intelligent. We ended up closing the bar and coming back to my place, and I've been on cloud nine ever since."

"He stayed over night?" asked Timothy, shocked.

"Well you do it, don't you?"

"Yeah, but Linda, you're my aunt."

"Yes, and I'm not dead yet. Just because I'm forty-two doesn't mean life's over, you know."

"Sorry. It just seems different when you're talking about your own aunt," said Timothy.

"Well, are you happy for me, or what?"

"You bet. You're very special to me, and if he's making you happy, that's great. When do I get to meet him?"

"I think that will take a little time. He seems, how do I put this, kind of preoccupied at times. Likes just staying at home with me."

"Do you know where he lives?"

"Look, I guessed you were going to ask me a lot of questions, and I understand why. Truth is, I don't know much about him. He's a traveling salesman. That's about all I know. I don't care to know at this point. He doesn't offer much about himself and I've chosen to leave it at that. Is that nuts, Tim?"

"In a way, yes. You'd think if two people are falling in love, they'd want to know everything about each other."

"I don't know about falling in love, we're just enjoying each other."

"Linda, I'd say there's more than that, from your side at least. Look at you. You're in full bloom."

"Here's my younger nephew explaining life to me," said Linda. She smiled and reached for his hand. "Thank you for caring."

"One more question, okay?"

"Shoot."

"You say he's a traveling salesman, but never leaves the house. Hasn't he worked since you met?"

"I had thought about that. He probably hasn't, but maybe he's on holidays or something. I'm just not looking for any answers."

"I'm sure you'll get around to it," said Timothy. "That was a great dinner, and the wine, well, almost as good as the company. Thank you."

"Ah, you charmer. Don't stop, ever."

On the way out, each were presented with a complimentary french stick, baked that day at the Sofitel. As they lived in opposite directions, they asked for two cabs. Timothy and Linda embraced warmly and said good night.

"Don't worry about me," said Linda. "Talk to you soon."

But Timothy was troubled. On the ride home he kept going over Linda's story. Here she meets some guy and he simply moves in and takes up residence. She doesn't know where he's from and apparently he hasn't worked for the last two days. It just didn't sound right.

He was staring at the picture of the taxi driver when he thought of the other pictures he had seen lately. In his section at work and in the cafeteria, actual photos and composites of some serial killer were posted. There was information attached to each picture. He didn't want to let his imagination run away, but it couldn't be helped. Radio and television had been running this story for about a week now.

It may seem like such a stretch, but he couldn't let it go. Surely Linda had seen the same newscasts and photos. If it had been him, she would have recognized the likeness. Guess it can't be. Still...

47

Jack had prepared breakfast. After a week he had finally done something for Jennifer. He had missed doing the little things for her and was pleased that Brett's arrival had him back on track, at least for this morning. The three ate together and Jennifer, who was delighted to see Brett again, was even more thrilled to actually have a meal with her husband.

Brett defended Jack, knowing the pressure of this case, and Jennifer let it be known she understood. Jack promised her they would take a trip when the case was over, hopefully soon. He reached over, cupped her delicate chin in his strong hands, and kissed her warmly.

They arrived at the office just in time for the morning meeting with the team. Jack introduced Brett and explained the connection. The number of incoming calls sighting the killer was increasing. While each had to be followed up, so far none had proved helpful. Half an hour into the meeting, Watson came in.

"Lieutenant, line 2. Urgent."

Jack went out to Watson's desk to take the call.

"Petersen here."

"Jack, it's Sven. Hope you're sitting down. Kurt's body floated and came to shore about twenty miles from Phil's camp. A couple of fishermen saw it washed up against some rocks. Coroner's already been there."

"What did he say, Sven?"

"Death by drowning. Been dead for quite a while. Matches Phil's story."

"Jesus Christ."

"I know, Jack. Feels like we're starting all over again."

"Sven, we've got the whole team here. I'm going to go over this with them now and get back to you later."

"Understand, Jack. See you." They hung up.

"Bob, call David Folk. I have to see him as soon as possible."

Jack returned to the meeting. This would not go over well.

"That was Sheriff Larsen from Brainerd," said Jack addressing the group. "Kurt Schmidt's body washed up on shore. Coroner confirmed death by drowning. He's been dead about a week."

The room went completely quiet. The stunned silence hung heavily. For minutes the only sound was the ticking of the institutional wall clock. Everybody knew what this meant. Gradually the conversation started up, punctuated with innumerable oaths.

"Okay, we now know there's a second killer," said Jack.

"What is this? We got a copycat and a look-alike?" asked one of the detectives.

"Why do you say that?" asked another officer.

"Well, didn't we get a make on the hooker's killer? The one in Minneapolis Monday night? Folk altered that composite taken from...a bartender wasn't it? Changed the hair and moustache or something. It looked like Kurt. And the knife work was sure similar to the other killings. As I said, copycat and look-alike."

"Not only that," said Jack. "We have the Jensen woman who swears it was Kurt in the mall yesterday."

"So if this guy's good with wigs and stuff, maybe he's good with makeup too. Makes himself look like Kurt. Hell, there's been so many composites of the guy, everybody knows what he looks like."

"And all his victims are connected to Kurt," said Jack.

"All except the hooker. How do you figure that?"

"Yeah, that one's out of the pattern," said Jack. "So we have a sicko who makes himself look like Kurt. Goes around cutting up people who have seen Kurt. Then strays and does a hooker, but again with a knife. Makes it look like the same suspect. Why?"

"Probably just trying to throw us off. This is the worst kind of killer. Guy uses a knife...bad character. That's 'right in your face' killing. Too personal when you use a knife," said another detective.

The discussion continued for another thirty minutes. New assignments were handed out. At least some of the ambiguities of the case were gone. The question remained whether or not there was a connection between Kurt and the new killer. Jack explained that David Folk was looking into Kurt's background. Hopefully he would find some answers. Despite the setback from the news of Kurt's death, there was a renewed purpose for the team.

"This ties up a lot of loose ends," said Jack. "However, it still leaves us with a nasty killer at large. Make sure you take every precaution with this guy. He's responsible for four murders that we know of, probably more. For the time being we'll keep protection in place for the same people. We have to assume it's all connected. Any questions?"

Fifteen minutes later the team was on its way with their new assignments. David had arrived so Jack asked him and Brett into his office.

"Have you heard, David?"

"About Kurt? Yes, Watson just filled me in."

"David, I've got some calls to make but there's a number of issues I'd like to go over with you. Give me a few minutes will you?"

"As if he could make one phone call in only a few minutes," said David.

Jack shrugged and started calling. He gave the Commissioner the news and explained the need for an all out search for the new killer, involving every level of policing.

"Is this good news or bad?" asked the Commissioner.

"It wasn't the best scenario for us, sir, but at least we now know what we're dealing with. There is a new killer, but Kurt has been eliminated."

"We need this one solved, Jack. Frank Wilson called me immediately after his wife was attacked. No doubt he called Senator Johnston as well. You'll continue to have the highest priority for the remainder of the case, but get him soon."

"Yes, sir." He hung up and called the Jensens.

Luckily, Sharin answered the phone. Her mother was at home and coming along nicely, with a full recovery and no complications expected. However, her parents were returning to Canada as soon as possible. The doctor recommended she not travel for a couple of days. Jack brought her up to date on Kurt's death.

"Then who was that in the mall?" asked Sharin. "I only had a glimpse of him, but he sure looked like Kurt."

"We don't know yet. He may be using makeup to look like Kurt. At least it's resolved a number of issues for us, so in many ways it will help the investigation. We're now able to focus on one killer. We'll need some time with you to get a description of the guy in the mall – preferably today. Your mother or father may have seen something as well," said Jack.

"I don't know how much my parents can help, but we're all here now."

"We'll be there in a couple of hours." Jack hung up and completed the rest of his calls, including Sven Larsen, before calling David and Brett back in to his office.

"As soon as this is done, we're going to the Jensen's to get a description of the new suspect. Okay, fill me in, David."

"Actually the news doesn't upset me, as I'd assumed that Kurt wouldn't resurface. No pun intended. I don't have anything for you yet, but we're getting a lot of info from Brett's office. I've been working with a colleague there, putting together a file on Kurt. I know you're pressed so we've been concentrating on this case. We're just not there yet."

"Did Brett tell you about the theory that it might be a copycat using disguises?"

"He did but I don't like it. There's too much anger here. The autopsies on Fred Pearce and Phil Lundquist proved that, with the excessive force used and the number of wounds. No, I've always maintained if there was a second killer, it had to be someone close to Kurt. A friend, relative, lover – somebody emotionally involved with him. There are other reasons." David took a file from his brief case.

"Jack, when looking into William's murder, you were trying to determine if Kurt could have made it out to L.A., commit the crime, and return here. I believe with Mrs Jensen's report you knew exactly when Kurt was actually here. Therefore you could work out if it was possible for him to make such a trip."

"That's right," said Jack. "We knew he couldn't have left any earlier than Monday morning as he was in the house with Sharin at three A.M. As for the return trip, we met up with him at ten o'clock Tuesday night outside William's house. The latest he could have left L.A. would have been early afternoon, because it's about a three and half hour flight with a two hour time difference. That would make it two-thirty at the latest. So it's possible. We've been checking with flight crews on all flights within that time frame." He checked his notes from the case file.

"Incidentally there were sixteen outgoing and nine returning, that fit this schedule. That's non-stops only. So we started with those. Officers have been interviewing the flight crews, showing them Kurt's picture. So far, no luck."

"If he didn't make that trip, we have a second killer," said David. "Let's leave that for a minute. During Kurt's residence in William's house, you said there were daily phone calls received over a two week period. These were traced to L.A., I believe. Now, when Brett was investigating William's murder, and following up on these phone calls, he continually received the same information. All the witnesses he met identified the suspect as Kurt. The one that really had me puzzled was the girl in the store." He checked his notes again.

"Yes, Marie Coster. She said the guy making the phone calls looked like Kurt," continued David. "Now maybe, maybe, Kurt made the trip to L.A. to eliminate William. But, he couldn't have made those phone calls. He was in Clearwater, receiving them. So, gentlemen, I believe you have somebody in L.A., or who was in L.A., that looks an awful lot like Kurt."

"Christ, David, you're not suggesting..."

"I'm not committing to anything right now. I'm leaving for L.A. tonight."

48

Sharin was preparing lunch for the family. Yesterday's phone call from Jack had received a mixed response. One monster was gone, only to be replaced by another. Outside the kitchen window she could see Eric playing frisbee with King and Kayla. What a contrast. The dogs concentrating on their game without any concerns, while Eric must be dwelling on their situation.

She felt such warmth and love for his confidence and support since this ordeal began. Isn't it curious that an event such as this could strengthen a relationship, make you more aware of your feelings, and have their deep love grow even more? It was an immense source of comfort.

This was one of her mother's favorite soups. It had been created by her grandmother. Mix a can of tomato soup and green pea soup with one can of milk, or half milk, half cream, and season with curry powder, salt, and pepper. Serve with fresh French or Italian bread and hard butter. A little heavy on the cholesterol, but as her father always says , 'nothing's harmful if taken in moderation.'

Sharin let everyone know lunch was ready. She had decided to eat in the kitchen. There was a cozy alcove with a bay window facing the wooded area behind the house. Frank helped Judy to the table. She was still a little tender but managing well.

"My favorite soup. Thank you," said Judy.

"One of mine too, Mom."

"Anyone care for wine?" asked Eric.

They all declined. Lieutenant Petersen was coming to talk to Sharin about the suspect in the mall. Now that they knew it was not Kurt, he needed more information to help identify the new criminal.

"You're quite incredible, Sharin," said Frank. "I'm amazed at your inner strength and apparent calm. Despite all the disturbing news, you still manage to keep a positive outlook and look like a million every day."

"Thanks, Dad. I'm not so sure about looking that great, but I do appreciate all your help. It makes it much easier to cope with all of you there for me. Now, even Mom is a victim. I hate the thought of it, but none of us seems exempt."

"You're probably right, honey," said Eric. "We're all at risk. But you've been the main focus of these maniacs and Dad's right, you're handling it so well. I love you so much for your strength. And even if you don't look like a million, it's at least a thousand...."

Sharin gave him a playful backhand smack. "Okay, several thousand..." Another smack. "Okay, okay, a million." He blew her a kiss. Sharin grinned.

She got up to get more soup. "Who wants seconds?"

Everybody did.

"Who could this new maniac be?" asked Eric. "Does Petersen have any ideas?"

"I'm sure they have some theories. I mean, they thought that Kurt might not survive."

"Isn't it bizarre that the man in the mall looked so much like Kurt?" asked Frank.

The dogs started barking and ran to the front door. It was Petersen and Callahan. They were invited to join the family at the kitchen table.

Jack introduced Brett and explained his involvement in the case. He asked the Wilsons if either had caught a glimpse of the suspect in the mall, but neither had.

"I guess I'm it, Jack," said Sharin. "It's strange, but I was sure it was Kurt. Now that I know it couldn't have been, it makes me wonder what I did see. Mom, since we're about to rehash the event, maybe you'd prefer not to hear this."

"Good thinking, Sharin," said Frank. "We'll excuse ourselves, Lieutenant."

Sharin stood to give her Mom a hug before they left the room.

"Lieutenant, I've been doing my best to recall that moment in the mall. My first reaction was, that's Kurt, even before I realized Mom had been hurt. I thought, why? The hair was totally different, like short and blond. I only had a glimpse of him, and in an instant he was gone. Yes, he was about the same size, but as I try to reconstruct the face, it just doesn't work."

"Yet, at the time you thought it was Kurt."

"I know. But what was the real sequence of events? Did I recognize him before Mom was hurt? Everything happened so fast. My mother's falling against me, I turn, there he is. He's big, he's gone. I had seen enough of Kurt to never forget that face. There certainly was something familiar, but was it just my imagination at the time? I'm afraid I don't know anymore."

"With the help of our artists and the computer, we'll be able to put a new composite together," said Jack. "We'd like to do that right away. With your input added to the attendant's composite and tapes from the mall cameras, we'll have a positive ID on him."

"Okay. Eric and I can drive down together. We'll follow you."

49

Jack and Brett were in St Cloud at division headquarters. It was late Thursday afternoon. Brett couldn't believe Jack had just put away his fourth burger of the day.

"How do you do it?" asked Brett.

"What? Oh, I only do this when I'm excited."

They had heard from David Folk, who was on his way from the airport. The team had been rushed in for the evening meeting, which had been moved up three hours. David had all the answers. Finally the issues had been resolved. There was an identity to the mystery killer. More than an identity.

The detectives went into the meeting room as soon as David arrived. The room was alive with chatter, most of it speculation on who the killer was. They quieted when the trio entered but there were a few comments and oaths still audible. One stood out.

"He must have a fucking twin."

"Your prescience is remarkable," said David Folk. "I must admit, it couldn't have been timed any better. We've been investigating Kurt Schmidt's background through sources in Brett's office. I've just returned from L.A. where the trail finally led to the identity of our killer." David removed several documents from his brief case.

"Here are copies of two birth certificates, one for Kurt Schmidt, born August 2nd, 1947. You know who he was. The second is for a Karl Schmidt, born the same day, thirty minutes later. Report lists the births as identical twins."

Pandemonium broke out. Several, 'I thought so's,' a few, 'I'll be damned's,' and many others. Forty-two detectives reacting to the stunning news.

"In addition, our suspect has a rap sheet. These are photos of Karl, taken two years ago by the LAPD. They indicate he's six foot three, weighs two hundred and twenty-five pounds. Three witnesses in L.A. connect him to William's homicide. He lived in a house with Kurt and findings there proved his presence at the murder scenes. We also have his prints which are being compared with those found recently in the hotel room in Minneapolis where the hooker was murdered. Of some interest is Karl's nose, which you will note has been broken. That is the only feature distinguishing him from his brother, Kurt. We have a file for each of you."

As the files were being passed out the mood changed. Gone were the ambiguities in the case. It was now clear cut.

"Now we know who we're after. This guy seems as psychotic as his brother and he's bent on making everybody pay for Kurt's death. He's killed at least five people including a police officer. These new photos will be circulated immediately throughout the system and the media. Any questions?"

A lively discussion followed for thirty minutes, then the assignments were handed out.

David and Brett joined Jack in his office.

"Good work, David," said Jack.

"There were just too many coincidences in this case and you know what I think of those. I decided to proceed on the basis that Kurt would not survive. That meant a new killer, and one highly motivated by anger, to revenge Kurt's death. Couple that with the strange likenesses to Kurt at the latest homicides and I thought he might have a brother. Didn't necessarily think twin, but that certainly iced it."

"The broken nose also explains the bellman's problem with identifying the suspect," said Brett. "Remember he said something wasn't quite right with the photo, and he had spent twenty minutes with him on that bus ride. Of all our witnesses, he was the most qualified to make the guy."

"That was a lucky break for us. We could use a few more to help catch him before we have another homicide," said Jack. "I need a little time, then I'll treat you to the best burger in the state, if not the country. Consider yourself invited as well, David."

"He's all heart, Brett. Have you noticed?"

"Maybe we make a deal, David," said Brett. "Today it's his burger joint, and tomorrow we have a huge smoked meat on rye at your favorite deli. How's that?"

"Finally a detective with a little taste. You're on, Brett. Let's get to this case while Sherlock gets caught up."

Jack shooed them out of his office and started calling. He gave the Commissioner the news then dialed the Jensen's home number. Sharin answered and Jack gave her the news about Karl.

"So it was Karl in the mall," said Sharin. "I only had a glimpse of him, but he sure looked like Kurt."

"Now we know exactly who we're after. We'd like to move you to a safe house, Mrs Jensen."

"I'd rather be here with my dogs. Besides, with this little army you have here, there's no way he's getting inside. We'll be okay."

"I can't force you," said Jack. "It would make our job easier, and your life safer."

"I might think about it after my parents leave, but not now. Thanks anyway."

Jack completed the rest of his calls, including Sven Larsen. The three left for Pete's, which Jack assured them would be their high point of the week.

At the same time, another lunch of significance was about to begin.

50

Timothy had spent a restless night followed by a morning of being preoccupied with his dilemma. He couldn't help thinking of his aunt and her new friend. All the while it seemed the entire office was discussing the serial killer who was loose in Minnesota.

Just before noon, one of the girls in the office had received a phone call from a friend who worked at a local police station. They had found the body of the original killer, only to later learn he had a twin brother who was responsible for the last four homicides. A massive search was underway and anyone having any information was urged to call the police.

Timothy fretted over what to do. Was his story too far fetched? He didn't have any idea what Linda's new friend looked like. He was only suspicious because it seemed strange that a person just happens into town, has no place to stay, says he's a salesman, yet doesn't go to work for two days. He was glad to have booked lunch with a close friend who had a cousin working in one of the homicide divisions. They would decide together what to do with his story.

They had agreed to meet in the cafeteria in his building where lunches were reasonably priced, which suited his budget, and the quality and selection were exceptional. While waiting he couldn't help but overhear several conversations, most of which centered on the serial killer. People were generally sickened by the stories and some were unashamedly afraid. How can anyone avoid the police for so long? With all the publicity and his photograph everywhere, you would think somebody has to turn him in. Similar sentiments verbalized over and over.

Timothy's friend, Reg Wolford arrived. They joined the line to pick up lunch. Conversation was kept to the weather and women. Reg was also a young bachelor so the two had lots in common. After loading up with the daily special, dessert, and large glasses of milk, they found a vacant table and began devouring lunch.

"Reg, I need some advice, or at least an opinion from you."

"Heh, this sounds serious. Got anything to do with girl problems?"

"Indirectly, but not the way you might be thinking," said Timothy. "It's actually my Aunt Linda. Have you ever met her?"

"I don't think so, but you talk about her so often, she feels like an old friend. What's up?"

Timothy went over last night's conversation with his aunt. How she was head over heels for a complete stranger whom she had met in a bar only last Sunday night.

"Tim, come on. Boys and girls do meet and get involved, some quicker than others."

"That's not all. He arrives in town but has no place to stay. Says he's a traveling salesman but hasn't made a call in two days. Hell, he doesn't even have a car."

"Look, maybe he's so enamored with your aunt he's decided to play hooky for a couple of days. Who knows?"

"A traveling salesman without a car or a place to stay?" asked Timothy.

"How do you know he didn't have a hotel reservation somewhere? And if he's from out of town, he probably uses taxis while he's here."

"I suppose, but it has an odd feel to it, at least for me. I can't explain it logically but something tells me it just isn't right. Can you buy that, Reg?"

"Even if I can, I still don't understand the problem."

"Surely you've heard of the serial killer that's been responsible for five or six deaths in the last week. It's all over the news," said Timothy.

"I've seen the odd clip on tv but didn't pay too much attention. There's always some crime going on somewhere. Tim, you're not thinking..."

"That," said Timothy, "is exactly what I'm thinking."

"Whoa. Your Aunt meets some guy, they fall for each other and are having a hell of a good time, and you have him pegged as this serial killer. Nah."

"And why not?" asked Timothy.

"Because, because there's just not enough there. I mean, what have you got really? He's male, doesn't work, or hasn't lately. I don't follow the rest of this. Why do you think he's the killer?"

"I didn't say he was the killer. It's just a lousy feeling I have. And suppose he is."

"Hmm. Well I guess he could be. It's a bit of a stretch, but maybe. So what do you want to do?" asked Reg.

"Don't you have a cousin working in one of the homicide divisions? Do you think we could call her and ask if I should be going to the police with this?"

"That wouldn't have been a problem, but she's no longer there. However, I have an even easier solution for you."

"What's that?" asked Timothy.

"There are pictures of this guy everywhere. Why don't you simply take one to your Aunt and ask her if this is her new friend?"

"I've thought about that. Problem is, how will she take it? I mean, suppose it's not even close. Here she gets involved for the first time since her divorce and her nephew accuses her of shacking up with a serial killer."

"What if you just bring it up in casual conversation? You know, 'have you been reading about this maniac on the loose here? Pictures everywhere, etc.' Just see how she reacts. If she's seen the photos, surely she'd know."

"The problem is we had dinner just last night and we normally see each other only once a month. If my hunch is right, it could be too late to wait till next month."

"Then my friend, you have no choice but to confront her now and take your chances. If you're wrong she's going to forgive you, even if it bothers her initially. If you're right, you may save her life."

"What are the chances that I am right?" asked Timothy.

"You want me to quote you odds? Probably something like a zillion to one against you being right. Does it matter?"

"No it doesn't. Thanks for leading me to the right decision. I'll get one of those pictures and meet Linda before she leaves work this afternoon. Thanks, Reg."

"Want me to go with you?"

"Let me think about that. Nice of you to offer. I'll call and find out when she's leaving today and arrange to meet her. Then I'll let you know later this afternoon."

"Good luck, Tim. Talk to you soon."

When Timothy returned to his office, there was a message to see his supervisor immediately concerning a project they were working on. He gathered up the file and headed for his office. It was four o'clock before he had a chance to phone Linda. He dialed her office number.

One of her co-workers said he had just missed her. Linda had left for home about half an hour before.

51

Linda decided to leave work early. She needed extra time to shop for their meal tonight. It was going to be a special dinner and she wanted everything just right. The grocer had put aside two choice salmon steaks which she would serve with asparagus in a hollandaise sauce, mashed potatoes, a light vinaigrette salad, and the fresh french bread from the Sofitel. A bottle of Chablis was already in the fridge.

The evening newspaper was on the front porch and she managed to put it in with the groceries while leaving one hand free to unlock the front door. Her car was not in the driveway, but she remembered he might take the car for some business today. Imagine, Timothy was worried last night because he didn't appear to be working.

Linda did not notice the picture of the wanted man on the front page as she laid the paper on the kitchen table and began putting the food away. She spread the marinade on the salmon, peeled the potatoes, prepared the hollandaise sauce, and cleaned the lettuce. The Chablis was indeed in the fridge and chilled properly.

Plenty of time for a hot bath, after which she would put on her lounging pyjamas and eagerly await his return. While drawing the bath she decided to pour herself a glass of sherry which would go nicely with the hot bath. It would help take away the fall chill as well as prime her for the coming evening. The newspaper was tempting but with a full bath it might get wet, so she would leave that till later.

The hot bubble bath was a treat and she could sense the Epsom salts soaking into her pores. She imagined the toxins being evacuated from her body. The sherry warmed her insides as it slid down smoothly, complementing the tingling of her skin. Heaven.

The phone rang! What to do? The experience was so relaxing that to interrupt the moment seemed blasphemous. The damn phone kept ringing and ringing. Okay, okay. She decided to answer it, grabbed a robe, and scurried into the bedroom for the nearest phone.

"Hi," she said, a little out of breath.

"Linda, it's Timothy. You okay?"

"Yes, I'm all right, but you interrupted a wonderful hot bath I was enjoying," she said mockingly.

"Sorry about that but I felt I had to talk to you. Are you alone?"

"Yes, but I expect Kris back any minute. Why?"

"You get the Star Tribune, don't you?" asked Timothy.

"Yes."

"Have you seen this evening's paper?"

"I haven't looked at it yet, but it's in the kitchen. What's this all about, Tim?"

"Please do me a favor. Get the paper and take a look at the front page. I'll hold on."

"What am I supposed to see on the front page?" asked Linda.

"Just do it, please, Linda."

"All right. Give me a second."

As Linda went to the kitchen, she heard the car pull into the driveway. What timing. She had wanted to be ready for Kris, with her hair done and dressed in lounging pyjamas. Instead here she was, clad in a bath towel with her hair stringy and damp.

She picked up the phone and stared at the front page. It was Kris!

"Tim, what does this mean?"

"Is it your friend?"

"Yes, it's him. He just pulled into the driveway," said Linda. "What's this? He's wanted for..."

"Linda, get out of that house, now!"

"I'm in a bath robe."

"Get out of the house, NOW, Linda. Run. I'm calling the police."

She dropped the phone and ran. Decision. Should she lock herself in the bedroom? No. She ran to the back door. Out on the porch and down three steps to the backyard. The neighbor on her right was away. She went left. Luckily the car was on the right side of the house. There was a five foot cedar hedge separating their lots, but halfway down towards the back there was a small opening. She dashed towards the opening and ducked through to her neighbor's side.

Karl came bounding out the back door, looked left, then right, then stopped. Linda froze. If she didn't move he might not see her. If he did spot her, she'd have no chance without help. It was dusk. With the reduced visibility, she decided to ease towards their back door. She crouched below the hedge and began moving. She could see Karl scanning the area. He started to move towards the hedge. Linda panicked and ran. He saw her immediately.

She knew he couldn't get through the hedge, he'd have to go to the opening. She sprinted to the front of her neighbor's house. She banged on the door, rang the bell, and started screaming for help. No answer! Karl came flying around the corner of the house. He stopped. Twin red lights spinning wildly atop a police car were clearly visible. The car was half a block away and closing fast. They both heard the sirens. Karl glared at her, then turned and ran.

The next door neighbor came to the door. Linda collapsed against him. She was sobbing and muttered something about the police. His wife arrived.

"Linda," the wife said, "what is it?"

"Police. Get them please."

52

Jack took the call from Detective Francis Mulholland. His division had dispatched six cars to the address where Karl Schmidt had been identified. Two of the cars were there within minutes. Tactical Teams from the nearest boroughs were quickly assembled. Within half an hour over one hundred officers were in the area and another two hundred would join the search in an hour.

Officers in uniform controlled the vehicular traffic, restricting movement to emergencies or residents anxious to get home to younger family members. An area of four square miles, nearly four hundred city blocks, was cordoned off. All pedestrian movement was monitored and spot checked. The Tactical Teams began to sweep the area, evacuating homes and literally searching yard by yard for the suspect.

Jack and Brett were at Linda's house in half an hour where they met the emotionally shattered woman along with the hero of the moment, her nephew Timothy.

Her house and property had been cordoned off, while the neighborhood was alive with the curious. Linda had been seen by a doctor, given a mild sedative, and was now gushing over Timothy.

"He saved my life," said Linda. "How did you know?"

"I didn't," said Timothy. "It was a little imagination and a lot of luck. I was concerned you'd be upset with me for meddling."

"Thank God you didn't let that get in your way," said Jack. "We know you'll need to rest soon Mrs Strong, but we have a few questions if you feel up to it."

"Don't you think she's been through enough, Lieutenant?" asked Timothy.

"You not only saved Mrs Strong's life, Timothy, but you may well save many others if we can get on with our job. That means getting all the information we can, now."

"The Lieutenant's right, Tim. Besides, other than being a little groggy, I'm okay."

"How long have you known Karl?" asked Jack.

"We met last Sunday, so that's four days ago. God, it seems longer."

"Let's start with where and how you met. Take us through the last four days. Try not to omit anything."

An hour later Jack and Brett assured Linda she would have round the clock protection until Karl was apprehended. They made their way to the command post to get updated on the operation. The coordinator said there were over two hundred officers involved in a door to door search. Dogs and their handlers combed the area. Another seventy cars with two officers each had blocked all the intersections to the area. So far there was no sign of Karl. It was as if he had dropped through a crack and vanished.

Jack was called to the phone. It was the Commissioner.

"Petersen here."

"Do you have a positive ID on this guy?" asked the Commissioner.

"Yes, sir," Jack replied. He went on to explain Karl had stayed with a woman who hadn't realized who he was. A nephew alerted her to the possibility he might be the killer. He had her check the photo in the Star Tribune. She confirmed it was him. The suspect, Schmidt, arrived at her house. She hurried out the back and headed for a next door neighbor. Two police cars arrived just as he was closing in on the woman. He was off and running before our guys were out of their cars."

"What's happened since, Jack?"

Jack brought him up to date on the operation.

"It's damn frustrating, sir, but so far there's been no sign of the killer."

"You have my authority to requisition whatever you need. We're already getting complaints from citizens who have to get to their homes. Some of the calls have been frantic as they have youngsters home alone, so they're naturally worried with this maniac on the loose."

"We'll have to live with that for now. The Tactical Teams have responded well. Anything else, sir?"

"No, just get him, Jack. We can't afford to lose him now." They hung up.

Jack and Brett decided to join the search. There was activity everywhere. Residents had been warned not to open their doors to anyone other than family, friends, or police. They had also been asked to report any unusual movement. Some homes had been evacuated, tv stations continually flashed pictures of Karl, and radio stations aired a full description of the fugitive. The Cities had never witnessed a manhunt of this proportion. Tracking dogs who had been taken to Linda's house to get Karl's scent from his belongings, were now on the prowl.

There were the usual number of false sightings. At one time or another Karl had been seen in all the suburbs of the Twin Cities. On some occasions, he was in two or three places at the same time. It was not only time consuming, an inordinately large percentage of the police force had to be involved chasing the false leads. At three o'clock Jack and Brett grabbed a power nap in a variety store. They were back on the job in thirty minutes. New shifts kept arriving as some officers had been on duty for twelve to fifteen hours and more.

Shortly past eight they received the devastating news. A young man working midnights had returned home to find his elderly parents brutally stabbed to death. He said their car was missing.

They lived exactly one block outside the containment area.

53

Karl bolted through Linda's backyard, hurdled a small fence, reached the back lane at full speed and turned right. He ducked in behind a garage as two officers reached the lane. They had to decide which way to go. One turned left, the other went straight ahead, into another backyard. Karl doubled back towards Linda's house, crossed her street only half a block away and slowed to a walk. Two houses away was an intersection. When he turned the corner it put him out of sight of her house and the police.

Three blocks away the first set of police cars arrived, converging on the street he had just passed. He saw a car pulling into a driveway of an obviously empty house. A couple got out of the car and headed for their back door. They were quite elderly. He slipped up the driveway and was in the house before they had shut the door. The knife worked quickly. He grabbed their keys, eased the car out onto the street, and slowly made his way out of the city.

The handy little retreat, complete with bitch, was lost, but that was no problem. He just had to find another before continuing with his project. Might have to add Linda to the list, but that was not a priority right now. Since he was in Edina, he worked his way through Eden Prairie, to Chanhassen, then continued west away from the Twin Cities.

As things were really heating up here, maybe he should keep heading west and lie low for a while. The old couple probably wouldn't be found for hours so he could keep this car without any risk. He pulled over and found a map in the glove compartment. Sioux Falls was about a four hour drive away, if he kept to secondary highways. From there he could take a bus and be back in L.A. by the weekend.

Karl started away again and was careful to keep his speed just below the speed limit, but not so slow as to attract attention. A check of the gas gauge showed he would not have enough to make it to Sioux Falls. Damn luck. Well, he'd just have to find an isolated gas station that didn't have too much traffic. Surely something would come up on these less popular routes. There was still over a quarter of a tank left, so no panic.

Less than an hour later he spotted a sign indicating a gas bar with restaurant, three hundred yards ahead.

'Take the first right,' it said. He slowed and turned right on to a dirt road, where another sign stated, 'Martha's 1/4 mile.' Perfect.

There it was, in the middle of nowhere. One gas pump in front of a small building, a weather-beaten sign with a barely legible 'Martha's,' and a half ton pickup. A small light with just enough wattage to show where the pump was, gave the only indication that maybe it was open. Karl pulled up to the pump and got out. No sign of anyone.

He entered the restaurant where the sound of a radio playing country and western music filled the one room. A lunch counter with six stools was it. Behind the counter a young woman was washing dishes. As Karl neared the counter she turned and started.

"Omigosh, I'm sorry," she said. "Have you been waiting long?"

She ran out from behind the counter, drying her hands on an apron. In her twenties and extremely attractive in a vivacious way, she literally bounced over to him. With a tight fitting blouse that barely kept her ample bosom in place, it was quite a sight. A mini skirt showed off well proportioned legs and with her engaging smile, it was difficult to know where to look first.

"What can I get you?" she asked.

"I don't know where to begin."

"Honey, a hunk like you comes in here, my guess is you could have anything you want. But if you want to eat, you better do that quick, 'cause I'm closing. Now where do you want to start?"

"What are you doing after you close?" asked Karl.

"Maybe having a couple of drinks with you, if you're interested."

"Let's get to it. I haven't eaten since noon, so what have you got that's fast and easy?"

"The grill's still hot so I could fix you up with some eggs and bacon. That's always a good meal to build up your strength. Sound good?" she asked.

"Are you saying I might need some energy for later on?"

"Let me fix this for you and we'll see." She whisked the eggs in a bowl, placed four rashers of bacon on the grill, and put two slices of whole wheat in the toaster.

"What's your name?" asked Karl.

"Cathy Ryder. What's yours?"

"Jack," said Karl. He liked the idea of using the Lieutenant's name. What a neat twist.

"Here you are, sailor. A nice evening snack."

"That looks great. Look, do you mind filling up my car while I tie into this? Then I'll help you close up so we can get down to some serious drinking and what all."

"Sounds great, Jack. I have only two grades of gas here. Do you want high test or regular?"

"Regular's fine, Cathy."

After Cathy had filled the car, they cleaned up and headed out.

"I've got a suggestion if you don't mind," said Cathy. "It may sound nuts, but I like to see Law & Order every Wednesday. If you pick up the booze, I'll provide the setting – my place."

"You've got a deal. Where can we find liquor out here?"

"There's a store in town, sells everything. It's right on the way to my house. I'll lead the way."

Karl followed Cathy into town which was only a five minute drive. What a break this was. Maybe he wouldn't have to go back to L.A. after all. When they stopped at the local store, Karl asked Cathy what her pleasure was.

"I can drink vodka anyway it comes. Martinis, screwdrivers, or straight up. Just love the stuff."

Karl picked up two bottles of Smirnoff, got back in his car, and in tandem they drove to Cathy's house, another two miles out of town. They arrived at a large bungalow, set back about three hundred feet from the road. The last house he had seen was over half a mile away. As they turned up the long curved driveway, Cathy activated the garage door opener, and Karl noted there was enough room for both cars. She signaled him to park beside her.

"Geez, how much land do you have here?"

"Half a section, that's three hundred and twenty acres."

"If you don't mind me asking, how did you acquire this much land with such a nice looking house at your age?"

"I was married to a rich prick who decided to take off with another woman. Left me the house and land. Not a bad deal huh?"

"Sounds like he's a loser," said Karl.

"C'mon in, Jack. My show's started already. You pour the drinks, okay? Kitchen's over there. You'll find mix and ice. Surprise me with the first one, but don't skimp on the vodka."

Karl took a while to find the ingredients he wanted but finally came out with his favorite Bloody Mary. Vodka, tomato juice, a dash of Worcestershire sauce, tabasco, wedge of lime, half a teaspoon of sugar, and three cubes of ice. Cathy loved it.

By the time Law and Order was finished, they had polished off four Bloody Mary's, all doubles. Cathy said it was time for some straight-up vodka. After another five drinks, vodka for Cathy and water for Karl, they headed for the bedroom. It was a memorable night for her. Karl could have cared less. He had a safe haven for the time being. He would decide for how long.

His only concern was the car. That would have to be dealt with tomorrow, as sooner or later, somebody might stumble on to it. Her pickup might prove to be his next means of transportation. That would be something to consider. Maybe he'd take her with him, back to the Cities. Nobody would be looking for her truck.

The next few days will determine what's going to happen. Cathy was asleep. Well, she'd drank twice as much vodka as he had. It's so easy. If Kurt was still here, it would have been even better.

They'll pay for that, all of them.

54

Timmy Crandall was a fun loving, free spirit. She was the life of most parties, but seldom over indulged. She was in excellent physical condition mainly due to the jiujitsu training she had begun several years ago. Her parents had been sure their first born would be a boy, thus the unusual given name for a girl. No one had minded. Her folks adored Timmy, and in turn, she relished her name. It was different and so was she.

Timmy attracted people, especially men, which was much to her liking. She was not a stunning beauty, but her manner of dress, hair style, and makeup, created an irresistible sight which constantly drew attention. Slight of build and full of energy, she threw her jet black hair away from her face with a toss of her head as she entered the bar.

It was Thursday night and Timmy had just completed a twelve hour day at the salon where she worked as a hair stylist. It was time for a few drinks at her favorite bar. Since tomorrow was her birthday she would not be working. She had an agreement with the salon owner, that she never worked on that special day. After all, she had been there for twelve years, had a steady clientele, and seldom missed a day's work.

Stan, one of the owners of the Silver Heights Bar & Grill, was working the bar. He had known Timmy for most of her adult life and had her favorite beer on the counter as she sat down.

"Big day tomorrow," said Stan. "Isn't it the dreaded three zero?"

"You had to remind me, huh," said Timmy. "Now Stan, do I even look thirty?"

"No sweetheart, but you used to."

Timmy snatched up her beer, and drew her arm back ready to toss it at Stan.

"Just kidding, Timmy. You look great kid. Incidentally, the beer's on us tonight."

He reached over to give her a hug and peck on the cheek.

"You're a sweetheart, Stan – most of the time anyway. Thanks."

While Timmy was sipping her beer with Stan, she received birthday wishes from several of her friends, mostly regulars, who happened by. The crowd was a little sparse this night, so Timmy decided to try something new.

"You know I appreciate the drinks, Stan, but I just feel like something different tonight. I'm going to head out on my own. See you Saturday."

"What's wrong with tomorrow night?"

"First I have my Black Belt exam, then it's off to my folks for dinner. Don't want to miss that, but I will come in for a night cap," said Timmy. "Hopefully to celebrate both events."

"Black Belt already? How long have you been taking jiujitsu?" asked Stan.

"I started November 1995. I'll be the first student to get her Black Belt within four years if I pass Friday night."

"Knowing you, Timmy, that's a lock."

"Thanks again, Stan. See you."

It had started to rain but there were always a couple of taxis right outside so Timmy was able to get in one right away without getting soaked.

"Isn't Jake's the place to go on a Thursday night?" asked Timmy.

"If you're looking for a lot of action and loud music, that's the one," said the driver.

"That's for me. Let's go."

True to its reputation, Jake's was hopping. Timmy was led to a table for two by a hostess. She ordered a Rusty Nail, which would get things going in a hurry. The combination of scotch and Drambuie was a deadly one, but as usual she would limit herself to one or two drinks. She wanted to be in control in case someone interesting showed up.

Timmy was so contented with her life. Blessed with good health, she thoroughly enjoyed her position in the salon and her co-workers. They were a strongly motivated team who worked well together and knew how to party when the occasion arose. Most of the staff would be in the Height's Saturday night to celebrate her birthday. She was still nursing her first drink when a tall, well built guy strolled up to her table. Was he good looking? Oh, yes. He flashed a boyish grin.

"There isn't a seat left in the house. Mind if I join you?"

There would be little hesitation here. After all, this is exactly what she had hoped would occur.

"As long as you don't smoke, you're more than welcome."

"Never have, never will. Can't even stand the smell of smoke. Name's Geoff."

Again the infectious grin, as he offered his hand. When Timmy reached out to shake his hand, hers simply disappeared. She had never felt a hand that large. While there was a sense of superior strength, his grip was firm but gentle.

"I'm Timmy. The name may seem odd, but there's a simple explanation."

They quickly fell into an animated conversation. It felt so easy, as if she had known him for years. As an added bonus, he was charming and bright. She didn't know where this was going but it was definitely turning into a fine birthday eve celebration. With tomorrow off, there was plenty of time to rest for her big test at the Martial Arts Academy. Timmy was ready for a long interesting night.

After a second Rusty Nail, Timmy suddenly realized she was starved.

"I don't know about you, but I haven't eaten since lunch. What do you say to some pizza?" asked Timmy.

"Sounds great to me."

"There's a place in the next block that makes the best wood oven pizzas. Interested?"

"Let's go," said Geoff.

The rain had eased but there was still a drizzle.

"Want to run for it?" asked Timmy.

He put his arm around her, and they sprinted down the street, giggling all the way.

They shared an extra large, loaded pizza, washed down with a cold beer. She was a little fuzzy around the edges but pretty well in control. They were lucky to find a taxi right away. Timmy gave the driver her address as they settled in the back seat. His advances were not a surprise as the two had really hit it off.

"Hold on," said Timmy. "I don't want to get too worked up till we get to my place."

She thought he reacted strangely for an instant, then became himself again. Ten minutes later they were in Timmy's high rise apartment.

"Let me get you a drink to tide you over while I get changed."

She poured Geoff a brandy, then headed for her bedroom. Timmy was just about to remove her blouse when she sensed something behind her. It was Geoff with a knife in his hand. Her reflexes were off. The knife carved into her shoulder. The force of the blow drove her head first onto the bed.

Slightly sluggish and stunned from the wound, Timmy still recovered quickly. She rolled off the bed to the other side just as he thrust at her again. The blade barely nicked her arm.

She was ready for him now. He came around the bed and drove the knife at her stomach. Timmy knew the drill well. She easily side-stepped him and grabbed the wrist holding the knife. At the same time she kicked him high on the right thigh, which numbed the nerve in his leg. He collapsed. As he fell, her hold tightened on his wrist. He was forced to drop the knife or have his wrist broken. The knife flew out of his hand. His head caught the side of her dresser as he was tossed violently backwards. He hit the floor with a resounding thud.

All movement and noise abruptly ceased. The room was still. Geoff lay motionless on the floor.

Timmy grabbed the knife and scooted out the door of her apartment. Luckily the wound had not been too deep. Although in pain and bleeding, she knew she could make it to the security guard in the lobby. Her attacker would be out for a while, so she had time to wait for an elevator which would be quicker and safer for her.

By the time she reached the lobby the effects of the knifing had taken its toll. She needed help. The adrenalin rush had got her this far. She staggered across the lobby. The Security Guard seemed so far away. Then there were two of him. Everything began to blur.

"Call the police and an ambulance," she said.

Timmy Crandall promptly fainted. The knife clattered across the tiled floor.

55

Jack received the call from Francis Mulholland at two A.M. His division had responded to a 911 call in Minneapolis from a Security Guard in an apartment complex. A woman had been knifed in her apartment. She had somehow got away from her assailant and reached the Security Guard who had put in the emergency call.

As luck would have it a cruiser was in the area. The officers had immediately sealed off two of the exits from the building. All others were monitored on close circuit tv. So far there had been no sign of the suspect. More police were on the way. Mulholland thought it could be Karl. They were taking no chances.

"I'm ten minutes from the apartment now," said Mulholland. "The woman was badly cut and has been taken to emergency. We haven't had a chance to talk to her."

"Give me the address. We'll be there in thirty minutes. Let's not lose him this time."

When Jack and Brett arrived, the scene looked like a war zone. There were police cruisers everywhere. They were ushered into the front lobby where Mulholland was talking to the security guard.

Mulholland excused himself and went to Jack, who introduced Brett.

"Morning, Jack, Brett. Good news is we're sure he's still here. We had her apartment checked first. It's been sealed off. There's an excellent security system here and all the exits are on the guard's monitor. He said that prior to Miss Crandall coming down to the lobby, there had been nothing showing. The search is being done floor by floor."

"How many officers here, Francis?"

"There's twelve, including those guarding the exits."

"What's been done with the other tenants?"

"They've all been alerted. There are seven apartments currently not occupied. Two are not leased. The other five owners are away. They've been checked and found empty," said Mulholland.

"I'd like a quick talk with the guard, then let's get at it. What's his name?"

"Dale Talley. He's shook up and angry. Has known the Crandall woman for a long time."

"How did she get away from him?" asked Jack.

"He'll tell you," said Mulholland. "Dale, this is Lieutenants Jack Petersen and Brett Callahan."

They shook hands.

"Dale, I know you've been through this before, but I'd like a quick rundown from you. This is an important case and what you have to say may be crucial."

"Yeah, okay. Timmy, that's Miss Crandall, came home about one-thirty with this guy. It's not the first time she's brought a friend with her. That's not my business. Anyway, about half an hour later she comes staggering out of that elevator, white as a sheet, and bleeding like mad. She starts to falter. I go to meet her. She says something about police and an ambulance before passing out. I dial 911 – ask for police and an ambulance. I know were going to need both. Then I call Dr Grier, he's in apartment 307, but he doesn't answer."

"Then what?" asked Jack.

"I'm trying to stop the bleeding when the police arrived. Timmy comes to and we asked her what the hell's going on. She said this guy came after her with a knife. I think that's it over there. Well Timmy's Black Belt jiujitsu, so she gave it to him. He had cut her twice but she finally knocked him flat and got down here. Said she left him unconscious. The ambulance arrived. The medics said she'll be okay but they had to take her to the hospital. Another two cops arrived so one team went up to Timmy's apartment while the other guys asked me about exits."

"Where did the knife come from?"

"Miss Crandall brought it with her. I was careful, picked it up with my handkerchief, then the police bagged it."

Jack showed the guard a picture of Karl.

"Is this the guy?"

"Can't really tell. He was a lot taller than Timmy, I know that, and bigger. But he was facing away, looking at her when they walked by, so I only saw the back of his head."

"What about his hair?"

"Sort of brown, medium length, I guess."

"What did the officers find in Miss Crandall's apartment?" asked Jack.

"No guy, but they did notice some blood. Some must have been Timmy's because it led to the elevator bank."

"If he's not in an apartment, where could he go without you seeing him on those monitors?" asked Jack.

"He could be in the garage. We don't scan the whole area. Also the furnace room and lockers."

"What about the laundry room?"

"That's covered. Monitor six, right there."

"Anywhere else he could hide?" asked Jack.

"He could get to the roof. There's a door at each end of the hallway on the top floor."

"Francis, where have your men been so far?"

"We have two teams in the lower levels, doing the parking garage and utility rooms. The rest of the search force started on the ground floor. They've been working their way upwards."

"How many sets of stairs, Dale?"

"One at the end of each floor. They go all the way to the parking levels."

"Have you got those covered, Francis?"

"Yeah, two officers at ground level."

"Right. We're going to the roof," said Jack.

Jack and Brett took the elevator to the twenty-first floor and went down the hall to the end exit, clearly marked. Although it was three o'clock in the morning, they occasionally heard noise from some apartments. Obviously the phone calls about the intruder had people awake and hopefully alert.

The officers drew their guns and opened the exit door, which revealed a narrow set of stairs leading to the roof entrance. There was a metal door with a safety release bar at the top of the stairs. They pushed open the door and waited. The wind and rain whipped into the doorway. It lashed the two officers.

Jack kept his concentration as he stepped on to the gravel surface. He quickly scanned the area. Brett was right behind him. The only sound was the crunching noise of their boots on the roof top, mingled with the wind and rain. All the elements seemed more severe at this height. The wind was stronger and colder. The rain more intense.

It was an eerie sensation. The roof area looked much smaller than Jack had imagined. There were only eight apartments per floor so he knew the building wasn't that big. He had the feeling they could fall off if they took another step, or be blown off by the wind. There was an assortment of sheds, and other protuberances dotting the surface.

They decided to circle the roof, working in opposite directions, then meet halfway around on the other side. For most of the time they would be out of sight from each other, so they agreed to call out immediately if they found him. Their suspect was big and dangerous.

It was rough going in the blustery conditions and the gravel was slippery. This was not a good situation. Jack took it a step at a time. The visibility was poor with the driving rain and darkness. He heard a voice and froze. Nothing. Then another sound. He couldn't place it. He moved a little quicker now, towards the noise. Around the corner of one of the sheds the shadow of a figure emerged, with the sound of another voice. It was Brett talking on his portable.

"Jack, let's go," yelled Brett. "They found some more blood. They're on the second level of the parking garage."

Jack and Brett ran down the stairs to the hallway. One of the elevators was still on the 21st floor. Jack took a quick look at the selection of floors available and chose P 2. It felt as though the elevator was hardly moving. They both stared at the lit up floor numbers as they descended. At the ninth floor the elevator stopped.

"Shit," said Brett.

The door opened and they showed their shields, telling the waiting couple there was a killer loose and to get back to their apartment and lock the door. There was a dull response. They had obviously been drinking.

"Get going. Now," said Jack as the door closed.

Too slowly for them, the descent continued. They reached P 2 and scrambled out, looking for other officers. For an instant all was dead quiet. The elevator door closed. As they began to move, the sound of their footsteps on the concrete floor was the only break in the silence. Then all hell broke loose.

They heard a car engine racing and tires squealing. The vehicle careened around a corner, accompanied by shouting and gunfire. As the car came into view, it suddenly swerved out of control and smacked into a row of parked cars. Instant quiet. The only sound was the soft hissing from the radiator. Steam emanated from the hood of the car.

With the officers appearing from the lower level, Jack and Brett hurried to the car to identify the driver, who still had not moved. He was slumped over the steering wheel. Jack opened the car door. The driver showed signs of coming to. Jack eased him back in the seat and stared at the face. His eye was cut and his nose was bleeding.

It was not Karl.

56

It was nine-thirty, Friday morning, October 22nd. In the last forty-eight hours, Jack had managed one hour's sleep, while Brett had done slightly better with two hours. First Karl's escape, then the attempted murder by a new felon. Twice in two days they thought they had him. The call from the Commissioner was not too welcome.

"How in hell's name did this creep find a way to outwit over four hundred police officers, Jack?"

"Commissioner, we're as frustrated as you. He must have got out right away. Firstly, as soon as our force was in place, I'm confident nobody could have entered or left the area without being scrutinized. Secondly, we're sure he killed the elderly couple, which was only one block outside of the area we had sealed off, as the coroner estimates the time of death between seven and nine last night. Our units had started moving in just after seven-thirty. He took their car and was probably out of there in no time."

"You put out an A.P.B. on the car?" asked the Commissioner.

"Right away, sir. Time was eight-twenty yesterday morning."

"And what happened last night?"

"An emergency call came into Mulholland's division early this morning. There had been a knifing of a young woman in a downtown apartment. It sounded like Karl. We covered the building and arrested the suspect. He's in custody now. Turns out he was a copycat. Liked the idea of mimicking Karl, but said he really didn't mean any harm. Meanwhile the woman who was seriously injured is going to be okay."

"Good work, Jack. Senator Johnston tells me the Governor may want to see us. I should know within the hour. You'll be in your office?"

"Unless Karl Schmidt is found, I'll be here. If he does turn up, I guess we won't have to worry about the meeting," said Jack.

"You've got that right. Talk to you soon."

Jack hung up and looked at the egg sandwich he had bought on the way in. Somehow it had lost its appeal.

David Folk came in, took one look at Jack and Brett and shook his head. "Sorry guys. You just aren't getting any breaks with this case."

"Dammit," said Brett. "Can't believe we could come that close without nailing him. Then we have that other nut case this morning. We really thought it was him."

"I do have some encouraging news for you, gentlemen," said David. "The hooker had managed to scratch her killer, so we found evidence under her nails that was tested for DNA. These were compared with fluid samples from Linda's house. They belong to Karl, putting him at the scene of the hooker's murder. Same thing with the car owned by Sam Hurst, the guy Karl killed after escaping from the mall. That's not all. Another match with hair and prints taken at Fred's house in Crosslake. We have Karl linked to all three homicides. We're still working on the murders at Phil's camp. Prints and samples from a place like that are so numerous, it's taking more time."

"What about William's hotel room? Any matches there?" asked Brett.

"Thank you, yes," said David. "Hair samples only, but they definitely prove Karl was in the room. Nothing on prints."

"Time for the morning meeting," said Jack. "David, I'd like you to update the team with this info. You have the new assignments, Brett?"

"Ready, Jack."

The mood was somber. They all realized how close it had been to nabbing him. Now the search area was going to be even larger than before. An overworked and exhausted team had to dig in again. Jack let them know about the Commissioner's call and a possible upcoming meeting with the Governor. If they thought there was heat before, it was nothing compared to what was ahead.

David's report put Karl at the scene of four homicides – Fred, William, Sam Hurst, and the hooker. Motive, opportunity, and style also linked him to Phil and the Brainerd police officer. There was little doubt how badly they wanted him.

"You'd think the Troopers would have spotted that car by now," said one of the detectives.

"Yeah. So far, not a sniff," said Jack. "We're circulating a photo of the car with the plate number to every gas station we can get to. The guy has to fill up sooner or later. He's going to make a mistake, you know that."

The team went back on the street with their new assignments.

Jack was told the meeting with the Governor was set for one-thirty. He took Brett and David to Pete's, the best place for him to brace himself for the coming session with the State's top brass.

He returned just after four o'clock, none the worse for wear. A lesser man would have looked like a whipped dog after what Jack had been through. Nobody would have predicted the coming events.

Days ran into weeks. The entire month of November produced little help. The trail was running cold. The longer they went without contact the more difficult the case became. It usually meant the suspect had moved out of the area. Jack had alerted other states and the F.B.I. He had all modes of transportation monitored. Airports, train and bus stations, and the Canadian border were all advised. All the leads resulted in dead ends.

In Minnesota they hadn't managed to turn up one gas station or attendant who had seen the car that Karl had stolen. It was frustrating and absurd. The suspect and car had just disappeared. Had he dumped it into the Mississippi River?

The operation was still active but there was some scaling down. With multiple killings including a police officer, Jack was able to keep most of his team involved. However, round the clock protection for the Jensens had been canceled. Life went on. New cases sprung up and with them new assignments. Of the original team of forty officers, he now had twenty-five working full time on the Schmidt case, with the remainder handling new assignments, but still connected.

The snow came. Christmas arrived and went. The New Year and new century began amid much flare. Millennium events and products were everywhere. None of the predicted disasters or glitches occurred. The world did not end.

Karl's vanishing was not unique. Jack knew this was a fact of life. Killers had been known to simply disappear. The murders stopped and they were not heard from again. Some may have died, others moved away to new countries or wherever. Still, he could not forget the Schmidt brothers. Neither would Brett, who had returned to L.A., or Sven Larsen. Not that the case was dead. There remained a good number of detectives hard at it, looking for the break that would lead to Karl's capture. Jack hadn't taken any time off for the trip with Jennifer. He knew he would, but for now, he had to stay with this case.

The Wilsons had left for Canada, which took some of the pressure off

Jack, but not all. Frank Wilson continued to communicate with the Commissioner and Senator. He would not rest until this was over. It was unfinished business that rankled.

Still there was no sign of Karl.

57

Winter had been an interesting experience for Karl. He had actually enjoyed the season, taken up cross-country skiing, and even participated in day long excursions with Cathy on her snowmobile. His long hair, full beard, and moustache gave him a new look. Occasionally there was a small news item on the killer who disappeared, but they were becoming less frequent.

Now and then he helped out at the little restaurant with maintenance work, but mostly busied himself at Cathy's house with renovating. She was quite a homebody who not only appreciated his work, but seemed genuinely pleased with his efforts. Every night there was some program on tv which she had to see. Luckily the evening news held little or no interest. Thus, with a plentiful supply of vodka, her addiction to these programs, and his artful skills on the connubial couch, a comfortable lifestyle had emerged.

As the restaurant stayed open later on Friday's, Cathy started at noon. There was a steady clientele every Friday night, when Cathy would serve fresh fish. She even had a high school student in to help out, such was the popularity of these weekly dinners. Karl dropped Cathy at the restaurant and headed east in her pickup. He figured it would be a four hour drive to Crosslake. That would give him plenty of time to accomplish his task and return before Cathy closed.

He had never seen this much snow. The drifting in the fields reminded him of sand dunes in the desert, that he had seen either in movies or magazines. In the country the snow was pure white. With the sun shining as it was this day, you definitely needed sun glasses. The glare off the snow was blinding as you could see tiny sparkles dancing on the drifts, like a sea of fire flies blinking on and off. Fortunately the roads were clear so he could maintain the speed limit with no difficulty.

How did they keep these roads open with all this snow? That seemed to him like an impossible task. Here he was, traveling on little used secondary routes, surrounded by mountains of this white stuff, yet the roads were practically bare. Well, that's their problem. He planned to be back in California in a couple of weeks so he could care less.

During the drive he thought about the early days, growing up with Kurt. The memories were not pleasant. Both parents were alcoholics. Their father had tried to take care of the four children but was never consistent. The beatings they received were not forgotten. His next memories were of the foster home. Then at age twenty he heard that Kurt was released from an institution. From that point on they had each other, only each other. Now they had taken Kurt from him. It wasn't fair. He'd make it up to Kurt and himself.

Karl chose a busy gas station to fill up. He didn't want any interruptions on his return trip. Next he stopped at a drive-through to pick up some greasy food. Had to have some nourishment before his early evening activities. As he pulled away, a soft dusting of new snow began to fall. By the time he reached the outskirts of Crosslake the snow fall had intensified and accumulations were building up on the roads.

With little experience in driving in these conditions, he would have to take extra care. The house was easy to find with their names carved on a stupid sign beside the mail box. He continued down the road, turned around, and drove back till he was a good hundred yards past their house. He parked facing in the direction of the highway. He didn't plan on staying around too long.

The snow fall was very heavy now, his foot prints were filled in and obscured instantly. He was thankful for the high boots he had brought along at the last minute. The snow fall would make the return trip more difficult but it was ideal for entering the house undetected. As long as the owners didn't come home for a while, there would be no sign that anyone had preceded them.

The back door was easy pickings as he slid quietly into a small area that looked like a utility room. A framed glass door looked into their kitchen. He waited, not knowing if a dog or anyone was home. The next step was to dust off any snow from his clothing. There would be no tell tale signs of his entry. He slipped into the kitchen and re-locked the door.

He would need the element of surprise if they arrived together, so he scouted the house to plan his ambush. It was now five-thirty and totally dark. It made his task more difficult, but in the long run, the darkness would be a bonus. He found what he wanted, discarded his parka, as well as the boots. It would be advantageous to be bare footed. There would be plenty of time to get dressed again before leaving.

He sat down to wait. The knife was ready.

58

Al had agreed to pick up Jan at work so they could leave for the family reunion as early as possible. They had a three hour drive to International Falls where the clan was gathering. This year his parents expected over a hundred family members would attend. It had become a popular event they had started five years ago. Only twenty had showed up for the first reunion but since then, every year had seen a steady increase in the number of attendees, as more family was reached.

He had met cousins he never knew existed, some of whom lived as far away as British Columbia, Canada. January had been chosen as most seemed to enjoy the winter activities available in northern Minnesota. Ice skating, tobogganing, cross-country and down hill skiing, were only some of the functions the family undertook with gusto in the week long get together. Ages ranged from four to eighty. There was no shortage of indoor games with fun for all.

Al and Jan had not missed a reunion yet. They were packed and ready to go right after Jan was through work. Al was particularly pleased with Jan's reaction to the family. She took on the week with the same enthusiasm as her husband. They were both discouraged when the storm moved in and dumped over a foot of snow in less than an hour, with more forecast to come.

Jan was ready promptly at five o'clock. They headed to Emily where they would pick up Highway 1 eastbound to Highway 169, then north to International Falls.

It was slow going with the snow fall and darkness. Visibility was severely reduced. The snow flew at the windshield giving a sensation of the car moving much faster than it actually was. Al was driving only twenty miles per hour, but the effect of the oncoming snow being picked up in the headlights, gave the feeling of moving at three times that speed. It seemed as if they were driving a wedge through an endless sea of white, that flashed towards the windshield, at the last minute parted, then whisked past. Gradually he had to continue to reduce his speed till they were managing only five to ten miles per hour, so restricted was the visibility.

Eventually Al was forced to pull over. Parked on the side of the road, they had the uneasy feeling of still moving forward as the wind driven snow was propelled at their stationary car. They realized the trip had to be postponed.

"No point in going on, is there?" asked Al.

"Definitely not. Why don't we go back to town, have some supper, and see what the weather does? If it stops snowing we can try again," said Jan.

"I guess we have no choice." Al carefully turned around and headed back to Crosslake. His disappointment was obvious.

"Even if doesn't stop snowing tonight, we can always leave first thing in the morning and be there for breakfast," said Jan. "We'll only miss the first night."

"Yup. You're right, honey. I've never seen it this bad."

The return trip of only twelve miles took an hour and a half. By the time they reached the restaurant in Crosslake, both agreed, the trip had to be canceled for tonight. One of the local police officers saw them pull in and was relieved to know they had delayed their trip till tomorrow. He reported most highways closed with numerous accidents already. Cars sliding off the road and general mayhem everywhere. The storm will be over in a couple of hours, so the roads will be fine by early morning, he told them.

Al and Jan were in a better mood after supper, now that they were resigned to heading out in the morning. It was after nine when they finally reached home. He didn't want to shovel the driveway the next day, so left the car on the road where it would be easier to get away. They also left the luggage in the car. No harm would come to the clothes and it would simplify things in the morning. They planned to leave at dawn.

Al phoned his parents to let them know they wouldn't arrive till tomorrow. They understood as they were experiencing the same storm. Tomorrow would be fine, as others were delayed as well.

Jan decided to have a bath tonight to save time in the morning. Al thought that was great and went downstairs to get a beer from the fridge. He'd have a quick look at the news before going to bed. He was excited now with the prospect of leaving bright and early. Maybe they'd stop for coffee and muffins in Grand Rapids.

He felt a scorching sensation in his back, then a hand clamped tightly over his mouth. The pain seemed to ease as the knife was withdrawn. Again another strike. He doubled over in agony. Al stumbled forward, knocking over a lamp. He fell face down on the living room carpet. He felt his head being yanked backwards. The pain in the back of his neck was even more unbearable. The sound of running water was faint, and slowly fading. He wanted to call out to Jan. He couldn't. There was a loud snap. It was the last thing he heard.

Jan who was in the tub heard the thump and called out. "Are you okay, Al?"

Nothing. There was only the muffled sound of the tv.

She turned the water off. "Al, what's happening?"

Again, nothing. Then footsteps on the stairs. Jan was paralyzed with fear.

"Al," she shouted.

The bathroom door opened.

"There's no Al," Karl said.

Jan stared in terror at the bearded figure.

"Kurt drowned, now it's your turn."

He bent over, placed a huge hand on her forehead and pushed her backwards under the water. Her head struck the bottom of the tub. She opened her eyes and could see him looming over her. She was not going to die without a struggle.

She grabbed his arm with both hands, then braced herself with her left leg against the end of the tub. With all her strength she brought her right knee up to crash into his face.

He fell back slightly. She was able to push up out of the water, gulp in some air, and bite his arm. Suddenly there was blood everywhere. She dug her nails in and bit him again. More blood. She could taste it.

Karl pulled one arm free, grabbed her hair and pulled her head back into the water. She tried to raise her head but he was too strong. She couldn't get at him as he was now behind her. Jan kicked furiously, splashing water, as she wriggled and twisted, trying to get free. Nothing helped.

Pain started to build in her head. She grabbed frantically for his other arm but couldn't reach it. She pounded the air with her fists trying for some kind of contact. Nothing. She was blacking out. There was no strength left. She gasped for breath. The water rushed in.

Jan choked on the water. Her death was painful.

59

Jack was at home when the call came in at nine o'clock Saturday morning.

"The bastard's back, I'm sure," said Sheriff Larsen.

"What happened, Sven?"

"Do you remember Al and Jan? They were at Roy's the night Ginny was killed."

"I didn't meet them but I recognize the names."

"We found Al dead from knife wounds and a broken neck. Jan was drowned in the bath tub. The B.C.A. team is here now. We've sent out an A.P.B. Got the Troopers alerted with Karl's picture. Figured it has to be him. You coming up?" asked Sven.

"Yeah. I'll leave right away."

"When you get here, go to the station in Crosslake. We'll have an officer bring you to the house. It'll be good to see you, Jack, but not under these circumstances."

"Ditto." Jack hung up. There had always been the concern it was not over. Still it was a major shock. The trail had just warmed up again.

Jack called Ed Brooker to set up protection for the Jensens. They'd meet at the office in twenty minutes to leave for Crosslake. His next call was to the Jensen's. He got the answering machine. Jack left a brief message bringing them up to date. Around the clock protection would be set up again to remain until the suspect was in custody.

Where were the Jensens?

Jennifer was at class so he left a note. He might not be home in time for dinner.

The road crews had done an amazing job of clearing the snow from the major highways. Over a foot and a half had fallen in the Minneapolis area, with more to the north. Jack and Ed elected to take Highway 10 for two reasons. Not only would they make better time on the divided highway, it would take them through Little Falls, where Jack happened to know a spot that used pure sirloin steak in their burgers.

Ed stifled a chuckle as Jack ordered two extra large specials to go, one with mushrooms, the second with cheese. Ed also realized he would be driving the second half knowing Jack believed you didn't insult a good burger by driving while eating. Since there wasn't time to stop, Ed was nominated. They arrived at the Crosslake police station before noon, where they were led to Al and Jan's house.

Sven and Jack exchanged New Year's greetings and got right to it. The house and property had been sealed off. As the investigative teams were finished, Jack had a look at the two bodies before the coroner signed off to send them to the Forensics Unit in St Paul. It was another brutal display by this deranged killer.

"This time we have blood which will give us DNA, as well as hair samples, and prints. If there's a match with Karl, it would be very conclusive," said Sven.

"You know as well as I do, it was Karl," said Jack. "And you also know we have the same problem – how to find him."

Sergeant Whelan came to the door.

"Excuse me, Sheriff, but we've got a witness who lives near Al and Jan. Said there was a vehicle here last night he never saw before."

"Send him in."

Joe Cooper was as friendly and talkative as they came. He had lived down the road from Al and Jan for nearly twenty years. The word had spread quickly about the latest homicides. Joe had been in Bill's Diner when the news hit.

"What do you have to tell us, Mr Cooper?" asked Sven.

"Yesterday I saw this truck parked a little ways from Al's house, not once but twice. First time was on my way home from work, around four-thirty. That was just when the snow started. Later I went out to bring my daughter home from her part-time job. That was about eight o'clock and the same truck was still there. It was snowing so bad by then, I had to creep along. Anyway, I knew I hadn't seen that truck around here before. It was a green, half ton pickup. Nice looking truck, maybe a year or two old."

"What else can you tell us about it, Joe?" asked Jack.

"Not much, other than it looked in real good shape," said Joe. "Of course, by the time I went out to get Gwen, that's my daughter, it was pretty much covered in snow. I do remember the plate though. Saw it the first time I drove by."

"You have the license plate number?"

"Yup. Not a number though. That's why I took notice, I guess. It was a name – 'CATHY.' "

"Minnesota plate?" asked Jack.

"Sure was."

"Ed, get on the horn and run that plate. Bring the Troopers up to date on the truck," said Jack. "Joe, have you talked to anyone about this?"

"Yup, I did. I hope that's not a problem," said Joe.

"We can't have this leak. When and where did you mention this?"

"Well, when I was in Bill's, everyone was talking about the murders. So I told them about seeing that truck last night, right near Al's."

"Who was there?" asked Sven.

"Only about five or six of us," said Joe. At that moment he looked down and started shaking his head.

"What," asked Jack, " is it, Joe?"

"That Jimmy Cronin kid was there, the young reporter. He sprinted out of Bill's like his tail end was on fire."

"Did you tell them what the license plate read?" asked Sven.

"Yup. I'm sorry. I see what I did wrong now."

"Christ almighty. Joe, do you have any idea where Cronin was heading?" asked Jack.

"I don't."

"Sven, do you know this Cronin kid?"

"I've heard the name but can't say I'd know him to see."

"I know him, Lieutenant," said Sergeant Whelan. "He writes for the local paper, as well as other regionals. Works out of his home most of the time. I can take you there."

"Let's go," said Jack. "Ed, as soon as you get the plate traced, get some officers out to the residence. If it's near the Cities, call Mulholland. I'd like him involved."

Jack got into Whelan's car and they wheeled away.

"Put your siren on," said Jack. "How long will it take us to get there?"

"Five, seven minutes. Maybe a little longer with the snow."

"Let's try to get him on the phone. Maybe we can hold him off till we get there."

Whelan called the station for Cronin's home phone number. It seemed to take too long. Jack was strumming his fingers and shaking his leg. Finally they had the number. Jack dialed it.

The phone rang and rang. After five rings an answering machine took over.

"Christ," said Jack.

They turned off the main drag and headed down a small side street that was all but impassable. After one block, they met a snowplow blocking the only open lane. The police siren was screaming. Whelan started honking his horn. Nothing happened. Jack leapt out of the car and ran to the plow. The driver, for some inexplicable reason, was not in the vehicle.

"How much further to his house?" asked Jack.

"End of this block. It's the last one on the right side."

"Come on. We'll have to leg it there."

They had about two hundred yards to go. Jack started running. Whelan followed. It was tough going. The snow was over two feet deep. He was wearing ankle high, winter boots, but they weren't enough to handle this much snow.

They saw several other tracks in the snow where people had come and gone on foot. One set of which most likely belonged to Jimmy Cronin. Jack tried to land in previously made tracks. When he missed, he sunk in up to his calves. Several home owners were shoveling their driveways and sidewalks. They all stopped to check out the two police officers who were gamely slogging their way down the street.

They reached Cronin's house, rang the bell, and pounded on the door.

Jimmy Cronin had just finished another phone call.

He hung up and went to the door.

60

Karl had checked into a motel shortly after three o'clock. He was only eighty miles south of Crosslake after nearly five hours of driving and finally decided that was enough. The motel was deserted and despite being awakened at the late hour, the owner sympathized with the plight of the driver, who with the weather conditions, had no choice but to stop for the night.

He called Cathy to say he had left to pick up a surprise for her but got stuck in the snow storm. He'd overnight in a motel, leave early in the morning, and be there to cook breakfast. She in turn was exhausted after a long, but successful day at the restaurant, so would welcome a good night's sleep.

Karl decided to have a couple of drinks. He was about to turn in when he heard a noise outside. A car was obviously stuck as the sound of tires spinning wildly in the snow echoed in the cold night air. He peeked through the curtains and saw a woman get out to stare disgustedly at her immobile car. Never one to miss an opportunity, Karl went outside to help the stranded motorist. He might just need her later on, who knows?

"What a hell of a night," she said as Karl approached.

"I'll get you out of here in no time," said Karl. There was a sight incline entering the motel's parking lot. She had hung up on a small mound of snow.

"Just put it in reverse and back down off this snow drift. Then take a longer run into the lot."

He pushed the car as it easily backed down onto the road. He waved her forward. She gunned the engine, cut the corner too fine, and ran into the same drift. She smashed the steering wheel with both hands. Karl opened the car door.

"I can't take any more of this," she yelled.

"Look, just put the car in reverse. I'll get you off this again, but this time, I'll drive your car. You can go and check in while I park your car."

She nodded and seemed to relax. They moved the car back on to the road again, then she got out.

"Thanks. I'll take you up on your offer."

Apparently the owner was still up as the door was open and the lights were on. A few minutes later the stranded driver appeared and headed for her car, which Karl had parked next to the motel office. She had registered in the room next to his. Karl said he would help with her luggage.

"Moving around in this snow isn't easy," he said.

"Thanks again. I'm sorry about yelling back there, but it's just been a horrible drive."

Karl easily hoisted the bag, waited patiently while she fumbled with the door key, then eased into the open doorway. She was in her early forties and not bad looking.

"I've never seen a storm like this," said Karl. "I couldn't see anything out there. Where would you like this?"

"Oh, I'll take it now. Those roads. That was really nerve-racking. I just had to stop."

"Same here. When you get settled, if you'd like a night cap, I have some vodka with me," said Karl.

"I sure could use a drink. First I have to let my daughter know what's happened. Give me a few minutes."

Karl had seen a drink machine next to the office, so he bought two cans of Sprite, the only soda he saw that would go with vodka. He returned to his room, poured a small drink, and waited for a call from his new neighbor. Twenty minutes later there was a knock on his door.

"My name's Darlene. I'm ready for that drink now, if the offer's still open."

"It certainly is. They call me Jack. At the risk of sounding too forward, would you prefer my place or yours?" asked Karl.

She smiled. "This looks better than mine right now. I just opened my bag and threw a few things around. In any case, one drink will be enough for me."

Karl poured her a stiff vodka and Sprite.

"This is the only mix I could find to go with the vodka. Hope it's okay."

"Right now I could probably drink the stuff straight. Don't usually drink vodka, but here's looking at you."

They clinked glasses. She downed half her drink.

"I've never seen the roads this bad," said Darlene. "I make this trip twice a month and this is the first time I've had to stop. Where were you headed?"

"I left Sioux Falls this afternoon under clear skies. Didn't run into any snow till after I stopped for supper. Like you, I finally gave up. Couldn't see past the front of the car at times."

She accepted his offer of another drink.

"Well, maybe one more."

It wasn't long before the first bottle was empty and they had started on the second. Her drinks were more heavily laced with vodka while Karl was coasting. At this stage, Darlene didn't seem to notice.

It was five o'clock before the two found their way to bed. By this time Darlene, who had given every indication of being interested in a romp with Karl, was just too far gone. The stress of the night's drive coupled with the powerful drinks were too much. As soon as she was undressed and under the covers, she was asleep.

Karl could have cared less. He had seen her car, a new Mercedes, and as always was thinking ahead. If it took a little booze to have a safety valve, so what. He didn't care whether he got laid or not.

He was surprised it was after eleven when he woke up. He had showered and dressed before Darlene stirred. She bolted upright.

"What time is it?" she asked.

"Noon."

"God, I told Miriam I'd be in the Cities by morning. I've got to run."

She leapt out of bed and headed for the bathroom. Karl turned the television on and was stunned to see the program interrupted by a special bulletin. The police were looking for a green pickup truck with the license plate – 'CATHY.'

How the hell did they know that? He shut off the tv just as Darlene came out.

"Look, I hate to just run, but I've got to get going. I'll shower here then go to my room to get made up. I'll be back to exchange phone numbers later. That okay?"

"Sure. Got to get going myself."

His plans were made. He had to take the chance she didn't hear any news.

61

Jack and Brooker were driving as fast as conditions would allow. A few miles north of St Cloud they would exit on to highway 15 south. The license plate had been traced to a rural address southwest of Hutchinson, which was on number 15. With the road conditions it could take them two hours to reach the residence, listed under the name of Cathy Ryder. Jack was beside himself.

Brooker had called Lieutenant Mulholland who was on his way to the address. He had also contacted the local Sheriff who assured them there would be officers at Cathy's house within minutes. They all knew Cathy Ryder and were well aware of the serial killer loose in their state. If he was in the area, they'd get him.

They had an A.P.B. out on the car and once again police forces across the state were on alert for the killer. Jack kept getting the answering machine at Cathy's house.

"What the hell's happening there, Ed?" asked Jack.

"Maybe he didn't make it back. She could be out shopping, or whatever."

"Christ, Ed, he would have left Crosslake by eleven last night or earlier. Even in these conditions he'd be at her house by now."

"Maybe he couldn't make it through. That was a hell of a storm, Jack. Let's hope so anyway for Cathy's sake."

Jack's portable rang.

"Petersen here."

"Lieutenant, this is Sheriff Lindsay in Hutchinson. We've located Mrs Ryder and everything's all right here. No sign of the killer."

"Glad to hear that. When did she last see him?" asked Jack.

"She said he left yesterday in her truck. Didn't say where he was going. Then he called her last night from some motel. The storm had forced him to stop."

"What motel?"

"He didn't tell her, but we've got a trace on the call. Should know pretty quick."

"Good work. Send it to St Cloud as soon as you get it. Did she identify our suspect?"

"We showed her the composite we had from last fall. It's him, but she said he's changed his appearance since then. Grew his hair, plus a beard, and moustache. She can't believe he's a killer."

"Make sure she believes it, Sheriff. We'll need her place covered in case he returns. Can you handle that?"

"Kind of short of staff here, but we'll do our best."

"Will you also get a new composite done with her input and send it to us?"

"Yup. Good luck getting this guy."

"Thanks, Sheriff. See you." He punched 'end' on his portable.

"Ed, we've got to find that motel quickly. Karl's probably heard the news about the license plate and has changed his plans. Doubt if he'd go back to Cathy's now."

They stayed on Highway 10 and headed for the office. The motel had to be somewhere between Crosslake and Hutchinson. He called Watson and had him alert the State Troopers with the latest. They'd go right by Pete's on the way so Jack offered to spring for lunch. Jack picked up two specials and insisted they wait till they got to the office before eating. The extra chili sauce made the burgers difficult to eat in the car and besides, it was an insult to eat one of Pete's best while driving.

Halfway through the delicious repast, Watson burst into Jack's office.

"They got the motel traced from the phone call. It's about twenty miles west of here, just south of 94."

"We're on our way," said Jack. "Bob, update the Troopers with the specifics. Have them seal off every road and highway in the vicinity of the motel."

He took the address and phone number. The burgers were left unfinished. Brooker was driving while Jack called the motel.

"Andy's Motel, Andy speaking."

"This is Lieutenant Petersen from St Cloud division. Do you have a guest there driving a green pickup? License plate reads, 'CATHY.'"

"Sure did, but I think he's gone."

"What do you mean, you *think* he's gone?"

"Well, I had two guests come in late last night, or early this morning's more like it. It was the storm you know. People just had to stop."

"Tell me about them, Andy."

"Well, the first guy arrived in that truck you mentioned. That was about three this morning. And you've got the plate right. Saw it this morning. Then a few minutes later a woman arrived. Didn't even get back to sleep. She had one of the fanciest cars I've ever seen."

"Where are they now, Andy?"

"Well, that's what I was going to tell you. A little before noon I saw the guy monkeying around with his truck, like under the hood. Didn't know what he was doing. Next thing I knew, he'd gone back to his room. A little while later he came out with Mrs Gold, tried to start his truck, but couldn't get it going. It did get pretty cold here last..."

"Andy, what happened next?" asked Jack.

"Well, off they went in her car. Didn't say good-bye or anything. That's why I'm not sure if they've really left. I mean, wouldn't he come back for his truck if something was wrong with it?"

"Don't know. You said they left around noon?"

"Well, yeah. Like maybe a few minutes after."

Jack heard a slight commotion over the line. He could hear another voice. It sounded like a man.

"Is that the guy with the truck?" asked Jack. "Just say yes or no."

"No, it's a police officer, asking about the truck."

"Put him on the phone, Andy." Jack heard him call the officer to the phone.

"Patrolman Weiss here."

"This is Lieutenant Petersen of the B.C.A. You aware who may have been driving that truck?"

"Yes, Lieutenant. I heard the A.P.B., so when I saw this green pickup I came in to have a look. Sure enough it's the one. License plate reads, 'CATHY.' "

"Weiss, we're about twenty minutes away. Can you stay there till we arrive?"

"Sure can. You think this guy might come back here?"

"Don't know that, but don't take any chances if he does. He's probably armed and he's definitely dangerous. See you soon. Put Andy back on will you?"

"10-4, Lieutenant."

He heard the officer call Andy to the phone.

"What's happening here, Lieutenant?" asked Andy.

"We need a description of Mrs Gold's car."

"Well, it was a Mercedes. Fairly new one, I think."

"What color, Andy?"

"Well, it was kinda blue. Light blue. Pretty sharp look..."

"Did you get a plate number?"

"Well, no. I didn't see that."

"What size, Andy? Two-door, four-door?"

"Yeah, I remember that. Two-door, sorta like a sport's car."

"If you think of anything else about the car, tell Patrolman Weiss. He'll stay with you until we get there. See you in fifteen minutes or so."

"Lieutenant, this sounds serious. Am I in danger here?"

"I doubt if our suspect will be back to your place, Andy. Just be careful and stay with the officer," said Jack. He hung up and called the office.

"St Cloud Division, Patrolman Watson here."

Jack gave him the details of the Mercedes. "Bob, send out an A.P.B. on this vehicle. Have the Troopers concentrate on roads south and east of the motel. My guess is he's headed back to the Cities. He left there about two hours ago. Also advise he now has long hair, a beard, and moustache. As soon as you get the new composite from Hutchinson, send it out."

"10-4, Lieutenant." They hung up.

Ten minutes later they pulled into Andy's motel. The cruiser and truck were parked in front. They entered the office and introductions were made. Jack showed him a picture of Karl.

"Is this the man who stayed here, Andy?"

"Well, not really. He had more hair and a moustache. But I guess it could be the same guy."

"What can you tell us about Mrs Gold?" asked Jack.

"Well, she was not young, but not too old either. Rather nice looking actually."

"Did she list an address with you?"

"Well sure. I don't register anyone here without recording their name and address. Do that with all my customers. Let's see, here it is. Got her telephone number too."

"Ed, call this number. See if you can found out where she was going. Andy, we'd like to trace any calls made from the two rooms. You have a problem with that?" asked Jack.

"Well, no I guess not."

"We're only interested in the last twelve hours or so. Just the time when those two were here," said Jack.

"Okay, go ahead."

Ed had just completed his call.

"No luck, Jack. Another answering machine."

Jack was staring at a map of Minnesota that was mounted beside the reception desk.

"Do you like that, Lieutenant? I thought it was real handy for my guests. If they had any questions about where they were going, we could just study that map right there and point them in the right direction."

Andy had marked the location of his motel on the map with a red arrow and the words, 'You are here.'

"There, you see the red arrow, that's us right here. Got the idea from those maps you see in malls," said Andy.

Jack was suddenly highly agitated.

"May I use your phone, Andy? It'll be a collect call."

"Sure, Lieutenant. And don't worry about the charges."

Jack dialed the St Cloud Division. It was answered on the second ring.

"Bob, how many officers have you got at the Jensen's?"

"We've had a bit of a problem organizing that, Lieutenant, but we're..."

"Christ Bob, you get three cars over there now, and I mean now!" He slammed down the phone.

"Weiss you stay here and get some back-up. We'll contact you as soon as we can. Thanks, Andy. Come on, Ed, we're out of here."

Jack was out the door and in the car, with Brooker following as fast as he could.

"I'll drive, you navigate," said Jack.

"Where are we going?"

Jack had the siren going and careened out of the parking lot.

"I was looking at that map. We're only half an hour from the Jensen's. Guess where Karl's headed?"

62

Once Darlene was in the shower, Karl went outside to his truck. He didn't have much time. He had the hood up, removed the distributor cap in no time, ensuring the truck would not start.

Back in the room he waited till Darlene was finished showering. She came out of the bathroom wrapped in a towel.

"I need some new clothes, Jack. Don't think I should go outside like this. I left an outfit in my room. Would you get it for me? Then at least I'll be dressed to get back to the room for my make-up."

"Sure. You have the key?" asked Karl.

"Right here." She moved against him. "Did I have a good time last night?"

She smelled good, but Karl had no time for this.

"I certainly did. Be right back, Darlene."

He brought her the slacks and sweater along with a bra and panties.

"You think of everything, Jack." She dropped the towel and hesitated. "Guess we don't have time for anything do we?"

"I'd sure love to, but you're in a hurry and so am I," said Karl. "I'd like to watch you put on your make-up though."

"Sure, let's go." She dressed and they went to her room. Less than twenty minutes later they were on their way.

"Why don't we grab breakfast together?" asked Karl.

"Great idea. I'll follow you."

They got in their vehicles. Darlene had her car going right away. He tried repeatedly to start the truck with no success. He got out and slammed the door.

"What's the matter?"

"Ah, this thing's been giving me problems lately. Guess with the cold weather, it just isn't going to go."

"What are you going to do?" asked Darlene.

"If we head into the next town and find a garage, I'll get them to bring the truck in. They can fix it while we have breakfast."

"Sure. Do you want to drive?"

"Why not?" asked Karl.

He put the Mercedes in gear and pulled away smoothly.

"Nice car. What year is this?"

"It's this year's model. Picked it up in August. I came into a little money through my last divorce, so I splurged. Never had a two-door before. I've also never been so happy. I'm free, have enough money to go where I want, when I want, and am really starting to enjoy it."

"Sounds like a good deal."

"Then there's Miriam. She's as happy about this as I am. Matter of fact, we're going to look at taking a cruise together this spring. She's got some brochures from several cruise lines ready for me. We'll pick one today."

"Never been on a cruise," said Karl.

"Too bad you can't join us on this one. Kind of too soon for that. But maybe next time."

Karl turned north at the first intersection. He knew exactly where the bitch lived and he was headed there. Shouldn't be more than half an hour.

"Why are we going north?" asked Darlene.

"I saw a garage in the next town on my way in last night."

"I thought you said you were coming up from the south."

"Yeah, well I went past the motel before I decided to stop. I turned around just up ahead," said Karl.

The roads were quite good as the plows had been out on the job, probably since early morning. The snow was piled high on both sides of the highway making the route seem like a long tunnel. Skies were clear and the sun danced on the snow drifts. It was dazzling but hard on the eyes.

"Do you have any sunglasses?" asked Karl.

"I think so. They should be in the visor above your head."

Karl slipped the visor down and found the glasses.

"Much better," he said.

"How long have you had the beard and moustache?"

"Why the fuck would you want to know that?" asked Karl.

The sharpness of his reply startled her.

"I don't know. No particular reason. A little jumpy are we?"

Karl merely grunted.

They drove for a while in silence.

"Where is this town supposed to be?" asked Darlene with a slight edge to her voice.

"I don't fucking know any town."

"What's going on here. Why are you so rude all of a sudden?"

"Shut up."

"What?"

"I said, shut the fuck up."

"Listen, I don't need that kind of talk. I just don't take that anymore. Now, turn this car around and go back to the motel. You can call a garage from there."

"There'll be no need for that."

"What's that supposed to mean?"

"I mean, I don't need a truck now."

"Look, I don't want to get into this anymore. Let's just go back, okay?"

The Mercedes continued boring ahead, northbound. Karl kept his eyes on the road. He could feel her staring at him.

"I don't get it," said Darlene.

"You don't have to – get it."

"Heh, this is my car. Now I'd really like you to turn around and go back to the motel. I can go on to see Miriam, and you can do whatever you want. Is that unreasonable?"

"Not at all. Only we'll do what I want to do, from here on. You don't have any say in the matter."

"Now wait a minute. You're taking me against my will."

"Aren't you brilliant? Now shut up, I have to think."

"I'm not shutting up and you're going to stop this car."

The blow came fast and hard, jarring a couple of teeth loose and cutting her lip. Nothing happened for several seconds. He saw her fumbling in her purse. He grabbed the purse and threw it in the back.

"Don't even try to reach for that." Karl pulled the knife from his pocket and pricked her side. He held it against her ribs. "You move, I'll cut your tits off."

"Christ, you're mad. Wait a minute. You're not the killer? The one I read about last fall?"

"I'm famous. Isn't that great?"

"Look, what do you want with me? I've done nothing to you."

"Yeah, but I need your car, see."

"Well, take the car. Just let me go. I can't hurt you."

"If you shut up, I might let you go," said Karl.

The only sound was the engine purring and the hum of the tires on the snow covered road. Karl recognized the road sign and turned eastward. He could hear her whimpering.

There was hardly any traffic. They had met only two or three cars during the entire drive. A station wagon was approaching. The road was a little narrow with the snow pinching in from the sides. Karl had to slow down.

When the station wagon was merely yards away, Karl felt the wheel yanked to the right and the horn blaring.

"You little bitch."

He slapped her hand away and hit the brakes. The car skidded, first towards the snow bank, then back to the oncoming station wagon. He just managed to swerve back, barely missing the other vehicle.

Darlene had opened the door and was out of the car in seconds. The station wagon had stopped.

Karl had no choice. He gunned the Mercedes. The passenger's door slammed shut as he accelerated.

He'd have to hurry now. Only ten minutes or so to her house.

63

Sharin had just come back from the doctor and was elated with the results. Her size and weight were normal for the sixth month. Eric was in Minneapolis attending a trade show and would return Monday night. She decided to take the dogs out for their favorite treat, a long walk in the woods. It was a bright sunny day with the temperature hovering at zero. There was no wind, making the conditions perfect for their outing.

While she brewed some coffee Sharin thought of turning on the noon news, but the kitchen tv had been acting up, so she opted for a John Denver C.D. which would be ideal to set the mood for their walk.

The moment Sharin began organizing her winter boots and parka, the dogs knew what was coming. It was excitement time. She filled a thermos with coffee and packed the usual treats for King and Kayla. The exercise would be good for everyone. Last night's snow fall had left their wooded lot in pristine condition, so there would be many animal tracks to investigate. There was also the chance of a deer sighting.

They had just started out the back door when the phone rang. Sharin was already in a foot of snow so she'd have to take off her boots before reentering the house to get to the kitchen phone. By that time the answering machine would probably have taken the call so she decided to ignore it. Eric wasn't due to call till early evening. She could pick up whatever message was there when they returned.

They headed for the logging trail which wound its way through the entire fifty acres. Although the trail had not been used by loggers for over thirty years, it remained clear and defined, and thus served as an excellent cross-country ski area as well as a free and easy path for walking. The dogs, of course, were off on frequent side journeys into the woods in search of any and all interesting sounds and movement.

As expected, they saw numerous signs of wildlife with a variety of imprints in the fresh snow. The chatter of birds filled the forest in the clear, cold air. Then a startling sound just off the edge of the path. It was a thunderous, flapping of wings as a pheasant was flushed out by Kayla. The bird kept its flight path low and was soon out of sight in the heavy brush. It couldn't have been more than ten feet from Sharin at the edge of the trail, yet had not taken flight until the Shepherd had sensed its presence and forced it to flee. Such bravery for the bird to remain motionless despite the entourage coming its way.

After the flurry of excitement the walk continued. Silence took over. She recalled the story they had heard from a close friend who had taken a wilderness survival course last summer. She had related many of her experiences, one of which was stopping to listen to the forest. Sharin did that now.

After a few minutes the forest did indeed start to talk. It was strange but fascinating. A gentle breeze caused the trees to sway and groan. Occasionally a branch broke or a twig snapped. The cracking sound echoed through the woods. She heard the crunch of her boots on the snow, mixed with the natural sounds around her.

As often occurred, Sharin reflected on the events of last fall. The killer had not been heard from but Lieutenant Petersen had explained this was not unusual. There were many cases of serial killers who had virtually disappeared, never to be heard from again. A mystery to be sure. The files were not closed, but naturally police activity on the case would diminish. It didn't totally alleviate her concerns when she considered he might still be alive. Neither did the occasional nightmare go away.

Her parents had left early in November although she had sensed her father wanted to stay on. However, enough was enough. Everybody had to get on with their lives. Besides, her mother had difficulty coming to grips with her terrifying incident in the mall. Frank called frequently to see how they were and kept in touch with the Commissioner and Chief. He was tenacious and caring.

They did return for the Christmas holidays and stayed on to welcome in the new millennium. Judy did not venture out of the house but showed she was a real trooper by remaining in a happy and festive mood. Frank was the hit of Eric's company party which was held on the Sunday prior to Christmas. He had recited two Robert Service poems that had received the rapt attention of the entire staff. He had even rented a Klondike outfit for the occasion.

Sharin stopped to pour a cup of coffee. The dogs who had been off in the woods for another tour, returned immediately at the sound of the thermos being opened. It usually signaled a treat would be available. They were not disappointed as Sharin fished out a couple of dog biscuits. They gently took the biscuits from Sharin, then immediately crushed them. There was incredible strength in their jaws. The vet had explained that whereas humans exert seventy pounds of pressure with their jaws, domestic dogs produce two hundred and fifty pounds.

They were about halfway to the back of the property, the dogs had again bolted off into the woods, when she rounded a corner in the path and was confronted by a tall bearded man. He stared at her.

"Who are you?" asked Sharin.

"You don't know, bitch? I know you."

Sharin looked past the long hair, beard, and moustache and recognized him.

"King, Kayla," she shouted and started backing away.

"They're not going to help you."

He slowly moved towards her, smiling and cocky.

"What do you mean? Have you seen my dogs? King, Kayla!"

He laughed.

Sharin considered running into the woods. She knew her way, he didn't. But the snow was deep. Could she outdistance him? Unlikely. She looked for a weapon, anything, as she continued to back away. Christ, he was big. Just like his twin brother.

"You killed Kurt," said Karl.

"I did not. He was sick. He killed himself."

"Like hell. You were responsible."

"He liked me. Why would I want to harm him?" asked Sharin

"I see you're showing now. Planning to have a baby, were you?"

"You really don't want to hurt me. Besides, there are policemen everywhere. You'll never get away," said Sharin.

She was terrified. Her bladder released. Where were the dogs?

He lunged forward and knocked her to the ground. He pounced on her and took the knife from his jacket pocket.

"Now you pay."

King and Kayla burst from the woods and flew at Karl. He raised his knife. It caught Kayla in the chest. She yelped, then fell backwards, temporarily paralyzed. Sharin couldn't move with his weight pinning her down.

King grabbed Karl's wrist in his massive jaws. The knife flew out of his hand into the snow. Karl started beating the dog. He drove his fist repeatedly at King's head. The dog didn't flinch. He was on all fours and continued to hold Karl's wrist in a vice-like grip. He growled and snarled, staring at this adversary. Karl, who had been sitting on Sharin was forced over on his back. His wrist was bleeding profusely. The dog must have severed an artery.

Karl tried to grope around for the knife with his free arm. It had fallen in deep snow. He couldn't find it. He was pawing frantically but having no success. King would not let go. Blood was now everywhere.

With Karl on his back and half off her, Sharin managed to wriggle free and get up. She saw a tree branch, picked it up, and swung with all her strength at Karl's head. The branch simply broke in two. It was rotten through.

Sharin was frantic. Kayla was motionless, but breathing. How was she to save herself and the two dogs?

She wanted to look for the knife but Karl was too close to where it had fallen. She did find a sizeable boulder, hoisted it, and dropped it on his knee. He hardly reacted. Just glared at her and continued battling with King. Karl reached for one of King's legs and tried to pull him away, but his strength was waning. The dog would not let go.

Sharin again reached for the boulder but as she did, he caught her arm! She bit his hand, tasted his blood. He let go. She scrambled to safety.

Karl's movements were severely restricted with the one hundred pound German Shepherd fastened to his arm. Every time he tried to stand, the dog seemed to bite down harder. Karl finally showed some sign of experiencing pain. He continued to pound the dog's head in hope of him letting go. With the loss of blood his movements were becoming more labored.

Should she leave now and return home to call for help? Somehow, that was not going to happen. She would stay and find a way to overcome this maniac. He was definitely weakening and not going anywhere with King holding on. Then she remembered the sturdy branches left over from the bridge Eric had built. They were by the stream, only fifty yards from where they were. He had cut several pieces of wood, about two inches in diameter, varying from three to six feet in length. The wood was solid.

"Stay, King. Don't let go."

She hurried down the path and quickly found the area. Where was the pile of wood? With the snow fall she was disoriented and couldn't remember where he had left the pile.

Sharin groped around in the snow, clawing through it in the hope of finding the weapon she needed. She kicked at the snow in frustration and stormed about. Where the hell is it? She tripped and fell in her frustration. Dammit! "I have to find that wood pile."

The sound of King growling gave her comfort. He was not going to let Karl free. She was confident of that. She yelled for help while she continued looking. Nobody would hear but it made her feel better. She picked up a small branch and began poking around. There should be an obvious hump in the snow indicating where the cut wood was, but too much had fallen, obscuring her much needed pile of weaponry.

A shrill yelp resonated through the forest. God, was that Kayla or King?

"Where are you, you stinking pile of wood?"

She began kicking again, and stubbed her toe on something. Energized by what might be, she flew at the snow with both hands. There it was. She had never seen a more glorious sight. She brushed away more snow to reveal part of the pile, reached in and grabbed one of the sticks. She pulled. It didn't move. They were frozen under the snow.

Sharin knew this was her only hope. With all the patience one could muster, she methodically cleared away enough snow to give herself good purchase of the wood. She stomped on the pile and eventually created some movement. More yelping. Out of the pile came two sturdy pieces of wood, about five feet long. Sharin hurried back to the dogs and Karl.

As she neared, King was still attached to Karl but he had somehow moved closer to Kayla and was beating her. What was he trying to do? Distract King so he could get free? His movements seemed lethargic. The blood loss was taking its toll.

Sharin laid down one piece of wood several yards away, in case she lost the first one. She moved behind Karl, took a stance, and swung with all her strength. The blow caught him flush across the back of the neck. A resounding crack resulted from the contact of wood on skull.

She swung again, this time so hard she missed and stumbled. Karl reached for her ankle. King snarled and bit down harder. You could hear the crunch of bone. Sharin kicked free.

At least she had diverted his attention away from Kayla who was quiet, but still alive. The snow was crimson from Karl's blood and Kayla's. Hopefully most of the blood was his. He certainly didn't have the same spunk and energy as before. He continued to battle.

Sharin's next blow found its mark, smashing his ear and cheek. Another blow landed in the same place. And then another. Three consecutive strikes all found their mark. Finally he seemed dazed. Karl rolled over, face down. Blood now flowed from his right ear. He didn't move. Was he unconscious? She wondered if another few hits weren't a good idea, but her anger was beginning to abate as he lay quiet. Had she really beaten this man to a pulp?

King was still attached to his wrist. Blood continued to spurt from Karl's arm, covering the snow as well as King. For the moment there was not a sound. The three survivors were breathing irregularly. Kayla was quiet, King labored, while Sharin was slowly returning to normal. She was perspiring and exhausted, mentally and physically.

Sharin slumped to the ground, stared at the havoc, then started shaking violently. Was it finally over? Things to do.

"Stay, King. Good boy." She inched her way towards Kayla. She wanted to tend to Kayla even though her bleeding seemed to have stopped.

Sharin felt a searing pain. She saw the knife in Karl's hand, and felt the blade start to slice down her left arm. She tried to move away but he struck at her again, this time in the back. It stung and smarted. Although it didn't have the force of the first blow it was still nasty.

Her legs were pinned under his and he was ready to strike again. King let go of his right arm and grabbed the hand holding the knife. Once again King had a strangle hold on Karl's wrist. Karl lashed out at the Shepherd with his free arm which was badly mangled. The hand hung limply at the wrist, probably due to severe tendon damage from King's tenacious hold. White, shiny bone was visible. Karl tried to batter King with the hand and arm, but it was totally ineffective. The knife dropped harmlessly to the ground. Karl was helpless.

Sharin was free to tend to Kayla. The bleeding was minimal and she used her mitten to stop it completely. She heard sounds but they seemed far away. What were they? What was going on?

She was sure she could see several figures moving towards her. They looked vaguely familiar. Yes, she recognized them now. Police. It looked like a whole division. She was tired, cold, and in pain, but happy.

It was over now.

64

Jack and Brooker arrived at the Jensen's just as two other cruisers pulled up. They had surrounded the house. The back door was unlocked. After entering and discovering nobody was home, including the dogs, they headed for the woods. The Land Rover was in the driveway. Knowing Sharin's habit of taking the dogs for walks, they were confident she was out there somewhere.

Fifteen minutes later they sighted the group and hurried to Sharin. Both dogs snarled but Sharin quieted them. King was coaxed away from Karl, who was now unconscious. Sharin held her two pets and wept. King had been the hero, and would be none the worse for wear despite the battering he had received from Karl.

Sharin was concerned about Kayla and asked Jack to phone her vet. She gave them the number. While one of the officers made the call, Jack noticed the tear in Sharin's jacket.

"You've been cut," said Jack. "Let's have a look at that."

He removed her jacket. Luckily both strikes had barely nicked her, but there was some bleeding.

"Let's get you back to the house. Are you able to walk?"

"I'll be okay," said Sharin. "He's off the phone. What did the vet say?"

"He wants the dog taken out on something flat and brought to his office as soon as possible. He was just about to close, but he'll wait for her."

Sharin asked one of the officers to go back to the house. There was a toboggan at the back door of the garage. It wasn't long before the four officers had taken Sharin and the two dogs away.

Jack and Brooker remained with Karl.

"That dog sure did a hell of a job on him, Jack," said Brooker.

"Sort of convenient isn't it? This will save a lot of time and court costs. Guess we just couldn't get him to a hospital in time. Guy bled to death."

Karl opened his eyes and looked at the two officers.

"Need a doctor," said Karl, in a voice barely audible.

"You hear anything, Lieutenant?" asked Brooker.

"Something about wanting a doctor? Don't think they make house calls anymore. Anyway it's Saturday. Really tough to find one now, don't you think, Ed?"

"Yeah. Geez, Lieutenant, I don't even know if there's a phone around here."

"You...saved...fucking dog," said Karl.

"I'd say she was worth saving, wouldn't you, Ed?"

"Fine dog. No doubt about that. Guess we should wait here a while. You in any hurry, Jack?"

"I'll have to check my schedule, Ed. Let's see, this is Saturday, right?"

"Yeah, it is and the divisional playoffs are on aren't they?"

"That's right. Who do you like this weekend?" asked Jack.

They heard a groan. Karl lapsed into silence. They stared at the monster who had been responsible for so many senseless killings.

"I think he's gone," said Jack.

"Should we get a doctor, Lieutenant?"

"No, I think a coroner would be more like it."

Jack felt for a pulse. There was none. They called the coroner's office and were told he could be there within the hour.

"Congratulations, Jack. He was a piece of work, wasn't he?"

"About the worst I've encountered," said Jack.

Two hours later they were back in the Jensen house with Sharin and King. Their family doctor had arrived and treated Sharin's wounds. Kayla would have to stay with the vet for two days. The knife wound had caused temporary paralysis but she would fully recover. King had a few scrapes but otherwise was fine. Sharin had reached Eric and her parents. A celebration was in order and Jack was to be invited.

They took Sharin's story, then headed for St Cloud to complete their report. Jack looked forward to calling Brett and Sven. David Folk would be pleased. They stopped at Pete's but Jack ordered only one burger. He was going to have supper with Jennifer tonight.

They had everything wrapped up by seven-thirty when Jack set out for home. He was dog tired but it was a great feeling. He'd even book a holiday for just the two of them. Maybe a Caribbean island for a couple of weeks. Jennifer would like that. Could he leave Minnesota in January for two weeks?

He was halfway home when his car phone rang. He hesitated. The ringing persisted.

Jack finally picked up the receiver.